CONTEMPORARY AMERICAN FICTION

ORRIE'S STORY

Thomas Berger, who lives just outside of New
York, is the author of seventeen novels, including
Little Big Man, *Neighbors*, and *The Feud*.

ORRIE'S STORY

A Novel by

THOMAS BERGER

PENGUIN BOOKS

PENGUIN BOOKS
Published by the Penguin Group
Viking Penguin, a division of Penguin Books USA Inc.,
375 Hudson Street, New York, New York 10014, U.S.A.
Penguin Books Ltd, 27 Wrights Lane,
London W8 5TZ, England
Penguin Books Australia Ltd, Ringwood,
Victoria, Australia
Penguin Books Canada Ltd, 10 Alcorn Avenue, Suite 300,
Toronto, Ontario, Canada M4V 3B2
Penguin Books (N.Z.) Ltd, 182–190 Wairau Road,
Auckland 10, New Zealand

Penguin Books Ltd, Registered Offices:
Harmondsworth, Middlesex, England

First published in the United States of America by
Little, Brown and Company 1990
Reprinted by arrangement with
Little, Brown and Company (Inc.)
Published in Penguin Books 1992

1 3 5 7 9 10 8 6 4 2

PUBLISHER'S NOTE
This is a work of fiction. Names, characters, places, and incidents either are the product of the author's imagination or are used fictitiously, and any resemblance to actual persons, living or dead, events, or locales is entirely coincidental.

THE LIBRARY OF CONGRESS HAS CATALOGUED THE HARDCOVER AS FOLLOWS:
Berger, Thomas, 1924–
Orrie's story: a novel / by Thomas Berger. — 1st ed.
p. cm.
1. Orestes (Greek mythology) — Fiction. I. Title.
PS3552.E719077   1990
813'.54 — dc20   90–5999
ISBN 0-316-09220-7 (hc.)
ISBN 0 14 01.4994 5 (pbk.)

Printed in the United States of America

To Brom Weber

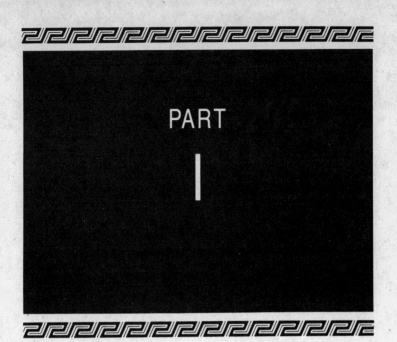

PART

I

1

⊡╱╱╱⊡

The regulars at the Idle Hour Bar & Grill, beer drinkers except for Joe Becker, who preferred stronger stuff and could afford it, and Molly McShane, who always drank sherry wine, were either too old for the service, medically disqualified, or, as in the case of Molly and her pal Gladys, of the wrong sex.

Augie Mencken had parachuted into German-held France in the wee hours before the morning of D-Day, got a battlefield commission at the Bulge, and ended up in Berlin itself. His latest postcard was Scotch-taped to the mirror behind the bar, alongside several years' worth of earlier cards, some now yellowing, and a newspaper photo of himself (though his back was to the camera) being handed a bottle of champagne by a pretty French girl as he liberated Paris in a Jeep.

That Augie had been the one to distinguish himself in the war was a surprise. He had not exactly been a success in civilian life, having failed as a businessman: his five-and-ten was a bust. He had been bailed out by his cousin, a guy nobody much liked (with the notable exception of Augie's wife) but who had done well in his own career, shady though it was said to be. Whether E.G., as he liked to be called, had enjoyed the favors of Augie's wife before his cousin went into the service was a matter of speculation by those at the Idle Hour, the males of whom thought Esther Mencken the sexiest-looking woman in town despite her age (late thirties) and her three children.

Of course if Molly and Gladys were present, the talk was suitably sanitized: in female company, the men were prudish, especially when the women were like relatives, Molly having always been plain and Glad an overweight widow in her fifties.

But everybody agreed that E.G. and Esther had been on intimate terms at least since Augie went to war.

Tonight, however, the ending of that war took precedence.

"Japs couldn't take another bomb like that," said Rickie Wicks.

Phil Paulsen, whose Regular Army brother had been listed as missing since the fall of Bataan and was thought likely to have perished in the Death March either from starvation or a more direct form of the notorious Nipponese cruelty to prisoners of war, was among the least bloodthirsty of the group. He now nodded soberly. "But what if Ralph's a prisoner in a camp near one of those towns that got it?"

This was a dispiriting thought, but Joe Becker said, "Our side would know where the Americans were kept. They wouldn't bomb our boys." Joe was the oldest of the men and the most prosperous: what he said had weight.

Al Hagman was at twenty-five the picture of health when sitting on a bar stool but had lost several of the toes on his left foot in an accident at the plant some years earlier. He now thrust his beer mug towards Paulsen. "Here's to Ralph."

Paulsen joined the others in drinking to that. "I still got my hopes. Mom believes he'll turn up, God bless her."

Hagman said, "Bill O'Hare got his at Anzio Beach, and Chuck Dunn got killed in the Battle of the Bulge."

"My wife's cousin, lived out West: he got it at Guadalcanal," said Wicks. "And then Howard Vedder was in a German P.O.W. camp till it was liberated, and a lot of guys from around here were wounded. This locality paid a price."

Bob Terwillen came in and stood beyond Joe Becker. He waved at the ladies, who sat as always at the short end of the bar, where it made a right angle and went to join the wall. Without being asked, Herm the owner and bartender brought him a bottle of beer and not a mug but a glass.

Terwillen drank some and then made his announcement. "Did you hear? Augie Mencken's coming home tomorrow."

Al Hagman chuckled. "Herm heard from him. We got a little party planned for lunchtime."

Molly's voice had a sarcastic edge. "War sure must have changed that guy. He wouldn't let butter melt in his mouth when he was around here."

Becker gave her a dirty look.

"Augie must be over forty if he's a day," said Terwillen, his eyes magnified by the thick lenses he wore. "And he's got those kids. He wouldn't have had to go into the service."

"Forty-two last April," Becker said.

"Probably had to lie about his age to get in," said Rickie Wicks, who was himself young enough to have gone to war, but there was something wrong with his heart. Unlike Hagman, who walked with a limp, Rickie could show no external reason why he was Four-F, and since Pearl Harbor he had been fair game for the abuse of strangers as a draft-dodger and did not dare go into a bar where he was unknown. "You know those kids who make themselves older to get into the Marines? Augie was the opposite."

Molly addressed Gladys, but spoke loudly enough to be heard by all. "I wonder what's going to happen with Esther and E.G. now?"

"E.G. better watch out," said Rickie. "Augie's done his share of killing."

Gladys was usually a listener, but now she spoke with obvious feeling. "She was the meanest little kid."

"That's right," said Molly. "Your family was neighbors with Esther's."

"My sister always claimed it was her poisoned our dog," said Gladys, "and while I don't know I'd go as far as that . . ." At this point she took a strenuous draft of what might easily seem the same cigarette she had lighted on entering an hour before but was rather the latest in a continuous series.

2

Ellie Mencken was sixteen but so underdeveloped she could have been taken as three or four years younger. Her mother, who had herself at the same age been voluptuous long since, considered her more or less hopeless.

Esther poured her a glass of orange juice from a can the top lid of which had been pierced twice with an icepick, one hole for pouring, one for air: a technique of E.G.'s.

"Are you going to school looking like *that?*"

"This is a clean blouse," said Ellie, glancing down at her flat chest through the bottom of her plastic-rimmed eyeglasses, one temple piece of which was cracked and wound with adhesive tape.

"How can you stand to keep wearing those ugly specs? Every time he sees you, your Uncle Erle begs you to get new ones at his expense."

Ellie set her pale lips. "They're okay."

"You're old enough to start wondering how you're going

to survive in life, you know." It was not the first time Esther had mentioned the matter. The orange juice was coming out too slowly into the little glass that had formerly held spread cheese. She shook the can. It was empty. Even with Orrie away at school, foodstuffs went quickly though at any given time the girl seemed to eat very little. "On your way home today, stop at Harriman's and get juice for tomorrow and some baloney for supper. Bread, I guess. This toast is the last of it, and I had to scrape some mold from that. And see if there are enough eggs. And try to hold the bill down, will you?"

The allotment Augie sent home from the Army was miserably small, and significantly, it came by postal money order and not in a government check. It was obvious that he somehow finagled the authorities into giving him the money instead of sending it directly to his dependents, thus enabling him to siphon some off for himself or maybe for a German bitch: he would have to buy his women. Esther now understood that she had despised Augie ever since he demonstrated his moral weakness by agreeing to marry her immediately on being told she was pregnant at sixteen, not even asking whether the kid was his own. She had already had other partners, foremost among them his cousin E.G., then called simply Erle, who a year earlier had been the first to make a woman of her, but at this time Erle was elsewhere in the country, in one of those periods of his life in which he went questing for greater opportunities than were offered locally. He had obviously made a go of it, whenever and wherever, though he was not the sort to reveal much unasked, and fearing she might learn something that would only make her jealous, Esther was not the one to pry.

He might even have been married at some point. Certainly, with his appetites, he would have had to deal with other women: a state of affairs that was bearable only so long as it remained abstract, without details. All that really mattered was that throughout the years he took her to bed whenever he was in town, and from the late 1930s on, he was more or less permanently at hand. At first they were discreet, but with the passage of time and a common contempt for her husband, his cousin, grew less so. It was not unlikely that Augie was well aware of the situation even before he decided to go to war: maybe that was one of his reasons for joining the Army. It was characteristic of him not to say, though he was voluble enough about his other problems, which were exclusively those of money, or rather the lack thereof.

Why then did she not leave Augie for E.G.? For a decade and a half, the children were too young. Furthermore, Erle had never said a word on that subject, and, as always, she was too proud to ask.

"If I were you I'd go to Sue Anne and see what she can do with that hair of yours, at least," Esther now said to her daughter, referring to the local beautician.

Ellie made no response to this. Instead she asked plaintively, "What I'd really like to do is stay home and wait for Daddy."

"Well, you can't," said Esther, removing the milk bottle from the refrigerator. She pried off the cardboard disc and sniffed at the contents, which only just could be called still drinkable. "He's not due at any particular time. He can't make his mind up on what train, I guess. Isn't that just like him? Uncle Erle would have been glad to pick him up. But *no*."

"I wish I could have talked to him," said Ellie.

"Don't flatter yourself," her mother said. "Think he'd name a specific time just for you?"

"Maybe he would."

"You have an exaggerated sense of yourself. Drink your milk."

Ellie shook her stubborn face. "It's sour."

"Then go without." Esther strode from the kitchen. She had no patience with the girl.

An Augie back from the service would be an unbearable burden on all concerned. Ordinarily, over the years, Esther had not bothered to answer his boastful letters — leave it to him to succeed only when he left home and family behind — but when he announced he was about to be discharged, she responded quickly, begging him to make the Army a career. He had made a go of it thus far, hadn't he, with the heroics and medals and promotions and all? Whereas what did civilian life have to offer? Would the postwar era be kinder to him than the pre-? She reminded him, as politely as she could, that he had no experience but that associated with the unfortunate five-and-dime. Why not stay in the Army and continue to prosper, maybe go on to become a general?

Augie paid as much attention to that appeal as he had listened to anything else she had said in all the foregoing years. But this time the laugh would be on him, and he would have only himself to blame. It was her idea, but E.G. agreed quickly enough, and anyway just thinking it up was the easy part. Making a plan of action that would allow for all the eventualities was much harder than the kind of thing you saw in the movies, which she only now realized were extremely sketchy about reality. Were it not for E.G., she might well have dropped the whole thing. He was much more practical than she: not only the means must be considered, but all that might result from each choice. A self-inflicted wound while cleaning a captured enemy firearm might rate high in plausibility but could they count on his coming home with a Luger?

E.G. said he had known returning soldiers reckless enough to bring along unexploded hand grenades. But how to detonate one of those without bringing down much of the house as well? There were obvious objections to nonmilitary means: hit-and-run by car (hard to set up without being seen by *someone*), murder by an armed robber (a crime unknown in their town), an assisted plunge down the cellar steps (might, with a healthy war hero, result only in some bruises), rat- or weed-killing poisons (even if undetected by the victim, how had they got into his food or drink?).

Esther became more savage as the quest proceeded. She now professed to be furious with herself for not doing away with him before he had gone off to war — and so saved Gena's life.

"A kid her age, hitchhiking by herself on a highway." E.G., next to her in the tourist-cabin bed, closed his eyes. He was not hearing this for the first time, but it had to be said. "She wouldn't have run away if he hadn't suddenly decided to join the Army. I couldn't do anything with her when she heard her Daddy had left. He always pulled the wool over those girls' eyes. They thought the world of him, no matter what. Like it was me who had anything to do with him going bust with the store."

Now E.G. showed anger. "Don't remind me of that. You know where the money should have gone. My dad never forgave his." The grandfather he and Augie had in common had been outrageously biased in favor of Augie's old man and against E.G.'s own, leaving the latter almost nothing when he died but providing the funds for Augie's father to open the five-and-ten at the edge of the business district. It had never done well during what was left of Theodore Mencken's life, in later Depression days, but when bequeathed to Augie it lasted only another two years. Of course Augie complained that he had inherited more debts than assets, but to Esther, and E.G., the reason was simply Augie himself.

On Augie's death the U.S. government would be obliged to pay the beneficiary of his G.I. insurance the sum of ten thousand dollars.

They finally settled on the plan only the night before Augie was scheduled to come home. He would die in the bathtub, by electrocution. An end-of-the-summer heat wave was in progress. It would not be unreasonable for an electric fan to be operated in the poorly ventilated bathroom with its one small window over the toilet, which furthermore could not be opened wide and still provide privacy. The fan might easily be dislodged from the rickety shelf high on the wall at one end of the tub and fall into the water below. On the other side of the wall was the master bedroom: a sudden blow against it, at the right spot, would do the job with dispatch and without incrimination.

"Ellie has got to be in the house," said E.G. His chest was covered with ape hair. Augie's was not nearly so hirsute, but, at least the last time she saw him, he had a full growth of hair on his head, whereas E.G. showed a long spear of skin where each temple joined the crown. Augie was taller, and actually better-looking in most particulars when taken superficially, but there was no authority in his weak chin and his brown eyes were soft as a dog's.

E.G. pointed a finger at her: it was his ringed pinky. "The timing has got to be just right."

"Okay, he's in the tub. So I listen till the water stops running. I go in the bedroom then and hit the wall at the place where we measured and —"

"No, first, before all of that, you went to the bathroom and moved the fan to the front of the shelf."

"That's right."

"And switched it on."

"Okay," Esther said, "I would have done those things. . . . So how long before I can go in and find the body?"

"Depends," E.G. said, "if he makes any noise or not. I still say we ought to try it with a stray dog or cat, see if they make any noise. My guess is someone doesn't when electrocuted. I think they're paralyzed immediately."

Esther had a special regard for animals: she could never have agreed to experimentation of that nature. "All right, so if he makes noise, I'll go in right away. But if he doesn't, as you think is probable, I'll wait awhile."

E.G. had lighted a cigarette from the pack on the table at his side of the bed and now blew a spurt of smoke at the ceiling. "I got to be someplace where I'll have a good alibi just in case somebody might think I have a connection with this. So I'll be at that bar where he always hung out. You know, the Idle Hour. When it's all over you first call me there and ask for a Mr. Reynolds. The bartender won't recognize your voice, will he?"

"I never set foot in that place," said Esther, taking the cigarette from him and drawing on it.

"Then you call the ambulance. I'll give them time to get there before I show up. Everything's got to happen in the right order. If you call the ambulance first, there might be some reason why you can't get through to me, maybe somebody's tying up the line." He pointed again. "When things go wrong it's because accidents haven't been allowed for."

E.G. had had no education beyond high school, but he was naturally shrewd. In acumen he made up for what had been lacking in his father, who had been so outwitted by Augie's dad. In the sons the situation had been reversed. While Augie was failing, his cousin had done very well. Precisely what he did remained mysterious to Esther, though she knew he had some real-estate interests among others. By contrast Augie on the slightest pretext would run off at the mouth on the subject of his own failure: he had softheartedly given too much credit; the wholesalers who distributed brand-name merchandise would deal only with the big chains, leaving the little guys like himself, in those days before Pearl Harbor, with made-in-Japan crap; the high-school kids whom he hired after school and on Saturdays were never of the caliber of those who set up pins in the bowling alley or caddied, he couldn't say why, though it was obvious to Esther that the reason was he did not pay enough. But she would rather have cut out her tongue than say a word about his store unless asked, and of course never would he have done that. She was only a woman.

"So you show up just about the time they're carrying out the body."

"Yeah," said E.G. "It'll still be early enough for a visit under ordinary circumstances. What would be more natural than me showing up to welcome my cousin home from the war? And lucky I got there then, what with this tragedy, a time when you need all the help you can get." He reached for the cigarette in her right hand, his left forearm across her breasts. Both of them were naked on this unusually warm night for September.

With one hand Esther placed the cigarette in E.G.'s lips and with the other she pushed his fingers down over her belly and into the damp thicket between her thighs. In a moment, still with the cigarette in his mouth, he had flopped her over as if she were weightless and entered her forcefully from behind.

* * *

Next morning, after Ellie finally took her wan self off to school on the two-mile walk she preferred, even in bad weather, to riding with her uncle, Esther repaired to the bathroom to run through the procedure by which her husband would be electrocuted. There was an immediate bit of bad news: the temperature had fallen significantly throughout the night, which could have been expected, but as yet the air gave no suggestion that it would soon rise again. They had counted on another scorcher that began early and by afternoon would make an oven of the bathroom and so make obligatory the use of the electric fan.

But E.G. had warned her against capricious pessimism. "It's a sound plan, as long as we don't lose our nerve."

Like Ellie, Orrie ignored Uncle Erle as much as possible. E.G.'s holiday gifts, always in the form of cash, were invariably transferred by the boy to his mother, without deductions. She preferred to believe her son was being more generous to her than negative to her lover. But no such interpretation was possible when he spurned E.G.'s offer to help with college costs.

"What the scholarship doesn't pay for, I'll get waiting tables." Orrie's tone was causelessly bitter, and his chin was at a defiant thrust that Esther found disrespectful.

"Hell, Orrie," E.G. said, elaborately opening his wallet, "I've got some portraits of Ben Franklin here, burning a hole in my pocket." He began to extract and wave hundred-dollar bills, one by one. A couple of those would cover dormitory room and board all year, which was more than could be said for the job Orrie had been given by the college employment agency. The scholarship took care of only tuition, with a modest allowance for books.

"Go ahead, Orrie," Esther urged. "Uncle Erle means it."

E.G. began a movement that might have ended in his

forcing the bills into the boy's shirt pocket, had not Orrie backed up violently and balled his fists.

Infuriated, Esther shouted, "Don't you act like that!"

Orrie gave her one contemptuous stare and left the room, and not long afterward, without saying a decent goodbye, the house itself. It was by accident that she glanced out the window at the right time to see his departure for college, the shabby old suitcase of his father's in hand and, worse, wearing the jacket to one of Augie's old suits, a salt-and-pepper tweed, so out of style it was belted in the back. Orrie had the pathetic belief he could get away with this as a sportcoat when he wore it, as now, with a pair of green corduroy slacks that scraped the ground at his heels, in an era when the prevailing style for young fellows was "pegged" pants, the cuffs well above the shoes.

She was about to call to E.G. to come and have a look but was suddenly restrained by a feeling of loyalty, affection, and an uncomfortable pity for her son, which she soon enough however converted into a more convenient hatred for the father who had selfishly run off to war to try to prove his manhood while leaving wife and children behind to fend for themselves.

That had been several weeks earlier. She had not expected soon to hear from Orrie, given the nature of his leaving, and she did not. But he had already written twice to Ellie. Esther intercepted both letters, read and destroyed them. This was done to retain her power in the house, but she was not without a more tender emotion. She genuinely loved Orrie and therefore could be wounded by him, and she knew he loved her in return, and not just, conventionally, as a mother. They had always had profound affinities. Even when Augie was at home, Orrie displayed a marked preference for her company and a notable lack of attraction for his father's pursuits. After the boy had rejected a series of invitations to rabbit hunts, big-league ballgames, and shows in which stunt drivers crashed through burning walls, Augie wondered about Orrie's virility.

"He ought to get out of the house more, have fun like a man."

"He's a child."

"He's started his teens," said Augie. "I hope he likes girls."

Esther was pleased to notice that Orrie never displayed such an interest in her presence, not even when the Burchnal kid, two backyards away, sunbathed her precociously developed body in shorts and halter. "That girl's really a mess," Esther had said to her son, who had given every evidence of not disagreeing.

To Augie she protested. "I don't want him coming home with a disease from one of the little chippies around this town. He's going to get somewhere in life!" Which of course was to make more of an attack on her husband than to express a hope for her son, though she was sincere enough as to the latter: she wanted Orrie not simply to succeed in the monetary sense, like his uncle Erle, but to have prestige of the kind that E.G. did not enjoy. She was aware that E.G. had no real friends but herself, whereas everybody professed to adore Augie — while taking their trade not to his store but to the nearest Woolworth's. People were such rotten hypocrites. E.G. was right in his conviction that fear was a more useful effect to evoke in others than affection. Nevertheless she did want Orrie to be a man of unimpeachable esteem, and that meant, in peacetime or war, anywhere in the world: doctor.

Orrie had winced and shaken his crewcut fifteen-year-old head when she first mentioned that. "God. Touching sores? All that blood? Getting coughed in the face?"

"They get used to those kind of things," said Esther. "It soon becomes just a job like any other. But you don't have to be a family doctor. There are all kinds of specialties, and they pay a lot more besides. Not all of them would be so bloody. What about the doctor who mainly takes X rays?"

Ellie intruded. "Or a nut-doctor. You know psy-uh —" Her mother told her to be quiet.

Orrie continued to grimace. "We're cutting up a frog now in biology, and I don't like it very much."

"Doctors are honored everywhere they go," Esther said. "Because everybody needs them. The President needs his. People will look up to you, Orrie. The greatest and strongest men in the world must obey their doctors."

"But Orrie wouldn't like making people take medicine," said Ellie. "He wants to be an artist."

Esther glared at her. "I thought I just told you to shut up." She resented Ellie's implication that he might be on closer terms with his sister than with the woman who gave him birth. She turned to Orrie. "I know he *thinks* that's what he wants to be at this point, but he hasn't yet had to face the world. Who's going to buy your art? The people around here don't even know what art is. They hang up calendars they get for free. So you go to the big city: who do you know there? And unless you know somebody, you're not going to get anywhere. They don't give strangers any breaks. The day of the free lunch is long gone."

"I don't know what I'll be in the future," said Orrie. "I just like to draw."

Ellie would not be stifled. "Mrs. Taviner hangs all his pictures up in the art room. You ought to see them."

With his usual modesty Orrie said, "She puts up a lot of stuff by other people, too. It's just a school in a little town."

"She gave him a book!" cried Ellie.

Orrie corrected her. "She *lent* it to me. It's full of oil paintings by Rembrandt and others. God, I've never yet even painted the right kind of water color."

"What's the right kind?"

"Not muddy! I'm hopeless." He ducked his head.

"No, you're *not!*" cried Ellie.

But with justifiable self-righteousness, Esther said, "There you are. You're probably not cut out to make art more than just a hobby. If you become a doctor you'll be able to buy all the art your heart desires."

He was irritated. "Buy? That's not the point. I like to make things of my own."

"As a doctor, you'll make people well," said she. "That's the greatest kind of making there is."

Orrie not only loved his mother. He honored her judgment. When the time came for him to go to college, though the actual departure was unpleasant, she had the comforting knowledge that he intended to take the premedical program of studies. The matter with which she had had no success at all, however, was in persuading him to be more friendly with E.G., and that was unfortunate, insofar as Orrie's conception, unlike that of either of the girls, happened during one of those periods when Erle was in town. He was gone again before Esther knew she was pregnant and did not return until Orrie was half grown, at which time E.G. first entertained the suspicion, since become a conviction, that he was the boy's father.

3

The returning hero was touched to see a homemade banner draped across the top rank of bottles: WELCOME HOME, AUGIE. It seemed to be part of a bedsheet, lettered probably with a shoe-polish dauber cap.

Behind the bar as he was, facing the door, Herm naturally saw Augie before the others did, and without telling them why, suddenly demanded silence.

He lifted the glass of ice water he always kept under the bar and said, "Here's to your friend and mine . . ." Because he was staring over their heads, by the time he had pronounced Augie's name they had all spun around on their stools.

Rickie Wicks stepped down and was first to shake Augie's hand though he had not been that close a friend before the war, whereas Joe Becker, who of all those present had known Augie best, was the last of the men to greet him and was least demonstrative though not for lack of regard.

Augie, still holding his suitcase, nodded at the ladies. "Hi, Molly. Hi, Gladys."

"You look fine," said Gladys. "Just fine, with the ribbons and all."

Molly wore a little smile that just barely raised the corners of her mouth. "You leave any live Germans behind to clean up the mess? Or did you wipe 'em all out?"

It was dispiriting to Augie to find her with the same sarcastic manner she had displayed prewar. Not much was left of Molly's looks now, but when they had been in high school together, she was, if not exactly pretty, attractive, to a painfully shy kid like himself. At least her skin had been clear. They became pals, walked home together, and routinely consulted each other on homework. His parents called her his "girl," and he himself began to think of her that way too, but when he finally got the nerve to take her hand in that phase of their homeward route when they cut through a little stand of trees where no one would see, she drew hers away as if it had been burned, made it into a fist, and shook it at him. He got the bizarre feeling that she believed him a pervert, as if she had been a boy with whom he tried to hold hands. From then on his feeling for her changed. In return she became wry. Not all these years had changed her.

Herm had drawn him a beer. "We'll go in back for lunch after a while. It's on the house." He handed the mug over, then said, fingers twitching, "Let's have that valise."

Augie gave him the suitcase, which Herm stowed behind the bar.

"How's that stack up with German brew?" asked Rickie Wicks.

"A lot better," Augie said, having taken a swig. "Can't beat *anything* American. You learn that right away wherever you go." He spotted his postcards fastened with yellowing

Scotch tape to the lower right corner of the back-of-bar mirror, and pointed. "Hey, you kept them."

"Proud of you, Augie boy." Herm leaned into the bartop. "Now tell us about them ribbons."

When nearsighted Bob Terwillen began to examine them at close range, Augie identified the most important.

Al Hagman called down to Joe Becker at the far end of the group, asking him whether he had ever seen a Silver Star. Joe said he had not, but stayed where he was.

"Must have been darn rough."

"Let's put it this way, Al. I didn't do any more than any of you would have done in my place." There were good-natured jeers of disbelief.

Molly shrieked, "Since when are you gettin' so modest?"

Terwillen hoisted his glass. "Here's to you, Aug. God bless you. Just glad you got home without leaving any part of yourself on a foreign field."

Later they all except the women, who professed to have duties at home (Glad had to feed her cat), went into the back room where meals were served and ate lunch, Augie's being a thick T-bone steak smothered in onions and paid for by the others (each chipping in a quarter; on the way home later on, Hagman reflected that Herm had made money on *that* deal). The rest of them ordered the blue plate: today, hash topped with a fried egg. The high point of this phase of the celebration was when Herm's wife, Gwen, who was the chef, brought out a layer cake that Rickie Wicks had got from the local bakery not an hour earlier, with just time enough for the baker to do a rush decoration job: stock rosebuds of frosting, much the same as used for weddings and birthdays, around the rim of the top, but framing "Welcome Back, Augie," handwritten in edible red script, beneath which was planted a miniature paper replica of the American flag.

Nobody asked Augie for particulars of his combat experiences, though he had been prepared to give such from what he had learned frequenting a bar near a big Army hospital down South where wounded veterans returned from foreign action to recuperate. He had bought the officer's uniform and captain's bars and ribbons from the legitimate owner thereof who had lost heavily at craps and poker. Any genuine holder of a decoration could obtain a replacement from the War Department if the original was lost or stolen, so nobody had been deprived.

At the time the United States got into the war, Augie's business had failed and his wife was having an affair with his cousin. He was in no position to make trouble when it was only by means of the same relative that he avoided bankruptcy. Only some desperate measure could save him. Harold Banks's son Jerry, often on the wrong side of the law, had escaped prosecution for a series of petty thefts from auto-parts stores by agreeing to join the paratroops, and Sam Potter had a boy who enlisted in the Navy to evade final exams as a high-school senior. The war could be used for your own ends if you were young enough, but Augie was no kid. It had taken him a while to realize that the mere appearance of joining the Army might serve as well as the fact. All he really had to do to establish the premise was to leave home. Esther was unlikely to send the police to fetch him back, involved as she was with Erle, and certainly not if Augie sent her regular amounts of money in the guise of G.I. family allotments. That he might be able to get away with the imposture made the idea at first the more frightening. He had not previously been the least daring in any area of life. He had married Esther because she was the only girl who would go to bed with him. He had inherited the store on the death of his father.

But what of the children? He was closest to golden-haired Gena, who was just at the threshold of womanhood. He had little in common with Orrie, who had always been more Esther's son than his own. It was possible that Orrie would never be one hundred percent masculine: he seemed averse to certain male pursuits by nature, for example, hunting and football. When tackled gently by his father, a very young Orrie burst into tears as his little body hit the grass. It could not have hurt; the boy took worse spills all day long. Later on, when old enough to go out for high-school teams, Orrie was saved by his size, having not then grown beyond five-four and a hundred ten pounds. As for hunting, an unfortunate thing happened the first and only time his father had taken him for pheasant. Augie brought down a bird with a poor shot that only disabled a wing. The creature dragged itself into the undergrowth and when discovered, with heaving body and the anticipation of death in its glittering eye, was admittedly not a happy sight for a normal hunter, let alone a squeamish youngster. But much of manhood consisted of dealing with responsibilities irrespective of prevailing conditions. Bagging game was to bring meat to the table. To put a wounded thing out of its misery was a human obligation. Augie opened his clasp knife and, working as quickly and mercifully as he could, cut off the pheasant's head. Wiping the knife on the ground and his hands on the legs of the old pants he wore when hunting, he heard Orrie running away through the field.

Later on, in the car, Augie said, "If you think hunting's wrong, then you oughtn't eat meat at all. Because this is the kindest way any animal can be put to death. You know how they kill and butcher cattle?" But like so many of the moralistic (most of whom were women), Orrie wanted to indulge himself in easy emotion and not to face the issue.

Not long after Augie went presumably to war, Gena had herself run away from home and had never been heard from since. Esther wrote him a vicious letter in which *he* got all the blame. As if Gena had needed another example than her mother to go wrong! Augie as it happened did not take such a bleak view. He thought it likely that the girl had gone to Hollywood, to try to become one of the blonde stars like those whose movie-mag photos she clipped out and pasted on the wall over her bed. Gena was pretty enough for the screen, but you needed more than beauty to succeed there, as you needed more than brains to make a go of business, which Augie had discovered the hard way. You needed luck. He had never had any — until he began to make his own.

He had got off the bus in a Southern city that offered a choice of defense-industry plants, all of which were eager to hire workers, no experience asked, and pay them what on the heels of the Depression were remarkably generous wages: on an aircraft-engine assembly line, with overtime, he was soon making in excess of a hundred dollars a week, more than twice what only yesterday would have been a nice income. His room, in a house of such, was overpriced by a rent-gouging landlord of the kind that was created by wartime, costing half a week's pay per month, and he had to eat most of his meals out, except for canned soup heated on a hotplate that was illicit on those premises, running his expenses even higher, for you could not fill yourself up at supper for much under six bits. But he spent little on anything else except nightly beers, and was able not only to send Esther a monthly "allotment" that was equivalent to the one the government would have paid, but also put something aside in the form of war bonds, for which an automatic deduction was made from his paycheck.

After three and a half years, he was prosperous relative to what he had been hitherto, and he had found a good woman as well, though she was in years but a girl, having left school as soon as she was legally able to do so, to work in the same plant as his, wearing women's powder-blue overalls and hair tied up in a Rosie-the-Riveter kerchief. Augie had met her in the company lunchroom when an apple she dropped rolled right up to his heavy work shoes.

Though her hair and blue eyes were reminiscent of Gena's, in character Cassie could not have been more sensibly down-to-earth. She too had accumulated savings and rapidly was overtaking him though having started work later than he and not receiving wages as high. But her expenses were almost nil, her parents refusing to accept more for room and board than twenty dollars a month and taking that only because Cassie threatened to move out if they did not. Like them a devout churchgoer, she neither drank nor smoked and was not supposed to dance but was sometimes prevailed upon to do so by Augie, not someplace in public where they might be seen, but in her own home, to radio music, when her parents were out. Even so, it bothered her conscience to be doing a sinful thing in their own domicile, behind their backs, and it took all the feeling she had for Augie to gratify him in this way, which aside from some closed-mouth kissing was the extent of their physical association. In the earliest phase of their friendship he once tried to touch her clothed breasts but had been so decisively rebuffed that he never even attempted anything below her waist.

Here he was, more than forty, father of three, married to a whore, in love with a nineteen-year-old virgin with whom he had no fleshly connection. He sometimes thought about the possible absurdity of the situation but never questioned the rightness of it for his peculiar wants. Cassie was the perfect antidote to Esther. And beneath that truth was the more plangent reference to Gena. He could only pray that his daughter had not, wherever she was, come to grief, that she had a lover as kind and gentle and fatherly as Cassie's.

With great trepidation, he had, in the old-fashioned way that seemed appropriate, asked Cassie's father for her hand before applying to the girl herself, and Mr. Pryor, a truck mechanic who had not gone to high school, assented eagerly, seeing Augie as a sound man and a step upward in culture, and asked no uncomfortable questions. When Augie did propose to Cassie, he was already furnished with a ring as well as a plan for their future together: using their combined nest eggs they would take a mortgage on a little house in the same neighborhood in which she had lived all her life, or as near as possible. Two bedrooms would do, one for them and the other as a nursery for the children. For his part, he would give up the drinking of any liquid containing alcohol, but (with a squeeze of the hand and a wink) he probably would like a slow waltz with his wife now and again, with the shades lowered if necessary.

"Why," Cassie said in the accent that never failed to make him melt, "thin everbody'd *know* we were up to no good." But her eyes were moist, and her betrothal kiss was the sweetest he had ever had.

Not once did either she or, in his presence anyway, her parents refer to the marked difference in ages, though Augie himself was wont to mention it frequently, if only to be reassured, for he could count on Cassie's absolute moral support. Never before had he known a woman he could *rely on*. He had had to live four decades to apprehend the basic truth that a man could not go it alone. Neither could he survive if he were in an alliance with a bitter enemy — as only now could he admit Esther had been for most of their marriage, and had he not finally proved man enough to leave, he would still be helplessly serving as the object of her scorn.

Whenever he thought about that matter he sent home another bogus account of an exploit of his in combat, taken either from soldiers he met in a bar where he still drank an occasional beer when Cassie was otherwise occupied, or from a current movie, though he was careful not to plagiarize the latter too literally, should Esther have seen the same picture, especially if it starred one of her favorite actors in a characteristic role: the cocky near-rascal who begins, owing to his exaggerated self-regard, without the sympathy of much of the audience but claims more and more of it as the film proceeds and then finally conquers all resistance by a demonstration of his readiness to lay his life on the line for the very comrades he had earlier upstaged.

The obvious problem was how to explain the domestic postmark and conventional three-cent stamp, on letters that were ostensibly mailed from foreign battlefields. At first this had appeared insuperable. To maintain such an imposture could simply not be done. But in his new life it had become routine for new possibilities to manifest themselves almost by magic. The letters to Esther need not be frequent, and the same was true of the messages, often on postcards, that he sent the gang at the Idle Hour. During the months of silence, then, he could be at the front, where the action was too heavy to permit even the scribbling on a V-mail form. In the intervals between these combat tours, he and his elite unit were flown back Stateside for a recharge of batteries. Anybody could understand that: thus his U.S. address.

And in fact, Esther had had no questions, dropping him a line only when the allotment was a few days late. He had phoned her but twice since he left: first, not long after leaving, and having been blamed so hatefully for Gena's disappearance on that occasion, he never called again until, four years later, he was about to return to say goodbye forever.

As to the gang at the bar, they were not on the alert to catch out a friend in a major lie, though any of them might be skeptical of something petty, like the length of a fish that broke the line and swam away before it could be netted, or the alleged sex appeal of one of the bachelors.

As far as Cassie was aware, Augie had never been married. Much of her value to him was in such an innocent approach to life, some of which was due to youth and lack of experience, but not all, not even most. He believed that she would be ignorant of certain things her life long, owing to a natural purity of heart, an inability to suspect the motives of another human being. For example, the supposedly blind man, with his cup of pencils, they encountered on an afternoon in the city: when Augie pointed out that after such people died, bankbooks were often found in their effects, listing sizable assets, Cassie could not begin to understand the implications thereof. How then would it have been possible to put his own history into terms that would have been intelligible to her?

Fortunately, she displayed little curiosity about how he had lived before they met. No doubt this was because she could not picture him in another existence, for she was utterly deficient in imagination of the common sort — another difference between her and Gena: Cassie had no dreams of Hollywood or any other place or milieu than that in which she had lived and expected to live until her death, at which time she would be buried near all the relatives who had preceded her. But if in this, her great strength, she was clearsighted, levelheaded, and stanch, she was also superstitious in the extreme, and not only as to all routine phenomena shared with the herd, the number 13, black cats, cracks in the sidewalk, open umbrellas indoors, but also some things peculiar to herself, products of the vivid dreams she experienced several times per month, not of the common sort, not mere wish-fulfillment like so many of Augie's (in which he invariably received large amounts of unearned money), nor the common nightmares he suffered once or twice a year, but rather visions of events to come in real life. Perhaps these, in the economy of existence, compensated for her lack of fancy when awake. In any event, they were not to be taken seriously as prefigurings of the future, for they always proved either at odds with what finally occurred or too vague for particular application. In a global war disasters were common enough. That Cassie claimed success in predicting a kamikaze attack on a U.S. battleship in the Philippine Sea, half a world away, because three days before, she had dreamed of fire falling from the sky, was the sort of idiosyncrasy in which she could be indulged if you loved her, as did her parents, who had heard its like ever since she entered adolescence and had survived several of her predictions of domestic doom by simply ignoring them, and of course Augie, who had taken pleasure as a boy in defying superstition, deriding Erle for cowering at home on Fridays the 13th and always walking under a ladder when he found one.

If Cassie saw in a dream that an outdoor picnic would

come to grief by way of flood (though there was no body of water near their place of choice), Augie was pleased to eat the chicken leg in a stifling kitchen, just as he washed it down with oversweetened ice tea rather than the cold beer he preferred. You made such sacrifices when you loved somebody. Unless the auguries were favorable you passed up ballgames, evenings of bowling, afternoon walks, and other such minor pleasures, because you consistently enjoyed the major rewards of love, which concerned not the senses but rather the soul.

There was nothing else about Cassie that could be called a foible. Her fidelity went without saying. She had had little enough to do with the opposite sex even before Augie's day. Now, with no urging from him (though he was certainly not offended), she interpreted the state of engagement as being one in which she looked no other male, except her father, straight in the eye, and conversed with none unless it concerned work at the plant. Aside from the board paid to her folks, she saved all her money for the marriage to come. She embraced Augie's opinions, when he had such, and when he had none, as in the area of religion, she continued to practice her own faith without demanding that he join her. Even after meeting him, her best idea for Saturday recreation remained baking several loaves of raisin bread. An accomplished seamstress, she made much of the clothing she wore.

Cassie readily assented to her fiancé's schedule for the wedding, which of course would be in her church, she in white, but not take place till the war was over. In her naïve way she accepted the patriotic argument — Augie couldn't take her off the assembly line to make babies instead until the peace had been won — but his private motive was a matter of personal responsibility and honor. A living hero did not come home before the enemy had been defeated. He would meanwhile continue to send Esther the monthly payment. But as soon as the war ended, he would return to his wife only to see her face when he said goodbye forever. Naturally he would miss the children, but his feeling for them must ever, unfortunately, be conditioned by his memory of their mother and her unceasing efforts to unman him. All his hopes now were with the brand-new family he would create with Cassie.

With the second atomic bomb the conflict was over at last, and here he was, back at the Idle Hour, where he could smile at Rickie Wicks's remarking it was (aside from a gray hair or two) as if he never left, for on the contrary it was as different as anything could be: he had left a failure, returned in triumph. Already he no longer felt uncomfortable in the decorated uniform into which he had changed in a toilet booth at the bus depot. He had not worn it during the trip lest other soldiers try to strike up conversations, which might have proved embarrassing, though the details at his command were sufficient to bluff civilians: e.g., the Purple Heart was for a wound he got from 88-shrapnel, couldn't show it because it had come too damned close to changing his voice; won the Silver Star at the Bulge, Xmastime there in the snowbound Ardennes, encircled by Krauts. In his cards to the Idle Hour he had claimed a part in the liberation of Paris and then, a year later, also in the occupation of Berlin, for who of the old gang was in a position to doubt him?

Augie was drunk by the time they all went into the back room for lunch, and throughout the meal he continued to drink, not beers after the first one but, given the occasion and that his tab was on the house, Canadian Club, which went down like sweet cream, all to the good because the steak was quite tough and the onions glistened with grease. He had been spoiled by Sunday dinners prepared by Cassie's mother, assisted in every phase by his intended.

The welcome-home cake was awfully nice as a gesture but it was dry and the icing tasted as though the butter had been skimped on. Also, after a couple of hours of these old pals, swell guys though they were, Augie began to wonder how, before the war, he could have endured their company. . . . The answer of course was Esther. He had had to go somewhere, have some companionship, home being unbearable after the kids went to bed and the evening stretched bleakly before him. But by now, with the best will in the world, he could find little in common with these fellows. The old times had not been good ones for him, unless you went back far enough, to before his marriage, but to reminisce of a happy boy- and young-manhood was depressing in the extreme, for any such memories proceeded inevitably towards what had followed.

It would have helped had he been able to reveal the new state of affairs in his life — the real one as opposed to the lies about the war — but that could not be done without possibly compromising his situation. Brazen adultress that she was, Esther was capable of making trouble if she knew of the existence of Cassie and even more if she was aware of the war bonds he had accumulated in four years at the plant. The job would probably soon be at an end. He would have to look for work elsewhere, and the pickings might be slim as the adjustment to peacetime was being established.

All Esther had to be told was that he wanted a divorce, on any grounds that suited her, even if he was legally to take the blame. She could keep their joint possessions, furniture and the like. The house she and the children occupied was rented from his cousin Erle. Augie had lost the previous place when he couldn't meet the mortgage payments and the bank foreclosed.

The guys at the homecoming lunch knew all these unhappy facts, but being real friends, never had made the slightest allusion to any even in the prewar time, before he had redeemed himself as a combat hero. Suddenly he felt guilty about being bored in their company. They were the brothers he never had. The alternative was Erle, always a rat and a sneak as far back as could be remembered.

"Hey, this has been terrific," Augie said now, pushing his chair away from the long table that had been formed by moving several small ones together. "But what time's it getting to be?"

"Have a cigar," said Bob Terwillen, sliding the cellophane-wrapped green cylinder past Rickie Wicks, but it was halted by moisture on the tabletop.

When the cigar had been pushed the rest of the way to him, Augie stuck it in one of the upper pockets of the officer's jacket, unbuttoning the brass button to do so. He had given up cigarettes for Cassie's sake and had never used cigars, but did not want to hurt a friend's feelings.

Of those assembled, Joe Becker was the one he had known longest, ever since they were little kids and the Beckers lived nearby. He and Joe built a lean-to in the woods and slept under it once in a while on summer nights, but never succeeded in weaving the leaves tightly enough to shed water in a heavy rain though it would withstand a mild sprinkle. At home Joe had bored a little gimlet hole through the back wall of his closet, through which you could peep into the bathroom, and if the closet door there was partially

34

open (this had to be arranged beforehand by hanging a heavy robe on the inside hook, so that the door would not close properly), you could spy on someone sitting on the toilet. By that means, Augie had seen, on Joe's older sister, the first female genital hair of his life. Joe would watch his own sisters through the hole: this seemed weird to Augie, but then *he* had no sisters.

Now, back here, far from Cassie and her parents, he felt absolutely alone. It was ironic that the welcome-home lunch had evoked this feeling. His morale might well have been higher had his return been ignored and he been permitted to maintain the stern resolve with which he had set out on the mission. To face up to Esther after all this approbation by his old pals would be harder than ever. Never had he drunk this much in the middle of the day. He was both so exhausted he could hardly keep his eyes open and jumping with nerves to the degree that he knew he could not go to sleep if given the chance.

Joe Becker waited behind him in the little men's room as he used the lone urinal. There was no room for anyone else.

"Aug, you okay?"

"I'm fine." He expected nothing to happen when he pushed the lever but was surprised to see a vigorous gush of water: they had finally got that fixed.

"If you come in here with your valise, then you ain't been home yet." Becker had fallen into the ungrammatical speech of their boyhood, when they believed he-men spurned school-teacher niceties of diction.

Augie was moved by the gesture of intimacy. "That's right." Having worked the flusher once more, he turned around. "I'm heading there now. . . . How's everything at your house? How's Pauline?"

"Good, great," said Becker. "Look, Aug, I really hate to get into anything like this, which might not be any of my business, but hell's bells, you and me go back such a long way . . ."

Having closed his fly, Augie fastened the lowest button on the skirt of the tunic and tightened his belt. In this attire he felt he really could have been as good an officer as any man alive. "I got nothin' to learn about Esther and Erle, if that's what you mean. I'm going up there and call it quits for good."

Becker stared into his face for a moment and then clapped him on the upper arm. "Good for you, pal. I won't ever mention the subject again. But listen, whyn't you go over to my place for a little nap first? I'll give you the key. I got to go back to work, and Pauline's at the hospital, so you won't be bothered."

"I'm all right, Joey. I just want to get it over with. Then I'll catch the next bus out and sleep on the ride back."

Becker was taking his own pee now and spoke towards the wall. "Gonna make a life of it down South?" He was not as surprised as he should have been. "Like that part of the world, do you?"

"I've got a fine woman there," said Augie. "Maybe when the dust settles and we're married and all, we'll visit back here sometime." This would never happen, and Becker knew it.

"I'm real happy for you," said Joe. "You need anything, any time, you count on me." He looked Augie up and down. "You make a fine-looking soldier. Remember when we were too young to go to the First World War and fight Heinies in the trenches and all? So you wait twenty years and go then, and you weren't exactly a kid any more. Damn it, Augie, I sure take my hat off to you."

Augie realized that Becker too was feeling the effects of the alcohol. "You really going back to work now? What'll the boss say?"

Becker smiled. Augie could remember how he lost that tooth. "*I'm* the boss now. Skillman sold out to me a couple years back."

Augie was human enough to feel envy here, despite the old affection for Joe just renewed. Becker was altogether self-made. He obviously had a knack for business.

"You know what that means," Becker went on. "I work twice as hard as anybody on the payroll."

Augie hated the memory of when he had last been an employer. That was the trouble with old friends: with the best will in the world, they could not help making unpleasant references. Rinsing his hands in the washbowl, he looked at a mirror image of his face for the first time since the day before. He badly needed a shave. "Why didn't you tell me?" he asked Becker. "I look like a gangster, for God's sake." Most of this growth of beard seemed to have occurred only in recent hours. He had not felt that much when he splashed water on his face at the seven-thirty breakfast stop made by the bus.

Becker used the washstand. "It ain't that bad, light-complected like you are."

Augie also itched at his back. "I could use a shower," said he. "I been in these same clothes for a day and a half now." His civilian clothing was in the suitcase. The uniform could be dispensed with, once everybody had seen it.

Becker again offered the facilities at his house, but again Augie declined with thanks.

"That's the last thing I'll ask of her," he told his old friend. "A bath. I guess I've got that much coming."

"Let me run you up there," said Becker.

Augie had got a lift out from the city bus terminal with a patriotic man who liked to help G.I.s. He intended to hire the local taxi for what remained of his journey, only another half a mile. Becker, who had done so well in life, probably had a car Augie could not have afforded. Therefore he declined the ride too.

Back in the bar, he shook hands all around without revealing to anyone else that this would be his final appearance on the premises. Joe Becker could provide that information at his convenience.

As Herm returned the valise, Augie told him, indicating the painted sheet across the mirror, that he could take the sign down now.

"Naw," said Herm, grinning with the discolored tooth that was next to another of gold. "It looks nice, jazzes up the old place. I'll leave it for a while and then save it for you when I take it down."

"I want you to know how much I appreciated this party," said Augie, leaning over to shake hands.

All the fellows were standing and, like him, ready to depart. Most of them worked. Some of those not on a night shift might drop back in the evening, and Molly and Gladys might return, though maybe not, for even nursing one drink for hours cost something.

Had Augie not gone off to war he would undoubtedly have been of the common run of this group, like Rickie Wicks, and not have joined Becker in success. By now the bar and the occasion had become desolating.

Toting the suitcase, he left the Idle Hour and walked towards the taxi office down in the next block, staring into the windows he passed, ready to wave at those on the other side, should they recognize him in the uniform he would soon take off, after one of the shortest military careers a man could have had.

But no one he could identify seemed to be looking back, not even Sal the barber, still working his scissors though he had already been old when Augie, a high-school freshman, had got his first crewcut. Perhaps advanced age was the reason why Sal though returning his stare did not recognize him now. Had the barber done so, Augie would have entered the shop and got a shave there and not arrived at his old home with a face full of stubble. All his life he had managed to do that which would only increase the contempt that had ever been the principal emotion felt for him by the woman he had married. But then there was some question as to what he could have done that would not have had the same effect. After all, so far as she knew, he was a war hero.

But to Esther, opening the screen door, it was as if he had never gone away: he could see that the first time he had met her eyes in four years. To pursue her respect had been absolutely futile. Immediately he was conscious of the fraudulence of the uniform and ribbons, as he had not been when they were being admired at the bar, where they were no less false, where in fact the display was more immoral, for some of those fellows had relatives and friends who had been genuine casualties.

"Sorry," said he to his wife, who had come only after prolonged ringing of the doorbell; he had not felt it right that he enter the premises without permission. "I didn't get a chance to shave." She remained silent and glanced at the suitcase. "Don't worry," he said quickly. "I'm not staying."

Esther moved back from the doorway, and he stepped over the threshold into the front hall. He followed her to a different living room from that he remembered, but whether the furniture was new or had merely been rearranged, he could not have said. Esther however looked like exactly the same woman of four years earlier. He even recognized the housecoat, which had apparently remained in mint condition, as if it had been put away when he left and not worn again until this moment.

Wouldn't she ever speak? He was too proud to ask. "Look, Esther." He stood in the middle of the room, not even lowering the suitcase. "I'm not here to make any trouble. I'll see the kids and leave. Your lawyer can handle the rest of it. Everything's yours. I'm sorry there isn't more."

Her expression went from disdain through amazement into something that had he not known her he might have called fear. "Lawyer?"

"I've given this a lot of thought. It wouldn't make much sense after all we've been through to go back as before, would it?"

She stared at him. "You're talking about a divorce?"

At last he began to feel more in control, at least of himself. What was so remarkable in the thought of divorce, when for so many years she had despised her husband and, since long before he went away, had been fucking his cousin? He put the valise down.

"Come on, you're not all of a sudden going to pretend you want me back?" He smiled; there was no reason why he should not be friendly. "Let's start off with a clean slate."

She had continued to stare at him. "You're drunk."

"No. No, I am not."

"You're drunk," she insisted, but now, amazing him, grinned. This was an expression at odds with her raven-black hair and strong mouth. She was handsome when her face was in repose and could even appear maternal if smiling at Orrie, but her grin, rarely seen, looked almost foolish without connoting a hint of good will.

He changed the subject, looking at his watch, and asked, "Ellie's due home soon —?" He touched his whiskers. "Maybe I have time to spruce up a little?"

"Take it easy," Esther said, grinning. It occurred to him that *she* might be drunk. "Have a seat."

He sat down at one end of the sofa, which seemed to have a new cover. "The boys at the Idle Hour threw me a little welcome-home party, including lunch."

"I *knew* you were drunk," Esther said. "Remember I know you, even though you've been gone all this while, and I know what liquor does to you." Her grin was now a kind of simper.

"I'm nowhere near drunk," said Augie. "I'm aware of what I'm saying. You get a lawyer and make it all my fault, desertion or whatever. I won't contest it. Furthermore, I'll pay for *your* lawyer. Is that fair enough?"

Esther moved slowly to the overstuffed chair that faced his end of the couch and sank into it. She crossed her legs. The skirt of the housecoat fell away, embarrassing him.

She asked, "How about more hair of the dog? There's a bottle in the kitchen."

"No, thanks." She was not taking him seriously. Perhaps he should have expected that, instead of so easily assuming that his new self would be immediately apparent to those who had counted on abusing the old one forever. "When does Ellie get home from school?"

"Lots of time yet," said Esther.

"I can't get over Orrie being old enough for college." He had learned that only on the occasion of the recent telephone call. He lacked the courage to mention the missing Gena.

Esther had uncrossed her legs and left her knees just far enough apart so that someone directly opposite her could hardly avoid noticing. Augie was revolted by the display. As yet he had had nothing from his fiancée but lukewarm kisses. Cassie was not a sensual young woman. Now and again throughout the years he had had his genital needs met by whores, but fear of disease and an utter lack of the personal in such connections made that almost as unsatisfying as masturbation. One thing he could say of Esther: even after he was aware of her flagrant infidelity, he had almost never been impotent with her. And she had never given him reason to believe that her disdain for him in his other husbandly functions extended to his performance in bed. Perhaps she was insatiable, and if so he did not really condemn her though it might be perverse of him. He could not have revealed this truth to anybody, including his conscious self, but was well aware of it in that part of the soul that is never taken aback by any erotic phenomenon.

"So," she said, smirking. "Nobody gets a divorce just to be alone. You bring back some captured German girl?"

At last he found the nerve to do what he should have done long since and stated a few details about Cassie.

"She's just a kid," said Esther. "You're robbing the cradle." Her lips were twitching, but he was not sure what that could mean.

"She's very religious," Augie said quickly, stiffly, in an effort to head off any assumption that his want was for young flesh.

"I'm sure," said Esther. "So you want to marry her?"

It was as awkward as he had anticipated to talk of the subject with this woman to whom he had been legally married for going on twenty years.

"Yes, I do."

42

"You haven't got her pregnant?"

"I've never been to bed with her. Neither has anybody else."

"Oh, for God's sake." Esther threw her head back and guffawed.

Augie was furious, but mostly with himself. He had given Esther every advantage over him. It was as if he had never gone to war, proved himself as a man, come home a hero! That he had not actually done these things was beside the point. It was terrible to realize that his wife would have been quite as disdainful of him had he been a genuine combat veteran.

"Let's be polite. I'm not going to say anything against Erle."

She bridled. "He saved your skin."

"Yes, and I happen to know he didn't lose any money when he took the store off my hands and terminated it."

"What's that supposed to mean?"

"That he managed to find a good many more assets than liabilities."

She had returned to her habitual sneer. "What do you think has been keeping us going these four years around here? Those shitty little checks you send?"

Augie was now very sorry that he had come back. He could have done what was required by mail, through a lawyer, and passed up the chance to strut at the Idle Hour. Cassie knew nothing of his existing wife and family, but in her superstitious way she had worried about his trip North, had seen in a characteristic dream that he would come to some grief there and never return to her. He loved her for such apprehensions: never had his existence been so valuable to another human being.

He stood up. "This was a mistake. I should have stayed away."

She rose and came to him. In high-heeled mules she seemed taller than he: he had forgotten that, unless she had grown in four years. She was somewhat fleshier but not unattractively so. She had been the most voluptuously built teenager in town: a pound more, breasts an inch larger, she would have gone over the line, he had then believed. But in fact she did put on weight once they were married; yet owing to the concomitant increase in height, had gone from being the kind of girl who at thirteen was ample enough to evoke the whistles and catcalls of passing male youth (and the leers of their elders) to a statuesque woman.

"Don't go away mad," Esther said now, her voice falling off on the last word, her eyelids lowering as if of their own heaviness. She was almost touching him with her luxurious body, and had to step back two inches to make room in which to raise her hand and run an index finger, with a nail conspicuously too long and colored maroon, across his ribbons.

"So you really were good as a soldier." She raised her dark eyes. "Did you kill a lot of them?"

He could remember the answer to a similar question he himself had put when buying the uniform from Captain Delaney, the debt-ridden officer who had earned the ribbons: "It's hard to tell, at the usual range." The captain had gone on to explain that, at least in the sectors in which he had seen action, hand-to-hand fighting was much rarer than you would think from motion pictures. But Augie suspected that Esther would not be impressed by the modest truth.

"It's not something I like to talk about. It's not nice and neat, like the movies."

"Nothing is," said Esther, looking intently at him.

44

At this moment he lost everything he had gained in four years, and of course she saw that immediately.

"Go take a quick bath," she said, and made a gesture as if pushing him slightly though not making actual contact. "I'll wait for you in our bedroom. We've got lots of time. She stays late at school today."

Augie found the bathroom to be what it had always been, small and without cross ventilation. And without a shower, which is what he really wanted, being in no mood to lie back and soak, then scrub . . .

Esther burst in without warning. "You'll need this. It's a warm day." She turned on the electric fan on the shelf above the end of the tub; its wire went to the female plug that had replaced the bulb in the old-fashioned wall sconce that was supposed to supply light to the alcove.

He was embarrassed though having as yet removed nothing but the officer's tunic, which he had hung on the corner of the linen-closet door.

She quickly left, but her intrusion had broken his rhythm. He now could not evade a horrified reflection on what he was doing. He was no longer as drunk in the mind as he had been only a few instants before, but, absurdly, his physical coordination now began to fail. He almost fell into the tub as, trying to balance one leg at a time, he struggled with his trousers. Apparently no one noticed that the uniform was not an exact fit. The jacket was a size larger than his, and the pants, of the same heavy, beautiful twill, though buff as opposed to the dark olive of the tunic, were slightly too long, touching the ground at the heel of the plain brown shoes he had had to buy separately, Captain Delaney not having had boots to spare.

He would bathe and shave and change into the civilian

clothes from the suitcase he had brought along to the bathroom. But it was clear that he must leave immediately thereafter, even if it meant not having seen Ellie. He could not conspire with Esther in his further unmanning. He began to run water into the tub.

4

Outside the bathroom door Esther was listening to the water filling the tub in which her husband was to be electrocuted, when who should appear at the top of stairs, frightening her for an instant, but E.G. Luckily the same water noise that had deafened her to his coming would have obscured the event from Augie.

She rushed to him, pressed his elbow, whispered and pointed, and led him downstairs and back to the kitchen, where, though now distant from their intended prey, she continued to speak in an urgent undertone.

"How did I know when he'd get here?"

E.G. was snarling. "Why'd you let him start the bath already? I told you to wait till Ellie got home!"

"He was ready to *leave*. He wants a divorce! He's got a girl he wants to *marry*."

This information did not have the visible effect she

anticipated. E.G. simply stared at his watch. "Here I am: my alibi is gone now."

In the kitchen they were directly under the bathroom, and the running water was more audible there than in the upstairs hallway. That the tub took a while to fill, what with the constricted flow through the corroded old pipes and faucets, was no longer to be deplored. Esther hated this house. Augie had lost the home she loved: for that alone he deserved punishment. But whether she could impose it upon him was another matter.

She touched E.G.'s wrist. "I don't think I can do it. I thought I could when it was only planning, but I can't."

"Sure you can. It's only hitting the wall. There's no blood, no mess. He won't even get hurt. We've been all over that."

"I can't do it."

He slapped her face so violently that she felt the single blow as a series, each more savage than the last. For a moment of horror she assumed he would go on striking her till she was dead.

But in fact the single blow had not been repeated: she was aware of that truth all the while she rushed towards doom in fantasy. It gave her a perverse satisfaction to believe that, so ready to murder someone of his own blood, E.G. was capable of equivalent treachery towards her, to whom he lacked any but an emotional connection.

However, his eyes were suddenly warm again, and he even wore a slight smile. "Settle down. You can do it."

And miraculously she knew she could. She had perfect license to focus her resentment, from whichever source, on Augie, who could conveniently represent all that was despicable in men, including their inevitable resort to brutality in moments of crisis, even though in banal reality her husband had never come close to doing such, was notorious rather for crimes of omission, but what did particulars matter when there were so many reasons for killing him? The pity was that he had not brought along his virgin, that saintly little whore, to share his fate!

She looked radiantly at E.G. "You're right." She wanted to fondle him but was concerned that he think it too sentimental a gesture and evidence, no matter what she said or what she proceeded to do, of implicit weakness. Her strength was what had held him over the years. He could have had a younger woman. No doubt he had had, did have, would have many to take, meaninglessly, to bed. There was some reason why he had been attached to her. She liked to think it was her resolution, her courage, her self-respect: her strength.

She turned to head upstairs, and just as she did so the sound of running water ceased. The silence changed everything. She had never before killed anything of warm blood. As a child she could not bear to watch her father take the live chicken, raw material for Sunday dinner, to the elm stump and gorily behead it with the same hatchet used for kindling, and even worse, though the bird was then beyond feeling, plunge the body in boiling water to loosen the feathers. Nevertheless, within two hours she was savoring a drumstick, in the self-righteous conviction that she should be provided for, irrespective of the measures required.

She appealed to E.G. once more, even though she might be struck again. "Can't you do it?"

This time he was not violent but simply contemptuous. "He's *your* husband, not mine."

Just as she reached the foot of the staircase, the nearby front door opened hesitantly and Ellie entered, hugging a brown grocery bag with her usual lack of grace, her eyeglasses slipping down a shiny nose.

The arrival served to distract Esther from brooding on relative mortalities. "It's about time."

Ellie protested. "It's early. They let me go early because my dad's coming home." With the usual resentment of voice and expression she directed part of this statement towards E.G., without having acknowledged him in any other way.

"Your father's upstairs," said Esther, extending a hand to restrain the girl from too passionate a reaction. "He's taking a bath at the moment and can't be bothered."

"He's *here?*"

Esther winced. "Keep your voice down. He's tired. He's been drinking. He needs peace and quiet. You can see him when he's ready."

Ellie shook the grocer's bag. "There's nothing much here but baloney and toilet paper. What are you going to give Daddy for supper? Shouldn't I go back to Harriman's and get something nice?" She did an awkward little dance step of elation. "I can't believe he's *here!*"

While Ellie was speaking, E.G. moved out of her peripheral vision and was making signs to Esther. Augie might be out of the tub if she did not get up there soon.

"Uncle Erle is taking us all out to eat. Now get that stuff put away."

"The toilet paper," said Ellie in her annoyingly high-pitched voice, "goes in the bathroom."

At first it had seemed that the interruption and delay had provided Esther with an extra moment in which to develop a resolution for the work at hand, but by now the anxiety had returned.

"*Later,*" she cried. "Get in the kitchen!"

She hastened up the stairs and into her bedroom. She went to the western wall and removed the framed picture that hung there, a print of an idealized hayfield in sunshine, thatched cottage and cart in half-shadow and no persons. By careful measurement E.G. had determined that the blow should be aimed dead center in the rectangle of clean wallpaper left when the picture was gone.

Esther made a fist and with its heel, as she had been instructed to do so as not to break bones, struck the wall with all her force. Something happened on the other side: there was a distant sound, muffled, unidentifiable. That electrocution was the cleanest sort of killing was why it had replaced the barbarities of hanging and the firing squad.

Esther left the bedroom and hastened to the bathroom door. Ear against a panel, she could hear nothing from within. She went downstairs.

E.G. lingered in the front hall. He did not look at her until she had reached the ground floor, and even then his face was expressionless.

"Be on my way," said he. "Be back later, after Augie's rested up."

"Wait a minute," said Esther, but her voice was too feeble to be heard by Ellie back in the kitchen. When she tried to raise it, what emerged was a kind of squeak.

E.G. responded to the emergency, but he sounded synthetic in the extreme. "Oh, he'll be down soon? Well, all right then, I'll hang around." If she had spoken too softly, his voice was much louder than normal and the words were enunciated as if being directed to the sort of family dog that has a passive vocabulary of three or four terms carefully pronounced.

Esther tried again to be heard, but her throat had closed so tightly now that it was all she could do to suck air through it.

Once more E.G. stepped in, but no more convincingly than before. "Maybe he went to sleep in the tub?"

Esther was humiliated to be in such a condition. It was so unfair: she had performed well in the hard part, had done the killing to perfection.

She had raised her finger to make some such point, though perhaps not in so many words, when Ellie came from the kitchen, carrying an armload of toilet-paper rolls.

"We're always running out, so I got some extras for a change."

Anger unlocked Esther's voice. "Oh, for God's sake."

"It'll be used," Ellie said prissily, clamping her bony chin on the topmost roll, to secure it, but too late. The cylinders seemed to explode from her grasp and went everywhere.

Esther lost control. "God *damn* you!"

"Nothing broke," Ellie said. She stoically gathered up the rolls one by one and made two equal stacks on the second step.

Toilet paper was kept in the bathroom closet. Esther suddenly recognized that this supply gave her the excuse she needed. "All right," she said when Ellie had retrieved the farthermost roll, that which had tumbled as far as the umbrella stand. "I'll take them from here on."

"I'll help," said Ellie, but was driven away with pantomimed slaps. Grimacing, she said, "What's wrong with you? I'm going up to my room, anyway."

"Just go then," Esther told her. This too was reasonable enough: Ellie's room was on the other side of her own, farther from the bath. "Just don't disturb your father."

Ellie shrugged and ascended the stairs, E.G. had disappeared into the living room. When the girl was gone Esther squatted to embrace the toilet paper, two stacks of three rolls each, and balancing them, rose and went upstairs. It took some doing to lower her burden without mishap against the wall alongside the bathroom. Perhaps because of this distraction she omitted an essential feature of the plan and did not knock at the door and through it loudly ask Augie whether there was enough hot water — only then, receiving no answer, was she to go within and find the body.

Instead she entered without pretext.

Chin lowered onto his chest, Augie was bleeding slightly from a gash in his scalp. The electric fan had never reached the water but had rather struck him on the head, bounced away, pulling its plug from the sconce, and hit the floor, where it now lay on the side of its deformed wire cage.

Still, if he was dead, what did the details matter?

He groaned.

Esther found, amazingly, that her first feeling was of relief: she could never be charged with a murder that had not occurred. This was followed immediately by anger with herself for not so positioning the fan that it would have missed Augie's head as it fell — though she now could see very well that it could not but strike some part of his body, for he filled the width of the tub. The plan had been defective, the plan that was an original creation of E.G.'s.

For an instant she had been alone with the problem, but now she left the bathroom and hastened downstairs.

E.G. stood in the living room, staring out the bay window from which they had watched Orrie leave for college. He did not turn to greet her arrival.

"Christ," Esther said. "He's not dead. He was just knocked out when the fan fell on him. What do we do now?"

At last he looked at her. "Nothing."

"What?"

"Let it go."

"There won't be another chance," Esther said. "If we

don't get him now, he'll go back down South and marry that little chippy of his, taking the insurance with him."

E.G. shrugged, offering no assistance.

"You just want to give up?" For the first time she began to doubt him.

"You got a better idea?"

"Plug the fan in again and drop it in the tub while he's still groggy."

"Jesus," said E.G. "You could go back up there and do that?"

"I was hoping I might get some help."

"With the kid right down the hall?"

"Oh, God!" Esther said. "Did I leave the door open?" She dashed out and went up the stairs, almost whimpering in anxiety, but reaching the bathroom, saw the door had been closed all the while. She had to take command of herself.

Ellie looked out of the doorway of her room. "What's all the commotion?"

"I just forgot something," said Esther, trying to catch her breath. "Is it any of your business?"

"Is Daddy going to be out soon?"

The innocence of the question took away Esther's pugnacity. "It won't be long now," she said in a nearly affectionate tone. "He had a hard trip, can use a good soak." But more was needed. "He's looking forward to seeing you, too." Fearful that Augie might groan loudly enough to be heard, she repeated, "It won't be long."

"Where are we going to eat?" asked Ellie.

Esther was immediately angry again. "Just wait till you're told!"

"You want me to change my clothes?"

"What I want you to do is run back to Harriman's and get some cold beer. That would be nice."

54

"Yes, it would," said Ellie.

Esther followed her downstairs and, when the girl had left the house, stepped into the living room.

"Come on," she said to E.G. "We've only got a few minutes."

"You mean, kill him?"

"Yes!"

"I don't like it."

"Neither do I," said Esther. "But I don't see any alternative." She was the leader now and preceded him on the route to the bathroom.

Augie lay as before, though he did not groan, not even when she touched his shoulder, at first gently and then with the stiff prod of an index finger.

"Hell," E.G. said, standing well back of her, "he's dead."

"He's breathing," said Esther. She picked up the fan and handed it to her lover, the wire dangling. He made no use of it, simply stood there. "Well, plug it in!"

He did as much, then lowered the fan as far as it would go. At the level of Augie's bare shoulder, the wire was taut, at its maximum extension.

E.G. straightened up. he had come out of his stupor. "Look at this," he said furiously. "It's not long enough to reach the water. It wasn't *ever* long enough to reach the water. You didn't even test it, did you? I *told* you to test it, and you didn't. For Christ's sake, *you didn't test it!*"

Esther felt only contempt for him. "I've had to do everything. All you've done is talk. Are you yellow? Is that it?"

His face was contorted, and his clenched fist was rising. She took no measures to protect herself, being incapable of dealing with physical violence.

Augie groaned again at this point and made a movement

of his trunk, too slight to alter his position but enough to catch the attention of his would-be murderers.

E.G. shuddered. For an instant Esther thought he might run away, but then, his face blanched, eyes rigidly focused, nostrils flared, he hurled himself on Augie's shoulders and head, forcing them under water. Beneath him, Augie now showed some life and, bigger and stronger, even though wounded and semiconscious he might well have saved himself had he been able to get a purchase with any part of his body, but his arms were trapped and the surface of the tub was too slick to grasp. He finally got his hands flat, under his body, and pushed up, but it was now that Esther added her effort to E.G.'s and together they managed, with their combined weights and strengths, to hold him under despite a savage and prolonged resistance that was amazing in a maimed man. But finally the last bubble had come up and burst.

Esther sagged against the far wall. She had not expected to commit murder in such a personal way. It was a nasty business even though there was no blood except the little bit at the head wound. For a few moments, eyes closed, gasping, dripping, she forgot all about E.G. and imagined that she had done the deed singlehandedly and was appalled and yet exhilarated by the revelation of a capability she had not suspected she possessed. But then she was chilled, as though the water had been iced and not still quite hot when Augie died in it. He had always liked his bathwater at a temperature too high for anyone else to bear. She was *freezing!*

She opened her eyes and looked towards the tub. E.G. was kneeling alongside it in an attitude of prayer, except that his fingers were not tented but rather flattened on his thighs.

She started to ask a question. "You think . . . ?" But forgot the rest of it. She would not have been startled to hear a posthumous groan from Augie, who had died so passionately, yet so quietly: he had some noise coming. But had his death been all that soundless? Was it rather that she had been deaf to the thrashing of legs, the bubbling of nose and mouth?

E.G. rushed, on his knees, to the toilet, the lid and seat of which he had hardly flung back when the vomit left him in a torrent.

Esther was revolted by this symptom of weakness, but then she was almost getting used to E.G.'s failures. He had not acted well since the beginning of this sequence, which by now seemed so long before. His part in Augie's death had been hysterical. If she had undertaken the murder so as to join herself indissolubly with E.G., she had been misguided.

Augie's upper half lay underwater, his legs as far as the calves protruding from the other end. E.G. pulled himself to his feet. She could smell the stench of his puke.

"Flush the toilet," she said in disgust. "And wipe your chin. Ellie'll be back any minute. We've got to fix our story." She turned so as not to see Augie's feet. "The fan fell and knocked him out. His head slipped under, and he drowned. There's not enough water in there now. Run it to the brim: that'll account for all of it that splashed out."

They were standing in water. The knees of E.G.'s pants were soaked. Esther's housecoat was wet, and her mules were probably ruined.

E.G. moved to follow her orders, opening the cold tap. "Use the hot," she said. "He always liked it almost boiling." That she remembered to call for such verisimilitude stimulated her self-confidence. In an instant she had formulated the rest of the plan. "As soon as we hear her come in, we pull him out onto the floor and give him artificial respiration."

"What if it works?"

"Do you know how to do it?"

"I've seen it in movies, but I don't really know how to do it."

"Good," said Esther.

He shrugged towards the tub. "Maybe we better start to get him out now? He might be heavier than we think."

"Let him be for a while yet. We want to be sure he won't revive."

E.G. was looking at her. "Jesus," he said, "you're a cool customer."

"It's taken me long enough," said she. "I wasted a lot of time on the way." At the moment she was not only more bitter towards Augie than when he was alive, but she resented E.G. as much.

The sound of the screen door reached them. For once Esther was pleased that Ellie had let it slam, something that in normal times, even when the girl's arms were burdened, never failed to startle and infuriate, for it was like a gunshot.

"Quick now," Esther whispered, and they went to the body and tried to lift it from the tub, she at the feet (which were still warm; a damp cornplaster was on the left little toe). But Augie's upper half proved too heavy for his cousin to move singlehandedly. Esther dropped the feet and pitched in at the shoulders, but as the tub butted against the wall, leverage could not be applied at its most effective place, so both of them grappled with one arm and shoulder as the lifeless head lolled on a limp neck.

Getting him out was as ugly an affair as killing him had been. At one point his upper back was across the rim of the tub but not yet so far as to outweigh that part of him still within, and unless strength was applied continually he threatened always to slip back. Then when at last the balance was effectively altered, he came out and over too rapidly, all at once, and hit the floor crown first, which had he been alive might have broken his neck in the lethal way but could do no meaningful damage now, and a great deal of water came with him.

Ellie was en route upstairs, her errand completed. The noises from the bathroom brought her at the run. By the time she reached the doorway, E.G. was straddling her prone, wet, naked father, hands on the bare back.

Her mother spoke quickly, before the girl could get past dumb horror. "Your dad had an accident in the tub. He's not breathing. Go phone the lifesaving squad."

Ellie did not move. "Go on!" Esther cried. "Don't you want him to live?" The question was inspired, and had the desired effect. The telephone was on the ground floor, in a niche in the passage between front hallway and kitchen. Ellie could be heard running down the stairs.

"Okay," Esther said to E.G. "You can stop pretending." She had begun to feel the bruises she had received in the struggle to hold Augie under water, to which she had been anesthetic at the time. No doubt the victim's body would show more. "Any marks on him," she told E.G., who was now rising, "got there when we had to pull him out to try to save his life." She sought E.G.'s eyes. "We've got nothing to fear. It'll take them a while to get here and set up the pulmotor. By then he'll be beyond reviving."

E.G. emitted a little groan that was reminiscent of Augie's last sound. "Oh, he's gone all right."

Esther thought of something. "Here," she said urgently. "Look through his pants pockets." She took the uniform trousers from the knob of the closet door and gave them to E.G. and herself began to search through the tunic.

"What are we looking for?"

"I don't know."

He found the wallet. "You don't mean take his money?"

"It won't be that much. Any pictures of his chippy? Name and address? We ought to notify her, so she won't come looking for him."

"There's a return bus ticket," said E.G., "and twelve dollars. Driver's license — it's expired." He lifted his arms as if in supplication. "Nothing else . . . Jesus, it's one thing to do the other, but to go through his pockets makes me feel cheap."

"Put the wallet back," said Esther. "They'll be here before you know it."

5

The members of the lifesaving squad were drawn from the ranks of the local volunteer firemen and included one of Augie's friends who had been at the welcome-home party. Despite his thick eyeglasses, Bob Terwillen served as both firefighter and lifesaver and in fact had at special times (such as carnivals) even been an auxiliary cop.

Terwillen had never gone to war but death was not an unprecedented sight to him. Fellow townsfolk now and again drowned or were accidentally electrocuted, and at least once in his experience there had been a local suicide-by-auto-exhaust. The squad was usually called in if there seemed any hope for resuscitation in such cases. Though all its members were employed locally, some worked on different shifts from others, so that part of the complement at any given time was available on the shortest notice. Those in bed kept their clothing nearby. But the men working in the factory, if they could hear the steam whistle that sounded the appropriate code identifying the part of town in which the emergency could be located (not always possible in the din), were almost as prompt to get where directed, which might be close enough to walk. Once in the proper quarter of town, you listened and looked for the ambulance, which was driven by Mel Furman, who kept it in one side of his large garage and could get behind its wheel within four minutes of the phone-call alert, less if the time was before he had gone to bed, for he worked out of the same garage, at auto repair.

Not everybody for whom the lifesavers were summoned died. In fact death was far and away the exception. Occasionally the squad really saved someone's life by its actions. At other times the men arrived to find their services un-needed — the subject was breathing again either by reason of God's help or interim first-aid measures taken by nearby loved ones. And then false alarms, sounded by the panicky, were not unknown.

Though having considered himself a friend of Augie Mencken's, Terwillen had never been in his home before; in fact, though in such a small town everybody knew where everyone else lived in an approximate way, he could not have identified the particular house as being Augie's, and the dispatcher (the police chief's wife) had not got a name from the individual who called in. So Terwillen had no idea of the identity of the victim until, with the other fellows, helping to carry the heavy pulmotor, he climbed the front steps, crossed the porch, and entered the front hallway, there encountering an urgent Esther Mencken, in a garment that was dripping wet.

"Upstairs, first door on the left," said she to Mel Furman, the leader of the squad. "Bathroom, fan fell on his head, passed out in tub. We gave him artificial respiration, but I think he was too far gone."

In the bathroom, the others got to the body before Terwillen did, and for a moment blocked his view of the head and trunk. He could see only the more pitiful half of the naked corpse, with the splayed feet and the skinny white shins and defenseless private parts.

From the edge of the closet door hung the beribboned officer's tunic. Protruding from the left chest pocket, erect against the decorations there, was the cigar he had given Augie not an hour earlier.

"Oh, *no*," he said. "*No*. This can't be. I just left him at the party." The others were silently going about what was necessary to get the pulmotor going: that was their job, they were not licensed to certify death, they would try to revive the body while one of them, Red Mercer, ran downstairs to phone the doctor on call for such emergencies.

Ordinarily Terwillen was capable of discharging his responsibilities, but he was useless at the moment, inconsolable, though he had not laid eyes on Augie nor heard from him in a personal way for four years. It was the injustice! To survive four years of combat unscathed, come back, and within hours drown in the quiet home tub, while family members waited unwittingly just outside the door.

Terwillen could not endure the bathroom. He left and wandered distraught along the hallway, passing several rolls of toilet paper in a stack against the wall. Through the open doorway of one room he saw a young girl sitting on the edge of a bed, her face in her hands. He knew Augie had several children but would have recognized none by sight in the absence of a parent.

He trudged to her. "Honey," he said, and when she lowered her hands to look at him, eyes streaming, he began himself to weep, had to remove his glasses, which meant he was almost blind.

He offered her his clean handkerchief, but she did not take it, so he finally brought it to his own tears. With the specs back in place, he could discern that, though so thin and pale, the reddened blue eyes providing the only color, her face showed a marked resemblance to her father's. "Honey," he asked, "what's your name?"

"Ellie."

He sat down alongside her, the bed sagging, and put his arm around her narrow shoulders. "Ellie, honey, I'm Bob Terwillen. I was one of your dad's closest friends." Without warning, he was shaken by a profound sob and gripped her more tightly. "This is a terrible accident. He was just at a party we gave him at the restaurant, not an hour ago. Oh, it's just awful. Oh, honey."

Ellie's body stiffened in his grasp. She wiped her eyes with the sleeve on her free arm. "It wasn't any accident," she said quietly, almost gently. And then escaped from him, stood up, went to the dresser and put on a pair of glasses of her own. Her eyes no longer seemed so pathetic. Still speaking in a low voice but now with ferocity, she said, *"They* killed him."

"Oh, honey," Terwillen repeated. "It's awful enough. Don't say things you don't mean."

Ellie was a skinny, white-faced young girl in rumpled clothing, her eyeglasses mended with dirty adhesive tape, but the hatred gave her remarkable presence. "They're murderers," she said.

Terwillen almost wailed in exasperation. "Who? There's nobody home but your mom." He assumed the girl, overwrought, was babbling nonsensically, and he rose and went back down the hall.

Esther Mencken had come upstairs by now. The noise of the working pulmotor could be heard from the bathroom. She asked him, "Do you think there's a chance?"

Against the light from the window on the landing, she seemed to be wearing nothing under the damp housecoat. In his current state Terwillen found this repulsive.

"You can always hope," said he and then, suddenly remembering what she had stated on their arrival, "You said 'we' gave him artificial respiration. Was somebody else here?"

"E.G.," said Esther. "He's still downstairs. He's in bad shape: he tried so hard, I think he hurt himself."

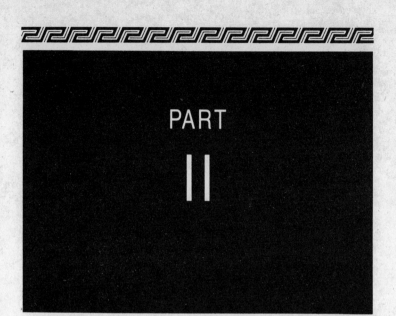

PART

II

1

To some, it did not seem right to drink alcoholic beverages in view of what had happened to Augie Mencken not an hour after the welcome-home party, and Rickie Wicks and Bob Terwillen had coffee as they sat at the bar in the Idle Hour on the evening of the day after the accident. But Al Hagman saw no disrespect in drinking his usual brew, and Joe Becker, who had been closest of all to Augie, was on boilermakers. Joe was taking it hardest of all, to the point that he was being disagreeable to the others.

"That's crap," he belligerently told Wicks. "You think not having a beer will bring Augie back?"

Rickie diplomatically stayed silent, but Bob Terwillen spoke up. He after all had the authority of having been at the scene with the lifesaving squad. "No, any more than getting drunk will bring him back."

"If you mean me," said Joe, glaring at him, "be man

enough to say so, and I'll be glad to step outside and give you satisfaction."

"For Christsake, Joe," said Herm, brandishing his wet rag. "You think Augie would want his pals to get into a fight before he's even put in the ground?"

Molly and Gladys were in place at the end of the bar. Molly now spoke up. "She's not going to bury him. She's going to cremate him."

This regrettable news diverted the men from the developing squabble.

"How do you know that?" asked Al Hagman.

"Sue Ann DeMarco," Molly said smugly, referring to the local beautician. "Bingman uses her to make up the faces on the bodies he embalms. But he's not going to have any work done on Augie Mencken. Closed casket, then immediate cremation. He'll be late in getting the body. They have to do a postmortem in case of an accident like that."

"God damn it to hell," Becker cried. "That's not right."

"You don't have to be foulmouthed about it," Molly said, scowling.

Becker flared up. "Listen, you —"

"All right, all right," said Herm. "Let's knock off the bad feeling, everybody. We all miss our pal."

"Hell if *she* does," Becker said. "She hated his guts."

"Now, don't you talk like that," said Molly. "Augie and I were friends since schooldays. There was a time when he was even sweet on me, I'll tell you that — long before he hooked up with that one. Just after I switched to the public school. Dad couldn't afford the tuition at Saint Catherine's, but Father Phelan got mad at him when he pulled me out, and the result was Dad wouldn't allow any of us kids to go to —"

Becker interrupted her with a dirty laugh. "Any time Augie was interested in you . . . !"

Molly jumped off the stool and pulled her purse to her. "I'm not staying here to be insulted." Alongside her, old Gladys desperately downed in one gulp what was left in her glass — most of it, for ordinarily she would have nursed it for hours.

"Sit down," said Herm, "and have one on the house while you simmer down." Gladys got a woebegone look, but he brightened her by adding, "You included, Glad."

"All I know is, Doc Spang determined he died of drowning," Terwillen said.

"I didn't know there was any doubt about that," said Al Hagman.

Terwillen looked at him through the thick glasses. "He was bruised a lot, like beaten up, you know. They had a tough time pulling him out of the tub. Then they tried to give him artificial respiration. If you don't really know how to do that, where to put your hands, you can do more harm than good. You can't just lean on somebody's ribs."

"You don't mean they could have hurt his chances?" asked Hagman, who had some beer foam on his horsy upper lip.

"I'm not saying that." Terwillen jerked his head left and right. "I'm saying he was quite a bit the worse for wear. But that was the explanation."

"It sure was a real lucky accident for them, wasn't it?" said Molly. "Came at just the right time."

Joe Becker leaned around Hagman and belligerently asked Terwillen, "So what's your opinion, Bobby? You were there just after it happened?"

"Mel and Dick and Red got in the bathroom before me," Terwillen explained. "There wasn't any room left in there with all of them and the pulmotor too, so I stayed out and tried to calm the girl down."

"Poor kid," said Hagman.

"What do you think?" Becker demanded again of Terwillen, but before the latter could answer, added: "I got my own opinion."

"It's not my place to say anything," Terwillen answered. "I was there in an official capacity."

"*I'll* come out and say it!" Becker shouted. "I wouldn't put it past them to knock him off, and now they want to burn the evidence."

Herm came to him and, leaning across the bar, said, "Keep it down, will you, for pity's sake? You could be sued for slander, unless you got some proof."

"Does it seem likely to you that a man who could survive all that combat would drown in his own bathtub? That's what I keep asking myself. I know he had a few down here, but he didn't have a load on by any means. That's what she's saying, isn't it? That he was stinking drunk. That's a dirty lie, and all of us know it."

"The fan fell on his head," said Terwillen. "There was quite a gash in his scalp."

"You're sticking up for them?"

Terwillen glared at him through the magnifying lenses. "Now don't you start on me. Your quarrel shouldn't be with your friends."

Becker glared back for a second and then grimaced. "You're right, Bobby. This thing's hit me harder than I can say."

"It's hit us all hard." Terwillen shook Becker's extended hand. "And maybe I shouldn't be telling you this, but the girl agrees with you."

"What's that?" Hagman asked.

"Still, a young girl will say anything. She was pretty worked up. She hadn't seen her dad for four years, and she never saw him alive now. Think of that."

"She believes they murdered him?" asked Becker.

Herm had stayed near them. He was uneasy. "What do you think, you guys? Should I leave it up?" He indicated the WELCOME HOME banner that was still draped across the mirror. "Maybe put some black crepe with it? Or just take it down, period, and reserve that corner there, with the post-cards and so on, in memory of Augie?" He looked wistful. "Be nice to add some of his ribbons, but I guess the boy will want them. That's his right."

Becker paid his tab and left the stool. "By God, I'm going to ask Howie Gross to look into the matter!" He went out with a desperate vigor.

At the mention of the police chief's name, Gladys came alive. "Howie's my second cousin, you know. He was the worst kid in town in his day, always in one pickle or another. Who would know he'd end up as a cop?"

Hagman said to Terwillen, "Still, Ellie's talking about her mother, isn't she? That's an awful thing for a kid to be saying about her own mom."

"It's an awful thing to *think* about her."

Molly called Herm over. "Joe Becker can't say a word without resorting to profanity. I don't care what his excuse is. We're all upset, if it comes to that. But this is no place for ladies, if you don't call him on his foul mouth."

Herm gave her a long look, then said, "I'll speak to him."

"You just do that."

"The girl," said Hagman, "she thinks her mother killed her father and she has to go on living with her?"

Terwillen nodded. "I guess so. Where else can she go?"

Hagman shook his head. "I don't think it can be true. It wouldn't make any sense, would it?"

Terwillen saw Phil Paulsen coming in the door. "Here

comes Phil. Do you think his brother will ever turn up?"

"It's hard to say," Hagman muttered, "but no, I don't. But I wouldn't ever mention it to him." He turned and greeted their friend with a hoisted glass.

2

"I never borrowed money from anybody in my life," Orrie told Paul Leeds. "I want you to know that." What he did not mention was that he refused the sum wired him by his uncle Erle. "This is a special situation."

"I told you not to worry about it," said Paul. "Just glad I can help out. I'm sure it's a tough thing to lose your dad, when your father is someone you admire a lot. I don't even like my own father, but I wouldn't exactly want to see him dead."

Paul habitually complained about his father, a manu-facturer — his son refused to say anything about him that was not disparaging, so Orrie was not sure just which product he manufactured — who was sufficiently rich to pay Paul a monthly allowance that would have taken care of Orrie's requirements for a year.

"I wasn't all that close to my dad," Orrie was careful to explain. He had always been literal, even as a small child, amusing his mother with, among many other things, a complex effort to characterize the weather with precision, when all she wanted was to hear simply whether it was nice or not ("It's not exactly raining, but it's not sunny either, and there's a lot of black clouds . . ."). "I think I probably disappointed him, wasn't much interested in the sports he liked, certainly wasn't very good at them, never big enough to go out for football."

"You're okay at tennis," Paul said, a tall tan fellow who was much better. He was being flattering, as usual. Paul looked and moved as though he himself were a natural athlete and could probably have been a football star were he not so lazy. Orrie had to admit to himself that Paul seemed pretty much of a ne'er-do-well: he had turned up at this modest state institution after having flunked his first year at a hallowed university in the Ivy League. He now was starting out as a freshman again.

Paul had taken an immediate liking to Orrie when they met in the line at registration time and (knowing how to do such things) arranged to replace the stranger originally assigned to share the latter's dormitory room. Orrie had no objection. He could see that Paul had his flaws, but there would seem to be no reason to spurn the proffered friendship of a likable and generous guy.

"I'm lousy and you know it," Orrie said. "But anyway my father would probably have thought tennis did not really qualify as a manly sport."

Paul shrugged. "Well, it's too late now to worry about that."

"But I guess I always will." Orrie had not been in any kind of communication with his father for four years. You would think a man might have found time, in spite of combat, which could not have been incessant, to send a card to his only son or at least ask about him in a letter. More than once he had made this point to Ellie, who of course though equally neglected stanchly defended her dad: "They keep them busy in the Army. There's a war to win." If he continued to make his point, she would run off in tears, and then he felt awful, not changing his mind about his father but regretting he had made his sister weep. He knew there were lots of people who fought with their sisters, but he was not one of them.

Paul, sprawling on the bed, took some crumpled bills from his pocket. Then he scattered them, hopped up, and gestured. "Take what you need. If it's not enough, I'll go cash a check."

"Just enough for the bus ticket and maybe a little extra to buy a shirt," said Orrie. "The only white one I own is too dirty to wear to a funeral."

Paul winced at him. "You don't have a dark suit, do you? Let me stake you to one. If you give Hymie a tip, he'll do cuffs et cetera in an hour or so." Paul was always going to the local tailor to get things altered. His serious wardrobe was custom-made, but sports stuff, sweatshirts and gym shorts, were acquired at the university co-op, and if there was one thing he couldn't bear it was ill-fitting clothes.

"No, thanks," said Orrie. "You've done enough." He chose a few bills from those strewn on the bed.

"When's the bus?"

"Six. Gets in at two A.M. after stopping all over the place."

"That's lousy," Paul said. "It's only a couple hundred miles, isn't it?" He punched one hand into the other. "Listen, I'm going to rent a car and drive you down."

Orrie protested. "Don't be crazy."

"The guy who owns the Sunoco's got that Ford he kept in fine shape throughout the war. Good rubber on it, and of course he's got access to plenty of gas. I've rented it for dates, as you know." Paul sometimes took a girl to the nearest city.

Having a car was against the university rules for a student, and gas rationing was still in effect. Orrie did not know whether hiring an automobile was also taboo. Paul could not have cared less. Keeping a coed out after the weekend curfew of midnight was illegal too, and yet he did it regularly. Thus far the girls if caught had as regularly taken exclusive blame and all the punishment: confinement to the dormitory every night for two weeks for every hour or portion thereof they were late in returning. Paul could get away with such stuff with the most attractive women on campus, whereas Orrie had yet to find a desirable girl who would so much as meet his eye.

"Jesus, Paul, you don't want to go to this funeral." To satisfy his conscience Orrie could assume he was thinking of his friend, but the fact was he would be embarrassed to have Paul meet his family.

"No," Paul said. "You shouldn't have to do this all by yourself. We're all stuck with our families, but at least we can choose our friends." It was unprecedented for Paul to play the philosopher, a role in which Orrie was, it seemed, cast by nature. But Orrie could at least reflect that it had been Paul who chose him as friend, not the reverse, and therefore Paul was speaking narrowly (as nonphilosophers usually did on the rare occasions when they appeared to be addressing universal issues) of himself. Which however did not mean he was being any less the friend: perhaps that is what friends are, persons whose selfish interests are complementary with one's own.

The fact was that Paul's companionship on this journey might mean much more to Orrie than it ever had thus far at college, for it would at least provide some distraction from his emotional predicament. Orrie did not know what he should feel with regard to his father's death. He had not seen or heard from the man in four years: the four years, furthermore, in which he himself had gone from child to adult and now taken the first step in the process of leaving home forever. It could be said without too much exaggeration that he had long since lost his male parent, that this recent event was anticlimactic, that though he might never have formulated it in conscious thought, he had never expected to see his father again anyway.

But being honest with oneself means nothing to one's guilt-making apparatus. If anything, the latter is stimulated to produce in higher intensity and greater volume. He had never really liked his father. He had joined his mother in thinking less of the man for failing in business. He had resented his father's abandoning his mother to the repulsive Uncle Erle — and yet of course the person in question was his father, the only one he would ever have, and now he was suddenly dead and in an awful, nonheroic way, and Orrie knew it was vile not to feel more grief of the good clean straightforward kind of the conventional man who has lost his dad. He could remember how Billy Creedy had sobbed, one day in high school, when telling of his father's death in a car crash, and some of the guys said privately, Yeah, it's a tough thing but crying is for girls, and Orrie defended Creedy, who wasn't even that close a friend. Yet now he himself not only could not weep: he would have been ashamed had he done so — and paradoxically it was because of this failure that he felt guilt. Could he have produced tears, his conscience might have been appeased, but his pride would have been mortally wounded: he would have been a better son but a lesser man.

"Just don't say I didn't warn you," he told Paul now. "You don't have to actually go to the funeral itself. I can't be sure how long I'll have to stay. Don't think you'll be responsible for the return trip." He took the money from his pocket, removed one of the bills, and thrust it at Paul. "I don't need this if you're renting that car."

Paul fended off the money. "You might need it for other things."

Orrie did remember something. "That's right. I guess I ought to buy some flowers of my own. I'm supposed to be grown up now. I don't want to be included with Erle."

"Who?"

"My uncle. He'll order an enormous wreath and put all our names on it with his own. He did that when my grandma died. . . . He's not really my uncle. He's my father's cousin, but pretty much the same age, so we were always supposed to call him uncle."

Paul made a face. "I've got an uncle I can't stand. He's just like my father."

"Erle is nothing like my father," said Orrie. He closed his old suitcase after throwing in the second pair of socks and swung it off the bed. "Any time you're ready, then —?"

Paul sauntered to the door. "I'm traveling light. I hate to pack. If I need anything, I'll buy it on the way."

"There's still some cash on your bed."

"God," Paul jokingly complained, "money's all you think about." He lackadaisically snatched up the crumpled notes.

"That's because I don't ever have any." Suddenly he had an insight. His father had never had enough money. He had heard that often enough as a boy, when it had meant little, but now, all at once, he understood that lack of money had ruined his father's civilian life, so the man had gone off to war, where no money was needed, then died immediately on his return from the Army, back to where money ruled. In the interim, in a milieu where courage and honor and selflessness were the operative values, and commerce was nothing, he had excelled.

"I'm a communist," he bitterly told Paul.

"What does that mean?" Paul asked, grinning. "You want to shoot my old man? Great!"

Orrie felt better now that he had discovered a way in which to think positively about his own father. "No," he said. "I haven't got anything personal against anybody. It's just that my dad had some rough times. But he measured up when it counted." Fortunately Paul was ahead of him, going out the door, for at long last there were tears in Orrie's eyes.

3

⌥⌥⌥⌥⌥

In all his years on the force, Howard Gross, first a patrolman and finally chief of police, had drawn his weapon but once in the line of duty: to kill a rabid dog. In his experience there had seldom been a local crime worthy of the name. Typical of the police work done by his three-man department (two of them part-time) was the current slow roll, in the cruiser, past the schoolyard. Mrs. Bly, a middle-aged widow with nothing better to do, had phoned in the information that two male adults were lurking there, probably with the intent of indecently accosting little girls. Gross expected it to be the usual false alarm, but as she had had one success in spotting a weakminded man who had exposed himself (though for the purpose of urinating rather than exhibitionism), the chief felt obliged to act on her call.

He saw them now, but they were not exactly adults. Both had crewcuts and the taller wore dirty white-buck, college-boy shoes. In their teens, they were very likely waiting for a younger brother or sister. He was about to increase his speed when the shorter boy turned to display a profile. It was Esther Mencken's son, Orrie, come back from college for his father's funeral.

Gross stopped the police car at the curb. Ordinarily he would have called the lad to the passenger's window, but in respect to Orrie's dead father, he got out and walked up to the edge of the schoolyard, where the boys stood against the high wire fence that enclosed the playground.

He cleared his throat at Orrie's back, and when the young man turned to face him, Gross said, "I'm real sorry about what happened."

"Yeah. It's too bad." Orrie was a nice-looking boy, if short in stature. Gross could remember feeling like a pervert when, as a senior of eighteen, he first noticed that Esther, a girl who lived on the next block up from his, was getting breasts at eleven or twelve years of age, and he made reference to it at confession, but very hurriedly so that old Father Phelan, always on the verge of napping anyway, would allow him to include it in the general category of impure thoughts, and anyway Esther was a Protestant. Gross and his wife had had seven children. Orrie now referred to the son nearest his own age.

"How's Frank?"

"My Frank?" asked the chief. "He's still overseas. Italy. That's right: you played ball against St. Iggie's."

Orrie shook his head. "I was on the debating team, in the all-county competition. Frank was with the team from St. Ignatius. We never faced one another. Both teams lost in the earliest rounds. But I got to know him to talk to anyway, while we were waiting around to go on."

"Oh, yeah," said Gross who, bored by debating, had forgotten about his son's participation in anything but baseball. He glanced at the tall boy who stood nearby. "Say, Orrie, could I talk to you in private for a minute?"

They walked to the police car, which Gross leaned against with the other hip than that which carried the pistol. "Listen," he said in a lowered voice, "do you know Joe Becker? He was a friend of your dad's."

"I know who he is."

The chief adjusted his cap. "He's okay. He's a good man. He's got a nice business over on the West Side. . . . Maybe he had one too many. I don't know." Gross scraped his lower lip with his upper teeth. "Thing is, he's doing a lot of wild talk. I wouldn't put any stock in it, if you happen to hear it."

Orrie frowned. "I don't have any idea of what you mean." Over the lad's shoulder, Gross could see that high school was letting out for the afternoon: young people were emerging from the arched main doorway of the building.

"Yeah." The chief rubbed his nose with his thumb. "I guess you come to pick up your sister, right? . . . This talk, there's nothing to it, believe me. Your dad passed away as a result of an awful accident. Your mom and E.G. tried to save his life with all their power. But it was just too late. He had taken in too much water."

"That's what she told me on the phone," said Orrie. "Why would anybody say anything else?"

Gross sighed heavily. "You know how people are when they get a few drinks under their belt."

Orrie was still frowning. "You mean that according to Mr. Becker something is wrong with that story? But how would he know?"

"Exactly!" The chief was relieved. "You put your finger right on it. He wasn't there. He just had a few drinks with one of the fellows on the lifesaving squad. It seems your sister had something to say. You know how loose talk starts! I want to

84

stop it in its tracks. It does not do anybody any good at all."
The first elements in the stream of students had almost
reached them. Gross patted Orrie's shoulder. "You calm Sis
down. That's the way to help the situation. You're a man
now. You got to help your womenfolk." He was well aware
of the irony here: E.G. would be boss of that house, as he had
been for some years. But the boy needed encouragement.
Gross went further.

"You need a pal any time, you come to me." He smiled.
"You're welcome any time. Come over and eat a meal with
us, soon, why don't you?" The chief did not include the taller
boy in the invitation, having no idea of who he was and
anyway thinking he looked too polished to be from around
this area, the way he wore a white sweater tied around his
neck on such a warm afternoon.

The Mencken girl was approaching. Not wishing to
encounter her, Gross told Orrie, "You remember what I said,
son," got into the cruiser, and was pulling away by the time
the girl reached her brother. According to Becker it was this
skinny kid who had started the stuff about murder, had acted
hysterical when Terwillen tried to comfort her.

"But," Becker had shouted, "who would say something like
that about their *mother* unless there was something to it?"

"Joe, I'm going to have to ask you to keep your voice
down. You oughtn't yell like that at me. You're in a police
station."

"Howie, I'm asking you a question." Becker had lowered
the volume but the indignation remained.

"All right," Gross said wearily. "I don't have to tell you
that the Mencken females, all of them, spell trouble. That's a
woman's specialty, as you and I know, but they take it to the
limit."

Becker shrugged. "Not this little girl. She's an A student.

Did you ever look at her? She's not the type to run around with boys."

"Just give her a while," said the chief. "She had the same mother as the other one. If that Gena got as far as Hollywood, she's walking the streets: you know that." He looked fraternally at Becker. "Now, come on, Joe, let's step over to the house and get a cup of coffee from the little lady. I'm supposed to be off duty at this hour." He had been listening to the radio when Becker called him away to hear this cock-and-bull story. That pair were a lot of things — what with Esther's low morals and E.G.'s known source of income coming from rent-gouging the trash who lived in the ramshackle houses he owned along the river — but they were hardly murderers.

Glancing at Ellie now as he pulled the cruiser away from the curb, Gross remembered he had been exaggerating when he projected for her the kind of shenanigans typical of her mother and sister: there was absolutely no means by which this woebegone kid could turn into a sexpot in the foreseeable future.

4

"Hi," Orrie said to his sister. He thought briefly about hugging her, but that kind of thing was not done by local people with their relatives, unless the huggers were grandparents and aunts and uncles of a certain age, with a musty odor, and those being embraced were under age twelve.

"Hi," said Ellie. She looked awful, especially about the eyes. "Have you been home yet?"

Other kids were passing them, and two guys said hi to Orrie. He answered Ellie's question. "Naw, we just got here." He pointed to Paul, who was still over against the fence. "That's a friend of mine named Paul Leeds. He rented a car, but it broke down twice. We had to stay overnight in a tourist cabin. He's a swell guy, lent me money too."

Ellie showed no interest in hearing about Paul. She stared at her brother. "Don't go home. If you've got some money, let's go away."

"What's got into you?" Orrie asked, and then was sorry

he had done so, for he realized that grief had probably warped her way of looking at things. She had always been a lot closer to their father than he, even though the man had been no more attentive to her. To all appearances he had ignored them both for four years. "That accident was a lousy thing," he said gently. "There's not much else to be said."

"Except it wasn't an accident." Behind those smudged lenses, Ellie's eyes were bright with ferocity.

Not until now did Orrie understand Chief Gross's cryptic suggestion that he calm his sister down. "If it wasn't an accident, then what was it?"

"They murdered him."

Orrie grasped her shoulders and moved her so that her back was towards Paul, in order to have more privacy for this matter, though as yet he could not really take it seriously. "Jesus, Ellie, I know you don't like Erle, and neither do I, but —"

"I'm talking about Mother too."

"Listen here, I know you're feeling a lot of sorrow about Dad. But you can't just take it out on the rest of the world." He had a protective impulse, and with a forefinger he pushed the glasses back up her nose.

"I didn't know they were killing him," Ellie said in her plaintive voice. "Maybe I could have stopped them. When I think of that, I wish I were dead."

As everybody knew, females were inclined to emotional excess, not to mention that adolescent girls went through an unpleasant process by which they got their monthlies, as opposed to boys, for whom acquiring pubic hair and a deeper voice was a tremendous improvement. Orrie could feel sorry for women when he thought about their lot in life:

in this turn of mind he had been influenced by his mother, who, particularly when he was younger, used to tell him her troubles, a practice that seemed to stop when "Uncle" Erle became a fixture. He detested Erle but he loved his mother despite his resentment towards her. Nothing in this complex of feelings could cope with what Ellie was charging. Yet she was the best sister in the world, and he was obliged at least to make her believe he was taking her seriously.

"What do you want me to do?"

The question took her aback. "Then you believe me?"

He frowned judiciously. "I'm not saying that. I'm saying I'm willing to listen to you." He turned and caught Paul's attention, then shouted, "Just a few minutes longer."

Ellie squinted towards his friend and asked suspiciously, "Who's he?"

"I told you: my friend from school, Paul Leeds."

Again she showed no interest in Paul, a fine-looking fellow like that. Perhaps she was still too young. She stared at her brother. "They got rid of me, you see, sent me out for beer. Daddy was supposedly taking a bath. I never saw him at all. When I came back from the store, there was a lot of running upstairs and downstairs and funny noises in the bathroom. When I got up there, Erle was on top of his body. They claimed they found him unconscious and underwater, and had to pull him out and try to revive him. But you couldn't believe that if you were there."

"But you still didn't really see anything but Erle giving him artificial respiration? You didn't hear Dad yell or anything?"

"How could he if he was unconscious?"

"Then you believe that part of the story, anyway? That he was unconscious."

"But how did he get that way?"

"The fan fell and hit him in the head: she told me that on the phone."

Ellie's thin mouth was distorted in a sneer. "Things like that just don't happen except in detective stories."

Orrie shook his head. "There you're wrong, El. If you found it in a book you wouldn't accept it, but stuff like that happens a lot in reality. How about England during the war, when a German buzz-bomb hit a chapel full of English soldiers, just during the only hour in the week that anybody would have been in there?" This event was memorable because it had been influential in Orrie's questioning whether God could exist and allow that to be done by the godless to the pious and in His house.

"She always hated him," Ellie said. "But why'd she have to kill him? He's the only father I had."

She was beginning to cry. Orrie was embarrassed enough as it stood. Gena had got all the looks. What Ellie had going for her was intelligence and, until now, common sense. If he had to introduce her to Paul, he wished she could at least get herself under control and speak normally. "Have you mentioned this theory of yours to anyone else?"

"That man," she said, "that man with the glasses on the lifesaving squad. I told him."

"You didn't go to the police?"

"Do you think they'd believe a *girl?*"

"Well," said Orrie, "Gross knows about you. He just stopped and warned me, so it's got farther than you are aware. An old pal of Dad's, Joe Becker, told *him.*" He put an avuncular hand on Ellie's thin shoulder cap. "You can be sued if you circulate accusations about people that you can't prove."

Ellie agitated her entire body. "So what was that big fan

doing on that little shelf? It wasn't ever there before. It was never used in the bathroom at all, ever. You don't get that hot when you're sitting in water, not even warm water. Think about it, Orrie!"

"Quiet down, will you please? Look, you're really going to have to —"

"She's already trying to get his Army insurance," Ellie cried. "I heard her on the phone. Daddy was gone *one day!*"

"I guess she really needs the money. He's got to be buried, you know. She never has had enough under normal circumstances." Orrie always felt guilty when he thought about how his mother had to struggle to make ends meet on the small family allowance paid by the Army. He had done his best to help out, ever since he became old enough to caddy, but she had generously insisted he keep most of his earnings for college, no doubt foreseeing that even with a scholarship he would have extra costs to meet, and certainly he did, for his job as dining-room waiter covered only standard room and board, not a doughnut and coffee in the evening or a hotdog at the Saturday football game which he felt obliged to attend with the other freshmen, not to mention dates with girls, of which he however was yet to have the first.

"She's got enough," Ellie said hatefully. "What about *Uncle Erle?*"

Orrie too found that name distasteful, but he avoided as much as possible bringing it to mind. "All right, maybe she's borrowed a little, but only when —"

Ellie interrupted. "It's not exactly borrowing, is it? It's payment for service rendered. Don't you even know that? She's a prosti——"

Orrie cut her off. "I'm warning you, Ellie. I'll have to —"

"Do what?" Her face had gone even whiter, with defiance. "Hit me?"

He was embarrassed. "Come on, don't talk that way."

"I'm only waiting for the funeral," said Ellie. "And then I'm getting out of here for good."

She was really in a bad way, but he did not know what to do about her. "Would you be satisfied if I talked to the lifesaving guys? I guess I could also see the doctor who signed the death certificate. But wouldn't these be the very people who would already have said something if anything looked fishy?"

"No!" Ellie said with heat. "They wouldn't notice. They wouldn't have any reason to suspect those two. *I'm* the only person in the world who knows about them. Well, maybe Gena does, if she's alive."

Gena was another subject he avoided thinking about. That she had never got in touch after leaving did not necessarily mean she had come to an unfortunate end. It was reasonable to assume that she had not been a big success, either. He had read that far and away most of the young girls who reached Hollywood each year never got close to being in a movie and ended up usually as car hops, usherettes, and so on, eventually returning home. Gena might be incommunicado because she was humiliated by the failure of her dream, but it was still possible she would come walking in the door one day.

"Gena hardly would be an authority on this matter," he said now, and held his head at an angle as if he were miffed. "What about me? I was there until only a few weeks ago."

Ellie grimaced. "You don't know anything. You're a *boy*."

"What's that supposed to mean?"

She lowered her eyes. "You better get back to your friend. It's not right to make him wait so long."

Orrie now took the opposing argument. "It hasn't been that long." But he walked over to Paul. "We're having this complicated family discussion," he said. "She's pretty upset. She was closer to my dad than I was."

"Don't worry about me," said Paul. He nodded at the playground. "If you're going to be a while, maybe I'll go over there and shoot baskets with those guys." Two high-school boys were beneath the netless basket mounted on a standard at the far end. Paul was a college guy and more than six feet in height: he'd be readily accepted.

Orrie returned to his sister. She might be personally unkempt, but her looseleaf notebook and the two texts she carried, bound together by a somewhat old-fashioned strap and buckle, were in perfect condition. Of course, school had been in session now only since Labor Day, but already most other kids' stuff would be showing wear and tear: Ellie's would be good as new next June. Her handwriting resembled those penmanship examples hung over the blackboards in grade school, whereas his own was awful, sometimes undecipherable even by himself.

"Okay, so I'm a boy. Does that mean I'm stupid?"

"No, of course not." She turned her head for an instant. Her spectacles had slid forward again.

"You mean I don't have *feminine intuition?*" This noncephrase was known to him from radio and the movies.

Ellie brought her eyes up to his. "Forget it."

"Come on, Ellie. What are you trying to pull?" Though the kids had gone by, in the habitual rapid exit of the homeward-bound, Orrie now lowered his voice as much in good taste as prudence. "You're outspoken enough to accuse Mother and Erle of coldblooded murder, but you can't tell me this thing?"

"Erle raped Gena," Ellie said flatly, as if with no emotion. "In the car."

"Uh-huh," Orrie said. He could feel the blood rushing into his cheeks. Nothing pertaining however slightly to sex had ever been mentioned by either of them to the other. He found the subject impossibly repellent when it came to relatives, but it was even worse with female ones.

Except for the burning face, Orrie kept himself in order. "I'm sure the first time he tried something like that, Gena went right to Mother and told her what kind of man he was."

"She did."

"Because," Orrie went on, using pomposity as a moral support, "she was a minor at the time, and that sort of thing is against the law. He could be sent to the penitentiary for that, no question about it."

"Mother didn't believe her."

"Well, there you are," said Orrie.

"She just called Gena a little whore."

Ellie wasn't letting up. He was outraged by her use of the word, though he had some familiarity with the charge. He had suffered a bloody nose once after he heard a larger boy make a like reference to Gena. Orrie got the worst of the fight, but won his point: with a victor's generosity, the other apologized. "You ought to have your mouth washed out with soap," he now told Ellie.

"*You're not listening*, are you?" Ellie asked disdainfully. "*That's* what I mean about being a boy. He got Gena pregnant finally, and Mother still wouldn't believe anything against him. That's when Gena ran away."

"Come on," Orrie said, but his voice seemed to be operated mechanically now, by someone else. "I was living right here myself. I would have known if it was happening, wouldn't I? Gena wanted to go to Hollywood and become a movie star."

"After she was gone," Ellie said relentlessly, "Erle turned his attentions to me. But I was prepared. I stole that hunting knife of yours. I told him I'd cut him if he didn't let me alone."

"I *wondered* what became of that knife," said Orrie. "I couldn't find it anywhere." He continued to mumble about the knife. He was scared of his sister now: either she knew too much about things too horrible for anybody but mature men, cops, physicians, soldiers, certainly for any female — or she was raving mad. A young girl like that, pulling a knife on someone: that was certainly crazy. He had to do something about her. He was now head of the family.

"You can't go around threatening people," he said. "You could be sent to reform school for that kind of thing." She was looking at him with an expression that might be interpreted as growing contempt. That wasn't right. She should respect her brother: he was male, and older. "Look." He kicked at the asphalt with his crepe sole. "You want . . ." He really did not care to hear what she wanted him to do. He just wished none of this had ever happened, because the fact was that a kid of eighteen, without any money or connections, without even a father for four years, could not do anything about anything. "If it was true, Gena should have gone to the police instead of running away. Nothing can be done in her absence at this late date. And I want that knife back! You'll just cut yourself with it. . . . And stop looking at me that way. I'm not saying I don't believe you. . . . Look, if it ever happens again, you tell me right away, and I'll take measures."

"I'll kill him," Ellie said. "I won't say anything at all. I'll just cut his guts out."

Orrie felt this threat in his own entrails. He spoke slowly. "I'm sorry, I'm taking a while, but my head's still spinning. Nothing like this has ever come up before."

"I can take care of myself," said Ellie. "Don't you worry any about me. What are you going to do about Daddy?"

Orrie winced. "That's a completely different matter, as I see it. Whatever Erle might have done with Gena doesn't mean he would be capable of murdering somebody."

"Remember he had Mother's help."

There she went again! It got no more acceptable no matter how many times it was repeated. Ellie was crazy. No wonder she kept to herself all the time and had no friends. The sex stuff was unbelievable as well. If she were interested in boys, it would take her mind off this morbidity. Basically she was a nice-looking girl, with fine features. She might even have a decent if slender figure underneath the ill-fitting clothes which seemed to be hand-me-downs from the more ample Gena, but of course that was not a brother's business, and anyway his soul had not ceased to writhe in shame since hearing her personal charge against Erle. Underneath his superficial references to the knife, Gena, reform school, and even his self-pity, he had been occupied only with Erle's advances to Ellie. What was so awful was that he believed her from the first but believed as well that he had a responsibility to pretend to disbelieve. She was too young to know that terrible things happened in life: they should therefore not be confirmed. He owed that to her! But he failed.

"When he did that to you, or tried to, you must have been only eleven or twelve."

Ellie's eyes changed. The subject seemed not as repugnant to her as to him, no doubt because she had not been overcome. "Yeah."

Orrie now gave way within. It was with a sense of loss, not triumph, that he said, "I'm going to get him."

Ellie seized his hand. "Not for me, please. I'm not a victim. Do it for Gena. But do it most of all for Daddy. He didn't have that coming."

5

"I looked everywhere," said Esther. "He wasn't wearing any dog tags and he didn't have any in his pockets or suitcase. He didn't carry any kind of identification that gave his Army serial number. All he had in his wallet other than the return bus ticket and twelve dollars was that old expired driver's license from here. I guess he didn't have a car down there."

E.G. and she were sitting decorously, across from each other, in the living room, keeping their distance. Neither had suggested going to bed together since the murder.

E.G. glanced around the room and moistened his lips with his tongue. He had two fresh shaving-cuts on his face. "They got him in a refrigerator now? I won't get a good night's sleep until he's cremated. I'll tell you that."

This was not the first time he had made that statement. "What are you afraid of?" she asked. "That he'll wake up and come gunning for us?"

E.G. winced. "How can we be sure the coroner won't find bruises or something that won't fit our story?"

She stared at him. "You said you didn't choke him. I couldn't see."

"I don't think I did. But it was hot and heavy there for a couple minutes." He lifted his left hand. "I think I broke a finger. It still hurts."

"That's the one where you usually wear your signet ring!" she cried. "You didn't scratch him with it, did you?"

"I'm certain I didn't. I looked him over pretty carefully before the lifesaving squad got there."

Esther returned to the matter of the insurance. "The Veterans Administration say they have to have a serial number before they can process the claim, and a legal death certificate, of course." E.G. seemed distracted by his own worries, and she reminded him, "This is important. He let his civilian policy lapse, you know. This is all I've got coming, this ten thousand."

E.G. did not react to the cue. Another thing they had not done since the murder was talk of their plans for the future. He got up now and went to look through the front window. "Orrie's supposed to show up soon, isn't he?"

"He's hitchhiking, I guess. I knew he would refuse the money you sent."

"Well, I keep trying," he said sadly. "I wonder if he'll change now?"

"He'll come around eventually."

He turned to her. "You've been saying that all his life."

She did not want to get into that subject at the moment. "Maybe I *should* begin to worry about him. I begged him not to hitchhike: you never know who might be on the road nowadays."

"He's all right," said E.G. "He's a pretty tough little egg, if you ask me."

Esther was annoyed. "He's not some roughneck!" She returned to practical problems. "How are we going to find out where this fiancée of Augie's can be located? I hate to have it hanging over our head: eventually the girl is going to come looking for him. She might make trouble. Whereas if we could get it out of the way as soon as he's cremated, we'll have nothing to fear from her tracking him down later and catching us by surprise."

"You can come up with the damnedest worries," said E.G. "Who cares about this girl? She can't do anything. You're still his legal wife, aren't you? She hasn't got any rights! I'm concerned about the postmortem. I don't *think* there's anything to find, but you can't really tell about doctors. If you'd just done it right in the beginning, he'd have been electrocuted once and for all, nice and clean."

She freely admitted not having checked the length of the cord on the fan, but it was also a fact that while planning the murder it had never occurred to *him* that the body would entirely occupy that end of the tub so that anything falling from above would necessarily be diverted from the water by Augie's upper parts. Things of that sort were male matters: as a woman she could not be expected to deal with them.

"It doesn't do any good to whine now. I want that insurance money!"

After a pause he said, "Get them to look him up by his name. There can't have been many August E. Menckens in the Army. It's not like Smith or Jones."

"Meanwhile," Esther said, "I'm in no position to pay for any of this."

"Any of what?"

"Cremation, to start with! What do you think I meant?"

"Don't raise your voice to me."

She was not ready to get into a real quarrel. "I assumed you would know what we've been talking about."

"You were talking about this girl of his." Then in effect it was he who capitulated. "Come on, let's not bicker." He turned back to the window. "When are you going to tell him?"

"This is hardly the opportune time," said Esther. She assumed a different voice, a witchlike falsetto. " 'Don't be too upset, Orrie. He wasn't really your father. It's more complicated: it was your real dad who killed him!' "

E.G. spun around. " 'And your mother,' " said he, in an ugly voice of his own, " 'she cheated on him for twenty years and then she killed the poor son of a bitch in the bathtub . . . when he had just come back from fighting for his country. That's the kind of mother you got!' "

In her fury Esther seized the nearest object that could serve as a makeshift weapon, the green glass vase from the drum table. It was almost always empty except on Mother's Day, when in recent years, after Orrie was old enough to celebrate the occasion, he bought such flowers as he could afford, with the money he made cutting lawns and caddying.

E.G. dodged the missile, which shattered against the sill of the bay window. Then he strode to her and struck her in the jaw. She fell to one knee. He seized the front of her dress, bunching it up above the bosom. She tried to get her legs under her.

"You do anything like that again, and I swear I'll kill you." He slapped her face with his free hand, going and coming. As it happened, this hurt more than did the punch, which seemed to carry its own anesthetic with it. "Don't you *ever* think you can do to me what you did to Augie." He was not speaking narrowly of the murder. "You try to cut my balls off, I'll cut your rotten throat."

Being in an impossible situation at the moment, she submitted, sagging in his grasp. He let her go without warning. Her head might have struck the floor had she not caught herself on her hands.

His rage having been expended, E.G. was suddenly less severe, though scarcely tender. "Go put some ice on your face. You ran into a door while carrying that vase. That's the kind of thing happens when a person's got a lot of grief."

6

⬛〿〿〿⬛

Orrie was not old enough to be served alcohol in a public place, nor did he look anywhere near twenty-one. Paul could get away with it, given his size and authoritative manner. He could also buy a bottle of whiskey, which is what he had done now at Orrie's request. They sat on their respective beds in the little tourist cabin, a mean place for such an exorbitant fee: two bucks. The bathroom was furnished with a stall shower and a toilet without a lid, and its door was not a door but rather a heavy curtain. Paul had suggested they stay instead at a decent hotel in the city, twenty miles away, but Orrie would not hear of spending even more on this mission, and when Paul amiably pointed out that he himself was uncomfortable and should be allowed to spend his own money, Orrie chided him for being there at all.

"It's not your affair. Go back to school."

Paul shook his head. "We're friends." He tilted the bottle

and drank from its neck, then wiped the top with his palm and passed it across to Orrie.

The first couple of swallows had been hard to take, Orrie not having a history of drinking hard liquor. He did not even like beer. But after a few mouthfuls he was getting inured to it. Paul had offered to get something to mix it with and to try to find a place that sold ice, but Orrie's pure and simple purpose being to get drunk as quickly as possible, there was no point in diluting the poison.

He felt the effects soon enough. His eyes were suddenly warm, and he was conscious of his tongue, wondering where he ordinarily kept it.

"Not bad." He returned the bottle to Paul. "I don't know much about whiskey."

"This is bourbon," said Paul. "It's sweeter than Scotch. I figured you wouldn't be a Scotch-drinker."

"My dad used to hang out at a local bar a lot when I was a kid, but I don't even know what he drank. Maybe I ought to go there and have one with his friends, in his memory. I guess they'd know what he liked. I ought to find out more about what he did in the Army, too. My mother never mentioned it unless we'd ask, and even then she wouldn't say much."

Paul drank more in each of his turns with the bottle than did Orrie, but as yet showed no sign he was affected by the alcohol. "I guess you're old enough to be drafted, aren't you?"

"Yeah," Orrie answered. "But I got a perforated eardrum. I didn't even know it till the physical. But now the war's over and there doesn't seem to be much sense in going to the service anyway."

Paul gave the bottle to him. "I'm Four-F myself," he said,

blinking. "Isn't that rich? I've always been the picture of health, all my life, been good at sports, never sick for a day. But it turns out I've got a heart murmur. Otherwise I would have joined the Marines. I'd a lot rather have done that than go to college."

"You would?"

"Yeah." Paul ran a hand through his hair. "Physical stuff. I'm better at that than books. I'm not stupid. I just can't get much interested in reading, and you've got to do so much of it at whatever college you go to. I thought it might be easier when I transferred."

"Listen," Orrie said with comradely feeling. "I'll help you out however I can. I really appreciate what you're doing for me here."

Paul accepted the bottle. "What am I doing? I just came along for the ride." He was a genuinely modest guy. Orrie thought: God, if I were tall and wealthy, I'd be unbearable.

"It would have been tough to go through it all alone. My sister, she's, well, she's awfully young . . ." He was still not drunk enough to begin to share what Ellie had told him with regard to their father's death. Paul might already be a good friend but he was still a new one. Being careful is not cowardice. Courage is not an exclusive possession of the rash. In fact, sometimes to move slowly and with care takes more guts than to rush in swinging wildly . . . or so he kept telling himself. What in hell did Ellie expect of him, to shoot Erle down in cold blood? He could not even bear to think of his mother in this context.

"She looks like she might be very smart in school," Paul said, generous as always.

"Yeah," Orrie said, drinking more whiskey. After he

swallowed, by now a smooth procedure, he went on. "She could stand to do something about her appearance: she's not bad-looking basically."

Paul genially chided him. "You don't mean get all painted up, I hope. That's the kind of sister to have. A lot of these young girls nowadays get themselves up like streetwalkers, with flaming lipstick and tight sweaters."

What he said had certainly been true of Gena — another subject Orrie had not mentioned. He had been quite a little kid when Gena, herself hardly twelve, had suddenly sprouted protuberances on her chest. At first this seemed like some kind of joke, and then when she persisted, it was embarrassing for him to be near her, especially when other people were also present. One day, by accident, passing the girls' room, he saw through the half-open door that she was stuffing a balled bobby sock into one slack cup of a pink brassiere.

"I can't stand girls who throw themselves at you," Paul added.

So as to seem sophisticated, Orrie pretended to agree, but in reality he would have been ecstatic had an attractive girl made advances to him — he would have been mighty pleased had any of the girls at college so much as glanced at him before turning their heads. As yet he had been invisible, a state of affairs that was no improvement on that in high school, where though he could have dated any number of plain-to-fair-looking females, he could never establish more than a passing acquaintance with any of the series of girls he had adored from a distance.

"The man should be the one to make the first move," Paul went on.

"That's right," Orrie said mechanically. He knew that

sooner or later he had to face his real problem. Even though he had seemingly more courage now, with a bellyful of booze, than just after Ellie had exploded her bombshell and then left it to him to pick up the pieces, he was aware that nothing would be changed when he sobered up. The situation was no less hopeless: it was simply easier to accept being without hope when you were inebriated. You might even get drunk enough to revel in your hopelessness. He had never before quite understood the allure of decadence, he who had naïvely assumed there was satisfaction only in being upstanding. So you just accept yourself as a coward, and if the heat is too much to bear where you are, you run away to somewhere else and start over. Who's going to follow you? God? The same God who permitted Erle to molest his sisters? To have power over Mother, the power of money? Erle owned the very house they lived in: chagrining but true. Orrie had enjoyed fantasies of making lots of cash in some quick fashion as soon as he finished college, buying the house and making a gift of it to his mother. That this vision was hard to relate to his vague intent to become an artist and suffer romantically for a while in legendary Bohemian style before being discovered by a wealthy collector with an exquisitely nubile daughter had not bothered him in the old days — that era which concluded with the death of his father the day before yesterday. But even that lamentable event had not changed things so much as had the meeting with Ellie.

God damn her. Why did she have to stick her nose in this mess in the first place? . . . An instant after the resentful thought had come and gone he did not believe he had summoned it up. . . . No, that was a lie: not only had he conceived it, he was proud of so doing: the little snot, she'd better not try any of that crap on him again or she'd be sorry. Making a fool of him with such cock-and-bull junk! As if a flabby jerk like Erle could have overpowered his father somehow . . . unless of course he sneaked up and took him by surprise: which was more or less what Ellie claimed to have been the case. But before you got to the details, you had to believe Erle had the kind of character it took to murder somebody. He was a businessman, not a gangster, had probably never even got into a fistfight his life long. He wasn't the type for violence. If he wanted someone murdered, he would undoubtedly have hired a lowlife of the kind he boasted of knowing.

Orrie could not remember a time when he thought Erle was anything but a phony. His mother always stuck up for the man, no doubt in the interests of family loyalty, though Erle was not her relative by blood, but Orrie had never, even as a little kid, felt the least respect for what was really only his second cousin. Maybe it would have been different had Erle been his real uncle. He had no uncles, and while he was supposed to have two aunts on his mother's side, if he had ever seen them it was only when he was a baby, because it was about then that his mother's sisters had both moved out of town and nobody had visited in either direction since. All his grandparents were dead. His older sister was missing, and now his father had died by either accident or . . .

"Ellie's got a wild imagination. You know how young girls are. She's got some crazy ideas about my father's death. I told her to forget them, but I don't know."

"How crazy?"

Orrie tried to approach the matter. "She was there at the time, right down the hall. She says Erle maybe killed my dad. She says it might not have been an accident."

Paul grimaced. "God."

Orrie hastened to say, "She was pretty upset, but to go that far . . . I just hope she doesn't go around town with a story like that."

"It looks like she has, though," Paul said.

"What?"

"Wasn't that the police chief you were speaking to today?"

"He was a friend of my dad's," said Orrie, "expressing condolences." But the whiskey impelled him to tell the truth. "Well, yeah, I guess she did say something to him. Isn't that awful? She's just going to embarrass everybody and get herself in trouble."

Paul rubbed his chin with a ring-bearing knuckle. "She doesn't look like a nut to me. Why would she say that sort of thing?"

Orrie needed another drink, but Paul had stopped exchanging the bottle, and he disliked asking for it. "She really hates Erle, you see. She's got it in for him."

Paul nodded. "She *must* have."

"Huh?"

"If she's more or less accusing him of murder. Isn't that what's involved here?"

Orrie laughed loudly but without mirth. "Yeah, that really makes sense, doesn't it?"

"Does it?"

"I was making a joke," Orrie said. "Why would Erle want to kill my dad — right there with my mother present?"

"They always got along?"

"Of course!" Orrie cried. "Erle helped my father out financially. My dad probably still owed him money."

Paul leaned back on his outstretched arms and stared at the ceiling. "Maybe she *is* a little off her rocker."

Orrie took quick offense, amazing himself. "There's nothing wrong with Ellie!"

"I meant just a temporary thing, because of what happened. You said yourself —"

"Erle tried to get fresh with her," Orrie said. "That's why she hates him so much."

"Oh," said Paul, "you didn't tell me that."

"No. It wasn't easy."

"You mean he —"

"Yeah," said Orrie, "but I don't know the details."

"He's an old man," Paul said. "He's more than old enough to be her father. That's disgusting. What's she saying: that he murdered your dad because he was afraid she would tell him?"

"No, she doesn't mean that, I'm sure." He finally brought himself to ask for the bottle.

Paul handed it over, but warned, "You ought to go easy if you're not used to drinking that much."

Orrie was resentful. "I can take care of myself." He slopped some whiskey into the glass but did not yet drink it. "I guess what she means is . . ." His voice trailed away.

Paul was thinking. "You don't suppose Erle would want to get your father out of the way because of your mother?"

Orrie leaped up and threw the contents of the glass in Paul's face, then raised his fists.

Paul wiped himself with the bedspread. He stayed seated. "You're stinking drunk," he said, "or I wouldn't take that from you."

"Come on," Orrie said, brandishing his fists. "You son of a bitch."

Paul rose and, brushing his friend aside with one hand, walked steadily to the bathroom, where he ran some water into one of the threadbare towels and cleansed his face. When he came back, Orrie was still standing in the combat position.

Paul put a hand on Orrie's chest and toppled him onto his bed. "Sleep it off."

Orrie shouted, "You can't talk that way about my mother."

"I didn't say a word about your mother personally."

Orrie was silent for a moment, and then he said, in as strident a voice as before, "You're right. I apologize."

"All right," Paul said. "Now get some sleep."

Orrie managed to get to a sitting position. "No," he said. "I've got to sober up."

"Why?"

"I've got to go home. I should have gone there in the first place, but I just didn't have the guts." He realized he was speaking too loudly and lowered the volume. He might be slurring his words somewhat, but he was thinking clearly. "Getting drunk really did help."

"Can't it wait till morning?" Paul's shirt was all wet in front. He was looking at his watch. "It's almost midnight."

"I'll drink a lot of coffee. I've got to go there now. That's my place. Under the circumstances, I can't invite you. I'm sorry about that. I'm sorry about the stupid thing I just did. You're the best friend I ever had."

"I'll be here."

"No," said Orrie. "Go back to school tomorrow. You've already done more for me than anybody I've ever known outside my family."

Paul shrugged. "Anything you need, just get on the phone and ask."

Orrie stood up shakily. "I don't know why you're such a good friend to somebody you just met."

Paul joked. "Neither do I." But then he said seriously, "This might surprise you, but I don't hit it off with many people. It might not seem like you and I have a whole lot in common, but we just seem to hit it off. Maybe you're the brother I never had." He jerked his head. "Come on, let's go find an all-night diner."

7

Despite the blow from Erle's fist, there was not much of a bruise on Esther's face, and what little there was could mostly be concealed with makeup. Ellie had apparently noticed nothing when she got home from school.

Not only did the physical effect of the punch prove to be of little continuing significance, but the moral import too was less than crucial. Esther was able to survive it so easily because she had lost all respect for E.G. in the course of committing the murder. She blamed herself for allowing him to get under her skin with the imaginary remarks to Orrie. Her only vulnerability concerned the job she had done as parent to her male child. She had been a good mother, just ask the boy himself! But she could afford no more emotional outbursts. Control had to be maintained at all times in a world of enemies, to whose company E.G. now could be assigned. Coward that he was, he would surely capitulate under any suspicion whatever.

He had left before Ellie came home. Ellie's manner was changed in the last couple of days. She had become silent, speaking only when questioned and then with the minimum. Could this be a result of Augie's death? But the girl had not seen her father in four years. How much could he have meant to her?

Given the strain she was under, Esther found it even more difficult than usual to be alone with her daughter. She had bought ground sirloin for Orrie. When suppertime came without his appearance, she told Ellie to open a can of corned-beef hash and, having no appetite herself, went upstairs to Orrie's room, where she sat down on the Indian-blanket bedspread, under the college pennants thumbtacked to the wall, and brooded over whether she should notify the police that he was overdue. If she did so, Orrie would be furious when he turned up. He had always hated what he saw as her tendency to meddle in his affairs. What she had tried to do, of course, was to compensate for a state of affairs in which, having two fathers, he had none.

They had been close when he was very young, but as adolescence proceeded, Orrie thrust his mother ever farther from him. That this might well be normal — as E.G. insisted, though here the source should be considered, for the boy had consistently, at whatever age, rejected *him* — made it no easier to accept. With Gena gone, Esther saw herself as fundamentally alone, despite the association with E.G. that finally extended to a partnership in murder. He was not flesh of her flesh. To be without strong blood-connections at her age, a woman was utterly defenseless.

The room still smelled faintly of Orrie, who as a child always exuded a natural bouquet and did not lose it even as an adolescent. Never had she detected the smell of sweat on him, as with Augie, or E.G.'s often strong breath. Her son was the most attractive male she had ever known.

After a while she lay back on the bed. It was serene here, in the growing twilight, between the silhouette of the desk he had acquired, with his own saved-up money, at a used-furniture store and the bookcase he had made from scratch in manual-training class, the titles of the volumes on the shelves thereof too dim to distinguish now, but she could remember many, having started him on the childhood classics at an early age, *Tanglewood Tales* and *King Arthur and the Knights of the Round Table,* with romantic illustrations of long-haired ladies and men in gleaming chain mail. They shared a love for stories about heroic animals like Balto the Noble Sled Dog who got the serum to Nome and Buck in *Call of the Wild.* There was a summer when Albert Payson Terhune, teller of true-dog tales, was the exclusive source of all Orrie's reading. Yet she had never got him a pet of his own.

Orrie was the sort of child to whom such things could be explained. When Esther was a kid her mother had no extra money to spend on a pet, but the girl adored the fox terrier that belonged to the next-door neighbors, which love was requited by Sparky, who spent most of his free time, in those leashless, fenceless days of yore, in her yard. To other people in the neighborhood, however, the animal was a pestilence, lifting his leg on prized zinnias, shitting on footpaths, barking at sunrise, and finally someone fed him poisoned food. He came to Esther to die in horrible convulsions. Never again could she expose herself to the risk of such agony. As to cats, she was as indifferent to them as they to her, and when nine-year-old Ellie came home once with a stray kitten found on a riverbank at the school picnic, it was Augie who had supported his daughter's cause, saying surely the creature had escaped from the bag in which, with the rest of an unwanted litter, it was supposed to be drowned. Such a will to life must be celebrated! All right, but it was up to Ellie to care for it. Which presumably the girl was still doing, for these many years later, the black-and-white feline could be seen now and again slinking about the yard. Esther had at least banned it from the house.

Like her, Orrie was cold to cats. He shared most of her tastes until, beginning to feel his oats as a growing man, he had believed it necessary to oppose his mother. Nevertheless, underneath it all, he cherished her. He had to. He came from her, and now she had no one else.

Though assuming she had stayed awake throughout her reveries, Esther must have drifted off at some point, for when next she became aware of the room the window had disappeared, taking with it all else that had been visible by its failing light.

She had just risen from the bed and started for the doorway when the gooseneck lamp on the desk suddenly came on. Its illumination of the room was indirect, its focus on the banker's green blotter beneath it and thus not blinding. Still, she had been in the dead dark, to which the introduction of any light would be oppressive. In this case it was also frightening: a male figure could be discerned but not instantaneously identified. Oddly enough, as she reflected later, she had assumed it was Augie, and believed she was not yet out of a nightmare. Then the moment passed.

"Orrie! God, I was worried." She stretched her arms towards him, but he stayed where he was. It had been some years since he let her embrace him.

"What are you doing in here?" He was scowling.

"I was worried. You were due hours ago."

He shrugged and at last lowered the suitcase.

"I've got a lot on my shoulders now, you know," she went on defensively. "I'm all alone."

"No, you're not," he said coldly. "You've got Ellie . . . and of course there's always Erle."

She had never been sure just what he believed about her association with E.G. In some ways Orrie was an innocent and yet in others he seemed to have a sophistication beyond his years. The trouble was in identifying just where one state left off and the other began. They had always been circumspect when Orrie was in residence. E.G. never stayed the night unless the boy was away at Scout camp or, during the school years, sleeping over at a friend's house. They had been less careful with Ellie, who was younger, insensitive to what went on around her, and had so little sense of herself that she was easy to ignore. . . . Perhaps it was time to be motherly.

"Have you eaten anything? I bought hamburger —?"

He waved the offer away. She thought it strange that he had thus far made no reference to Augie's death. She had told him the details on the phone, but such matters are normally reprised again and again, even with nonintimates. The neighbors on the north, a middle-aged couple named Neblett, had already visited twice, on the pretext of bringing food (molasses cookies, tuna casserole), but came really to hear repetitions of the story of the tragic event. And though Esther had no friends locally, some pretending to be such, e.g., Molly McShane, called with bogus sympathy but a ghoulish curiosity that was genuine.

"It was terrible the other night."

Orrie swung the valise onto the desktop and, careful to avoid the lamp, opened it and poked within.

"Everybody did everything they could," Esther continued. "But everything was useless."

Orrie found what he was looking for, a pair of pajamas,

crumpled and none too clean-looking. He closed the suitcase and put it on the floor.

He said rudely, "I'm going to bed now."

She stared at him for a moment and then asked, "Why are you acting like this?"

He tossed the pajamas onto the bed and defiantly returned her stare. "Like what?"

"What are you mad at me for?" She managed to feel like an authentic victim. "All I've been through the last couple of days, and you're being like this? Are you blaming *me*? He was drunk, Orrie. I hadn't seen him in four years, yet he stops first at the Idle Hour and drinks with his pals before he comes home. He was dirty and needed a shave. And you should know this: he told me he had a girl he met near the Army camp down South. But not only that: he wanted a divorce so he could marry this floozy."

Orrie remained impassive.

"You know what kind of girl hangs around Army bases. Imagine him coming back after all those years of not providing for his family, and talking about some little streetwalker with a social disease. He had no respect for me whatsoever, nor for his family."

"Well," Orrie said without apparent emotion, "he's beyond that now."

"He did it all himself!" Esther cried, realizing she was speaking too desperately but unable to restrain herself. "It wasn't even that hot a day to call for the fan. I guess he was overheated by the drinking."

"Where was Erle?"

"Here. Heard Augie got to town and wanted to see him — you know how close they always were. Ellie was here too."

"She went out to the store?"

Esther peered sharply at him. "Where did you hear that?"

"I saw her after school today."

Esther needed a delay in which to collect her thoughts. She turned the desk chair around and sat down on it. "Well now," she said, "this is the first I heard of that." The little bitch had not breathed a word. "Then you've been in town for hours."

"You were with Erle the whole time?"

"What's that supposed to mean?"

Orrie raised his voice. "Just answer!"

She pointed at him. "Don't speak to your mother in that tone of voice."

"Was he alone with Dad at any time?"

She stood up, pretending to greater resentment than she felt. "You're being silly. Is your sister trying to cause some trouble? Let me tell you about E.G. If we had only known, we could have saved your father's life. There he was, unconscious, head under water, filling his lungs, and we were sitting right downstairs."

"What did you care if he wanted a divorce?" Orrie asked. "He had not been around here for years, and you never had a good word to say about him when he was."

"Now, look here, don't you —" But she was not convincing, even to herself. "You're exhausted," she said. "God knows what you were doing, drifting around town all day. It must be way after midnight now. You get some sleep. You won't have these crazy theories when you wake up in the morning. We'll have a nice breakfast. Just what you like: French toast. I'll send her over to get some little sausages."

"Yeah," he said in the flattest of voices. "Ellie's used to running over to Harriman's."

Esther stuck to the high tone. "Goodnight, Orrie. Sweet dreams. I feel a lot better with you in the house. You have to be the man around here now." She suspected that any attempt on her part to come closer to him physically would have negative results and therefore turned and swept out the door. He was after all a kid of eighteen, whose experience of the world now amounted to a few weeks at college with other children of his age. She was well aware he had not yet known a woman sexually, though of course she had never exchanged a word with him on that subject. He was still a child, her child, and she knew he loved his mother. He had no alternative.

8

Orrie had only just discovered for himself that when conditions demand it, sobering up, at least sufficiently to meet the new situation, could be done in less time than it took to get drunk — insofar as moral and emotional matters were concerned. The physical effects were more persistent: he had a dry throat, an aching head, a sour stomach, and his eyes burned. To be sure, he had had no sleep thus far this night, which by now must have gone past three. Yet he stayed awake to wonder how drunk one must be to drown in a bathtub — even with a head wound.

"Are you sleeping?" It was Ellie, who had opened his door so quietly he had not heard her. His eyes were now adjusted to the darkness, which was not complete owing to the moonlight that entered through his uncurtained window.

As it happened, he had had enough of her today. "What do you want? You know what time it is?"

She sat down on the bed. "Keep your voice down, I don't want her to hear."

"She was just in here."

"I know," said Ellie. "I keep tabs on her."

"You stay up all night? Listen, you're just a kid. You need your sleep."

"I thought maybe she had *him* in here."

Orrie did not want to think about that subject. "She was worried about me. I just got in."

"I know. I was waiting for you."

"All right, but get back to bed now, will you? We can talk tomorrow."

"Can I stay? I get scared by myself."

"I thought you had my knife. Anyway, nobody's in the house now but us."

She merely repeated, in a plaintive whisper, "I'm scared." After a pause, she added, "Remember when we were real little? I was, anyhow, but you and Gena weren't very old, either. And sometimes we'd stay with Grandma and all three sleep in the same big old double bed? I sometimes think of the old days like that."

"What are you getting at?" he asked with a scowl. "We're way too old to sleep in the same bed, for God's sake. It might even be against the law." He softened his tone. "Go back to your room. I'm right down the hall. I won't let anything bad happen to you, I promise."

"Remember what else you promised," she whispered solemnly.

Not wishing to detain her, he did not ask for her interpretation of his so-called promise, which actually, if he remembered it correctly, was no more than agreeing to look into the matter of their father's death. Had he not done as much, just now, with Mother?

"Look," he said. "Apparently Dad had been drinking. You get mixed up when you drink. I found that out only recently!"

"Come on, Orrie. You're not joining *their* side!"

He clasped her forearm. "This is not a thing of sides, for God's sake. Can't you get that through your head? It's not some football game. It's life and death."

"You're telling *me?*"

He let her go. "All I'm doing is trying to find out the details of what actually happened. You may not understand this, or want to understand it, but to be taken seriously you have to deal with details. Let me tell you that so far the details I've heard from her could only be attacked by means of other details that contradicted hers." She started to object, but he said, "Now, you listen to what I'm saying."

She quietly burst into tears and threw her arms around his neck. When she could speak, she did so in the little depression defined by his collarbone. "If they get away with this . . ."

She was wearing pajamas of some smooth-finished fabric very like that of his own. Gena had been given to short, fancy nighties with matching underpants of which you could see too much whenever she moved. He could remember his mother's remonstrating with her for parading around the house like that, but Dad had pointed out that she was still just a child — which to Orrie seemed a loose use of the term. Yet it was unbearable to think of Erle's violating her. Maybe a stranger, if drunk, might, assuming from her mature figure and her manner — Orrie had been embarrassed to be seen with her en route to school, the way she had begun to walk — some grown male, full of drink, might take her for an older girl, one beyond the age of consent. But Erle knew how old she was. Beyond that, he was a relative.

"Listen," he said to Ellie, "would you be willing to testify about what *he* did to Gena? That's not only the thing with a minor but it might be incest or something too. He'll go to the penitentiary."

"Do you think I could mention that to anybody in the whole world but you? Anyhow, they wouldn't believe me. I'm just a silly young girl, and he's this big important man, with his big car and pocketsful of money and all."

"He's not that big," said Orrie. "But I guess to really make it stick, we'll have to find Gena. . . . She won't even know Dad is dead, will she?"

Ellie pulled her head back and said dolefully, "If *she's* still alive."

What a thought. "Why do you say that?"

"We've never heard *one word* in all these years. That's not like her. Maybe she didn't become a big movie star or anything else much, but she could always lie about how well she was doing. I know Gena: the truth never stopped her before. She lied all the time to Mother and Dad and the teachers. Why not now?"

Everything was so awful. "Go on to bed," he told Ellie, separating himself from her as gently as he could. "I'm really tired out. I can't think straight without some sleep." He rolled over, face into the pillow. Sometimes when he was small, sleeping in that position, he would awaken with the illusion that he was being suffocated but, hands paralyzed, could do nothing to save himself, yet knew all the while that it was a matter of the personal will: all he had to do to breathe was simply to revolve from prone to supine. But the struggle to achieve this end called for a heroic effort of which he was forever incapable. He was dying the most miserable and stupid death . . . then suddenly he would liberate himself! Turned face-up, gulping sweet air, he would be immediately embarrassed to reflect that as a crisis it had been phony and meaningless, a fantasy: nobody could accidentally perish as the result of having gone to sleep with his face involuntarily embedded in a pillow.

Drowning was an elaborate form of suffocation. Though his mind was clouded by alcohol and then a blow to the head, did Dad know in his soul that he was dying? Orrie hoped not. He found himself praying to that effect, to Something, if not the deity that he had no longer believed in as of the age when adult hair began to appear on his body and his sweat developed a strong odor. As he was asking now that his father rest in peace, it was not the moment to cry, God damn you, God, for allowing this to happen to him, to us, all of us!

He had no sense whether he actually slept or was rather in some other state of psychic suspension, but he found no rest wherever. At one point during the night he was stirred by the knowledge that unless he exerted the utmost self-discipline he would wet the bed, and he forced himself to rise but remained in the same coma into which he had fallen on saying goodnight to Ellie, else he might have reacted more strongly to being at the scene of his father's death. He could not of course ever bathe there again. He could not even bear to look directly at the tub.

He peed, having carefully raised both lid and seat, for failures to do which as a sleepy child he had been punished, though not once, despite close calls, had he ever pissed any bed. Punished — yes, his French toast ration, next morning, had been cut by half a slice, or something equally mild. He had always been his mother's favorite: he would have known that even if it had not been mentioned so often by Gena when she was in trouble. Ellie was not the kind to bring up such matters, for he was *her* big brother. Each family connection was different from the others: he had not thought of that before. Would he even have known any of these people had he not shared their blood? Would he even, like Oedipus, not have recognized his mother under certain conditions?

The drama society at college was preparing a production of the ancient Greek play, and on a whim informed by an urge to distinguish himself somehow so as to attract girls, Orrie had gone to the open auditions held for all but the major roles and read, in what he could helplessly hear was a quavering voice much higher-pitched than usual, for the part of First Messenger, "a shepherd from Corinth": "May I learn from you, strangers, where is the house of the king, Oedipus? Or better still, tell me where he himself is — if ye know." It went without saying that he was not chosen for the cast, but he anyway privately read the entire play, whose shocking theme had surely kept it from even being mentioned in high school. Right now he would be too embarrassed to tell the plot to Ellie, who in high school was reading the innocent and corny poetry of Felicia D. Hemans, Henry Wadsworth Longfellow, and John Greenleaf Whittier. She knew nothing of the great world beyond her small one . . . yet it was she who insisted that murder had been done in the very place where he was standing — for he did, after all, find the courage to go to the bathtub and stare into it, prepared to be numbed by horror but instead seeing it as only what it was, a banal receptacle for water, into which he had periodically immersed himself, though never without missing the shower they had enjoyed at their previous home, which had been lost through his father's financial failures, well known in the family even before his dad had gone to war. His parents had quarreled too much on that matter. It was only money.

Orrie had no intention of ever marrying, but he did very much want to participate in a love affair.

But to have such a thought at this place and time, was it not a desecration? He switched the light off and went back along the dark hallway blindman-fashion, orienting himself by frequent touches of the wall until he came to the open doorway of his room. He remembered to grope around for Ellie, but sensed that she had left even before he went to the bathroom. Now, finally, he slept.

9

"It just isn't right," said Molly McShane to Gladys. "First she didn't have a wake. Then she doesn't put him in a grave."

Gladys spoke resentfully. "I didn't go, and I'll tell you why: I liked Augie all right and I feel sorry for those kids, but the way I look at it, Augie's beyond knowing or caring whether I show up at a funeral of his, and I just didn't want to give *her* the satisfaction. I never liked her since she was a kid."

Molly sipped at her sherry. "Anybody who was halfway normal would have had people over to the house after the services, but not *her*. Not that I would have gone."

From behind the bar Herm spoke to them all. "I thought maybe I'd have something here, but the only people me and Gwen are close to are yourselves, and you'd come here anyway. Anybody's hungry, go back to the restaurant and Gwen will feed you."

They were all at the Idle Hour after attending Augie's

late-morning funeral. In addition to the regular gang, some of the wives had come along. Joe Becker's Pauline was a tee-totaler: a nurse, she was soon off to the hospital.

Al Hagman was talking with Becker. Betty Hagman listened to Rickie Wicks, who, conspicuously avoiding anything to do with the funeral or the Menckens in general, was speaking of the high-school football team's fall prospects. Betty anyway did not know the family well, for she had been reared elsewhere in the county, and her one child was far too young to have had any school-time associations with the Mencken children.

"That's right," Becker told Hagman, "they didn't find anything out of the ordinary at the autopsy." He was calmer now than he had been of late. "It's done now, and Aug's a handful of ashes." He looked into his glass. "Life is lousy."

"But better to go that way than like my mom," Hagman said, tears growing in his eyes. "Five months of pain, screaming all night towards the end, when the morphine didn't work any more."

A stool apart from the others, Bob Terwillen sat with his wife, a pleasingly plump woman with a face that was still girlishly pretty. She had been nursing one and the same glass of beer throughout their time there. Terwillen wore a sports jacket of green tweed, his dark suit having proved too tight to wear when he tried it on for the first time all year. Over the months he had put on more weight than he noticed.

He still felt guilty about his reaction to seeing Augie Mencken's body on the floor of the bathroom. He had in effect fled the scene. That no one but himself knew this — for the other fellows on the lifesaving squad had been occupied with their job — meant nothing. As a man of conscience he had only a superficial interest in the opinions of other people on moral matters pertaining to himself.

"I was thinking," he said to his wife. "Couldn't we do something for the little Mencken girl? Maybe —"

"Now, isn't that a coincidence?" May exclaimed. "I was thinking the very same thing. If the summer wasn't over, we could take her along to the lake."

The Terwillens were childless. For a week in the August just past, they had rented a cottage on Long Lake and greatly enjoyed the beach-antics of the children from neighboring cottages.

"And what about the boy? I was almost thirty when my own dad died, but it broke my heart. I didn't know I'd miss him so much. How we used to fight when I was in my teens! He rode me all the time, and I have to admit I hated his guts sometimes. I guess it was remembering those days and wishing I could have told him he was right and I was wrong, which I never did, though I got to be friends with him later on. You know how those things go."

"We always think of it too late," said May. "I tell you what I'd love to do with little Ellie: buy her a decent dress and maybe get her hair fixed. She could look very sweet. That was awful, that black outfit she was wearing at the funeral: cut down from some old castoff of her mother's, I bet, and she looked real anemic. I wonder if the poor little thing gets enough to eat over there?" She looked away and then back, lowering her voice. "I know you thought the world of Augie, but otherwise it's a pretty awful family."

"You can't blame that on the kids," said her husband. "And you could put it another way: they're all okay except Esther and E.G."

"And the girl that ran away."

"Maybe she knew what she was doing," said Terwillen. He peered at the rim of his glass, from which he had drunk nothing for some time. "I spoke to them both, got 'em aside after the services."

"I wondered where you went."

"I wanted to be confidential, you know. Got them back in the little hall off the rear parlor." He looked away as if embarrassed.

"And?"

"I guess I should have checked with you first, but I got the idea all of a sudden, and I acted on it. What I told them was — now you might disagree, but knowing you I don't think you really will. What I said to them was, if you kids ever need a place to stay, you just come right over any time, no matter when, to our house."

"That was nice, Bobby."

"You mean it?" He now peered at his wife.

"Why sure. You ought to know that. I just wish I thought of it first." She made a little fist and gently tapped his biceps with it.

Terwillen readjusted his glasses at the temples. "Actually, I went a bit further. I was inviting them to move in and stay permanently, if they wanted."

May continued to smile but was puzzled. "Why would they be needing a permanent home someplace else? Wouldn't Esther have something to say about that? I know she leaves something to be desired in many ways, but she's still their mother."

Terwillen briefly lifted the heavy eyeglasses and rubbed the indentations they had impressed into his upper nose. "I don't know. I just got a bad feeling in that house. I'd like to see the kids out of it before something else happens that we'll all be sorry for."

"Anything you want is okay by me, Bobby. You know

that, I hope. But maybe you just can't get out of the mood of what happened the other night." It was sometimes the case that a woman as maternal as May never became a mother, but found that her natural attributes did not go to waste if she had a man to comfort.

"Well, anyway, I made the offer," Terwillen said. "I don't know what the girl felt. She's changed since the night of the accident — which she then claimed *wasn't* an accident. I guess she was just in shock then. She's hardened up since. She acted like she didn't even remember me, just kept her eyes on her brother. But the boy, Augie Junior —"

"Orrie."

"Orrie — he gave me this funny look, and he said, 'Well all right, if you really mean it. We'll keep it in mind.' "

"He wasn't any politer than that?"

"Oh, he called me Mister and so on, and thanked me."

May moued and said, "I hope so. You know Augie, rest his soul, always had the nicest manners when you came into his store. I never forget that. E.G. doesn't have any manners at all. He pushed right past me today without a word, and I can't believe it's because he's so broken up by Augie's death."

Terwillen nodded. "He's never been known for being much of a gentleman, but he looks sick now, besides. You notice that? The black circles under his eyes, and he's got a bad color. Maybe yellow jaundice?"

"They all look awful except Esther," May Terwillen said, smirking. "I've never seen her looking better. I got to admit it, though she's older than me. Black seems to suit her. And how about that veil? No women around here wear veils. That's the kind of thing you see in the movies."

Herm was there again. "Everything okay, folks? You ought to drop in more often, May, not just when somebody dies. This is a respectable place for ladies."

"Well, I'm no drinker, Herm."

"You notice how awful E. G. Mencken looks?" Terwillen asked.

Herm rolled his eyes. "Never liked his looks in the first place."

"Listen," Terwillen said, "I saw the nice card on your floral piece." He reached for the wallet in his back pants pocket. "I want to kick in something: it's only right."

"No," said Herm, backing away with raised hands. "Don't make an enemy of me, Bobby. That was little enough." He left.

"What's that, Bobby? I didn't read it. Forgot my glasses."

"Herm bought that beautiful piece out of his own pocket, but the card read, 'So long, Augie, from all your pals at the Idle Hour.' I wish he'd let me kick in."

"Well," May said, "we did send our own flowers." She brought her purse from her lap and shifted her weight on the stool. "Time to go home and get a meal together." She had no inclination towards lunching on the premises, having seldom eaten a restaurant meal that came up to the quality of what you could do in your own kitchen.

Herm asked Rickie Wicks about Phil Paulsen. "I didn't see him at the funeral."

"Maybe he didn't go. Augie's death got him thinking more about his brother. There wasn't much in common between the two, but I guess he's superstitious, sees what happened to Augie as maybe a bad sign, I don't know."

"The preacher was doing her a favor," Molly said to Gladys. "None of the Menckens were ever seen in any church, according to everything I heard. This man had never seen Augie when he was alive — he came to town only two years ago — so he didn't have any idea of what to say about him, except that he was, quote, 'a pillar of the community.' "

She leaned to say sotto voce, "That's a laugh — with all respect to the dead."

"He *was* a war hero," Gladys noted reprovingly. "They can't take that away from him."

Molly nodded grudgingly. She didn't know about that subject, never having herself been under arms, and it was her way never to speak of things of which she was ignorant. Instead she referred to the unprecedented haste with which Esther had had Augie cremated. "She didn't want to waste time on a wake. What's the hurry? E.G.'s not going to marry somebody her age."

10

The funeral director told E.G. that Orrie and Ellie had left with the rest of the people and when last seen were turning the corner into High Street: an event he had noticed because he thought it unusual that they had not remained to join in the accompanying of their father's body to the crematorium.

E.G. and Esther drove through the business district but looked for the children in vain. Finally the time came when E.G. pointed out that the hearse would already have arrived at its destination and they'd better follow suit or the body would be burned with no family present. As if things weren't bad enough as it was.

They sat together in whatever the place was called, waiting room, parlor, or whatnot, just two people amidst all the empty folding chairs. Vases of flowers were on stands in the corners, and recorded funeral music was piped in through speakers embedded in the walls. Both windows were covered with tightly closed venetian blinds, so nothing of the day — a cool one with the winds that were especially strong up here in the hills, but bright — could enter to alleviate the oppressive atmosphere within.

Everything E.G. ate or drank became corrosive when it reached his stomach. This was true even of straight milk and American cheese. It was probably an ulcer, but he dreaded so much going to the doctor that up to this point he had tried to make do with baking soda, Bromo and Alka seltzers and the like. The condition predated the murder but was hardly helped by the effort that had been needed to kill his cousin, as opposed to the quick, neat, clean, and even almost painless means that had been planned by him. He could not abide anything slimy. He had puked after killing Augie, not in repugnance with the deed, but rather because phlegm had come from the facial orifices of the dying man.

He had no current interest in sex. He was sick and he was lonely. He realized that he probably should not have baited Esther into throwing the vase at him, but for her part she should not have jeered at him on the subject of Orrie. As to slugging her, he had no regrets about that. She could have wounded him badly, even killed him, in which latter case she would have dispatched both her men within the same week. The irony of this reflection did not amuse him.

"Christ," he mumbled now, leaning towards her and speaking in an undertone though aside from themselves nobody was in the room, "this is taking forever."

Esther stared grimly ahead and said nothing.

"I'm sick of that music," he went on. "If you're still around when my number's up, make it something else, will you? John Philip Sousa or something."

Esther continued to look at the back of the folding chair in front of her.

"I guess," he said, "you're still sore about the other day.

Well, those things happen. You hand it out, you can expect to take it."

At last she turned her face to him. "You're avoiding the subject."

"Huh?"

"What bothers me is I can't pay for this. How's that going to look?"

"You want money, right?" he asked, smirking and looking away and then back. "So why don't you just come out and ask for it?"

She was disgusted. "How about you asking once in a while if I need some? Figuring it out without me giving you a bill?"

"I should do that and pay for it too?" He showed a mirthless smile. "You got a warped way of seeing things. No, if I'm supposed to do the paying, then you do the rest."

She bit her lip. He had her there, and she knew it. She said bitterly, "I called the Veterans Administration again. They still can't find any records on Augie."

"That's crazy," said E.G. "You better go down there in person."

"What good would that do? I don't have any further information on what he did in the service. We've got to find that girl of his. She should know something about his Army career, if she was going to marry him. I guess he met her when he got back from overseas. She must live near the last camp he was at."

The same sober man who had welcomed them to the crematorium now entered the room. E.G. assumed that the cardboard box in the man's white fingers held what Augie had been reduced to: ash, presumably. He had no intention of examining the substance.

Putting on her air of bereavement, Esther accepted the container, and they left the place.

In the car E.G. said, nodding at what she held, "What are you going to do with that?"

"I was going to get rid of them, but I got a better idea. I'm going to give them to Ellie. Something's eating her. Maybe this will get her mind off whatever it is. She was close to Augie, though God knows he paid as little attention to her as to any of the rest of us. He was all for himself."

"Funny," said E.G. as he pulled the car out of the asphalt parking lot of the crematorium, "I thought she was acting a little nicer lately."

"She is. That's what's wrong. It's not natural. I told you Orrie got in late, really late, last night. We had an argument. Then I went back to bed, but before I got to sleep I heard *her* going down the hall and into his room."

He was on a steep section of the road, with a sharp turn coming up, but E.G. expressed his concern at what he heard. "They're getting too old for that kind of thing, aren't they? You ought to say something. Maybe nothing's going on, but still it doesn't look good."

She stared at him. "What are you talking about? For God's sake, don't be creepy. What worries me is what she might have told him about the other night."

E.G. negotiated the big car around the hairpin, then replied. "What could she tell him? She wasn't in the house at the time."

"She came back!"

"You know what I mean. He was dead by then. She went out for beer. By time she got back, we were trying to revive him." He did not bother to characterize the last phrase as ironic: that was self-evident.

Esther put the box of ashes on the floor, bracketing it with her feet. "I don't know exactly what she knows about *us*."

"Come on," said E.G.

"I mean it. She's not like I was at her age. She's a stupid kid — not at schoolwork but with everything about real life."

"What I wish I knew is what Orrie knows or thinks," said E.G. "But he's acting the same as always." He was struck by such a surge of self-pity that he all but gasped. "I wonder if that will change when we finally tell him." He glanced at Esther. He suspected her of wanting to keep the secret forever, even though she had had no respect for Augie. Of course, her motives were selfish: revealing that Orrie was a bastard would reflect on her reputation. Indignantly, even though he could anticipate her answer, which on the rational level made sense, he asked, "When are we going to tell him?"

She sneered. "I'll tell him I'm giving the ashes to Ellie because Augie wasn't *his* father. That should make him feel good."

"You really ought to watch that mouth of yours. I'm the only friend you've got." His tolerance for cunty behavior was reaching its quota. She was someone without a source of income except a G.I. insurance policy she could not collect on.

11

"No," Ellie repeated, her mouth set in that stubborn way he knew so well. "I'm not leaving."

Orrie started again to explain why it would be the right thing for her to accept the Terwillens' offer. "They're nice people. You can see that."

"That's got nothing to do with it," said Ellie. "This is my home. I've got as much right as anybody to live here. And I'm staying."

"I've got to get back to school soon. I'll worry about you living here."

They were in Ellie's room, Gena's former side of which was preserved pretty much as she left it, with fan-mag photos of movie stars thumbtacked on the wall. The chenille bedspread, which could have used a wash, was covered with things Ellie had dropped there.

His sister looked at him in disdain. "You're just going back without doing anything?"

He threw up his hands. "I don't know what I could do."

"Listen," Ellie cried, "I wouldn't go with those goddamn murderers to where my dad was burned to ashes. I hope he understands that, wherever he is now. It wasn't out of lack of respect for *him*."

"I'm sure he does," Orrie said gently.

"I'm not going to forgive and forget. You go on back to college, if you want, but I'm staying right here, you can rely on that. They'll make a mistake one of these days, and I'll be here to see it."

Orrie smiled. "You mean Erle is all of a sudden going to confess? Come on." Of course he had always rejected Ellie's accusations against his mother, but the fact was that neither did he seriously believe Erle was a murderer. He had just been humoring her. But he had discovered that it is difficult when you are around somebody with an obsession totally to avoid being touched by it. Still, he had not really gone further than allowing for the possibility that Erle had maybe bungled his attempts at artificial respiration.

He sat on the chair that went with her little knotty-pine desk. Ellie remained standing. Now she walked to the open doorway and listened for a moment. But it was obvious that Mother and Erle had not returned. She was really getting warped. There was a word for that state of mind, but at the moment it escaped him. When it came back to the memory, he should write it down. At school he had begun to keep a list of new terms, so as to improve his vocabulary now that he was a college student. Paul had seen it once and asked, "What's this?" When told, he shook his head and smiled admiringly. "You're going to get somewhere one of these days."

"I know you're older," Ellie was saying. "And more experienced and, since you're a boy, probably smarter, but —"

Orrie had to interrupt her there. "Your grades are as high as mine were in history and English, and you do better at the toughest stuff of all: math. Miss Sheely gave me a break in algebra, else I'd never have passed. I bet you're getting your usual A's in trig."

"But," she continued as if he had not said a word, "I wonder if you really know much about people."

"I suppose *you* do?"

"I know Mother and Erle are sleeping together."

Orrie had never admitted it to himself in so many words. He was staggered now to hear it from his kid sister. He rose from the chair and walked to the door of the closet and back. Of course he had *known* it — in the way you know you will be burned if you put your finger in a candle flame, so you don't go and verify your knowledge, you just let it be, you simply avoid bringing unprotected flesh near fire: you have no reason ever to talk about it.

"Why do you mention something like that?" he asked. "I don't like the way you have begun to talk."

"You're criticizing *me?*"

"One thing you don't seem to know is what to talk about and what not. *You're* the one who doesn't know about people." His anger increased as he spoke. "It's beneath you. Haven't you got anything better to do with your life? Why don't you wash your hair, for example? Or change the tape on those glasses? It's dirty, for God's sake. I don't know where you suddenly got the right to lord it over everybody else in creation. You're just a young kid in a little town nobody's ever heard of. All of a sudden you act like you're some kind of princess."

The appalling thing was that nothing he said seemed to have any effect on his sister. She should have run from the room or, staying, have been in tears, but her expression was almost serene. "Go on," she said, "get it out of your system."

He said, "Oh, hell," and put his hot forehead against the cool frame of the door to the hallway.

"Look," Ellie said sympathetically. "It's not your fault. I can tell you this: they've been doing it since long before Daddy went to the war. It was Gena who told me."

Orrie turned. "Will you stop? What's gained by this?"

"That's why they murdered him. Well, that and his Army insurance. She keeps calling the government and trying to collect."

Orrie covered his ears. "Stop it, just stop it!" Then he said, as calmly as he could, "If that were true, it would be the best argument against their murdering him. Why would they have to, if they got away with it anyway? And Erle doesn't need money." But to speak like that was mutilating to his soul. His mother could not be touched by filth: he besmirched himself even by submitting the matter to discussion.

Ellie shrugged inside the black sweater she had borrowed from Gena's abandoned wardrobe. With the old pleated black skirt and the black beret she had insisted on wearing, so as to cover her head as befitted an adult woman at a Christian ceremony, it had been her funeral ensemble. Almost obscenely snug at Gena's bosom, the garment hung sacklike from her sister's thin shoulders.

"Why," she said, "they got used to having Daddy away. They didn't want to go back to sneaking around, that's obvious."

Again he was offended by her juvenile smugness. Their father was murdered, Gena dead in exile, their mother a harlot and a murderess. Ellie produced such theories effortlessly. She, who had never so much as walked home from school alongside a boy, knew all about illicit, even perverted sex. . . . He had finally made up his mind: Ellie had some kind of mental problem. She was not exactly crazy, just not quite normal. It was probably only a temporary condition, nothing that required confinement in an asylum or electric-shock treatments, such as had been done to the goofy brother of one of Orrie's high-school friends, Jimmy Wendt, without doing any good whatever for the guy, who was kept at home thereafter, mowing the lawn and raking leaves: the mothers warned neighborhood children to keep their distance, lest they be seized and misused by the maniac, who Jimmy however insisted was absolutely harmless.

Orrie knew there was a type of doctor who just talked to patients with nonphysical problems and gave them things to quiet their nerves. He was no authority on the subject. It seemed to him that his father had had a nervous breakdown, so called, after the business failure. He could not recall what the treatment, if any, had been. Perhaps just the passing of time. Maybe that would work for Ellie. But if she meanwhile continued to slander all and sundry!

"I want you to go to the doctor," he now told his sister.

Her eyes quickened behind the lenses. "Say, that's a good idea," she cried. "And find out if an electric fan, falling like that, could knock a man unconscious enough for him to drown without waking up."

Orrie suppressed an urge to exclaim in despair, and replied as gently as he could, "That was already done at the autopsy. . . . What I'm talking about is that *you* get a checkup. Tell him you probably need something for your nerves." He grinned. "You're not nuts or anything — except in the normal way of girls your age — but this thing has been an awful lot for you to bear. He'll understand, I'll bet."

She was staring at him.

"He might even want to send you on to someone else, a specialist in nervous problems, who —"

"What do you think you're doing?" Ellie asked.

"Don't worry about the fees," Orrie said. "I'll work something out."

"Are you talking about a *psychiatrist?*"

"Certainly not. Not someone who deals with lunatics, for God's sake. But there's another sort of doctor, who just deals with the kind of upsets of the nerves normal people have when things get out of control."

Ellie grimaced in disbelief. "You mean, where you lie down on a couch and talk about your dreams?"

"Oh, you've heard about it? Well, I don't think it's only that." Ellie had always been intellectually precocious. She sometimes even read *Scientific American*.

"Do you realize?" she asked. "You're acting as if *I'm* the one with the problem."

"I certainly didn't mean to hurt your feelings."

"Don't worry: you haven't." But she said it so frostily he knew he had. He was relieved of the need to figure out where to go from there by the sound of his mother's return, downstairs.

He went quickly to his room and closed the door, but before long there was a knock, and his mother's voice asked, "Are you there?"

He opened the door. She was the most attractive woman he had yet seen in real life, slightly taller than he, and so far as he knew he had reached his maximum growth. He could not remember her ever before wearing a completely black outfit, though perhaps she had done so at the funerals of other relatives, which had all taken place when he was very young.

She was angry. "Will you please tell me why you two ran away? You embarrassed me, you know. That doesn't surprise me in *her* case. But *you*."

"I know it might have looked strange —"

"Is that the word for it?"

He beckoned her inside and gently closed the door. "Ellie's in a bad way," he said. "She absolutely refused to go, and I didn't want to leave her wander around by herself."

"We all lost someone, didn't we?" his mother asked, looking at him with angry dark eyes. "Why is it worse for her than for anyone else?"

Because she cared for him more than any of the rest of us did . . . But that would have been out of line to say on the day of cremation.

Instead: "She's got a delicate system. I think she should go to the doctor and get something for her nerves."

"That's crap," his mother said vulgarly, and loudly enough to be heard through a closed door. "She's putting it on to get attention, as usual!" She strode to the door and flung it open. "We've got to have a little conference and straighten things out. I'll meet you both downstairs."

When he reached the hall, Ellie was standing there. She had heard. They went down the stairway in silence, she a step behind.

Their mother stood at the table where the green glass vase had been for years. He noticed its absence. In its place was a cardboard box. She told them to sit down.

Orrie joined Ellie on the couch, which had a summer cover on it throughout the year because it needed reupholstering. But the room was seldom used. They never had guests unless Uncle Erle could be called such.

"We need to get some things straight," his mother said now, looking at the worn rug. "Life goes on and we've got to live it. You should know I am having trouble in locating your father's Army insurance, I don't know why. I haven't even been able to find his serial number. As it is, he's left us with nothing so far."

"I'm leaving school," Orrie said, "and getting a job."

"No, you're not."

"I'm not contributing anything. I can get hired tomorrow at the factory." He referred to the automobile assembly plant just across the state line, which had been occupied with military vehicles during the war but was expected soon to return to family cars. Several of his male contemporaries had gone there last summer, directly on graduation from high school, while they waited to be drafted.

"Don't talk like that. As it is, you're paying your own way completely, with the scholarship and waiting on tables. Hang on and you'll be a doctor and be able to name your own price. You'll *be* somebody, not some loser who lets everyone down."

He was really uneasy at being used for the purposes of adverse implication on his dead father and hastily said, "The work as waiter just takes care of the board. I'm going to look for something else that pays real wages. I got my nights and weekends."

His mother winced and at last sat down. "No," she said. "Absolutely not. You *must* stick to your studies. I'll get by. I just say it might be tough."

Ellie spoke in her high-pitched voice. "I'll try baby-sitting again." She had had little success at that pursuit. Though there were local girls who made good money at such work, Ellie had not been able to get hired by anybody but a young wife who had had a baby almost nine months after her husband had been drafted. Still a teenager herself, the girl found it hard to accept her new responsibility and wanted a baby-sitter to take care of the infant while she went out on the town, sometimes returning with a man. Ellie could not suffer such an offense against her personal moral code.

"Our problems are solved," their mother said with a smirk.

Orrie thought it regrettable that sarcasm was his mother's habitual response to Ellie. Which of course did not justify Ellie's believing her a murderess. But neither did it help.

"That's a good idea," he said, mollifyingly, to his sister and then, to his mother, "It's really lousy the way the government is treating you. A man puts his life on the line for this country, and that's the way they act. I'd better go down there and straighten them out." He was capable of a vigorous public display of indignation when the occasion called for it: somebody unjustly cutting into the head of a line, for example, or the way a postal clerk would shut his window on someone who had waited a quarter hour to reach it. Once as a passenger in a friend's car he denounced, at a stoplight, a driver who had dangerously swerved in front of them a mile earlier, a very large football sort of guy, who on Orrie's complaint climbed heavily out and challenged him to make something of it, and Orrie would recklessly have done it though a head shorter, but his friend was of less stern stuff and sped away. Orrie still believed that a righteous cause gave one the strength of ten, despite the exceptions to the rule that were cited by cynics.

"*You*," said his mother, "are going back to school. You can't miss any more classes."

Ellie suddenly rested her small hand on the back of his. She had never done anything of the kind before, and he was moved. He knew he was defying his mother, but he said firmly, "Not right away. I'm staying around here till we get things back on an even keel."

148

"What things?"

"Well," he said, "it was *you* who had that idea, just now when you told us to come downstairs for a talk."

She sniffed and stood up. "There's one thing more. . . . As you know, your Uncle Erle owns this house. It was only through his generosity that we've been able to stay here." She turned her back on them and spoke toward the arched doorway to the dining room. "He's been living in that apartment hotel in the city. It doesn't make any sense, when this place is his."

"He's moving in," Ellie said levelly, without apparent emotion.

"He *could* just throw us out. Not that he would ever do that, of course, good as he's been to us!"

Orrie asked, "He's moving in?"

Their mother turned to face them. "Would you prefer that he sell it? He's had an offer."

Orrie could not stay seated any longer. "Then Ellie and I are getting out." He grasped his sister's hand, and they both stood up.

"Sit down!"

"No!"

His mother breathed deeply. "Please sit down," she said. "Don't tell me we can't speak reasonably any more."

This sort of approach always appealed to Orrie, who believed in nothing more than reason. He was no authority on international affairs, but he suspected that if someone had spoken reasonably to Hitler early on, there might not have been a World War II.

But Ellie was tugging at him. "Don't listen to her."

This infuriated his mother. "Damn you!"

"All right," he said in his masculine role. "Everybody simmer down."

But now Ellie had become intractable. "Not me," she cried. "No more!" She tore her hand from his and left the room. He could hear her running upstairs.

"If this keeps up," his mother said, "she's going to find herself in some institution. I can't stand much more of it."

"*I'll* look after her," Orrie said with quiet authority. "But I'll tell you this: I won't let her live here if Erle moves in."

His mother shook her head. "What's that supposed to mean? You're not making any sense. Where then would she live? She's not an adult, you know."

"The Terwillens have offered her a home."

"You must be kidding. That pal of Augie's, Bobby Terwillen, on the lifesaving squad? He's *got* a home?"

Again the sarcasm, and about a decent man. "Yes," Orrie said, "and he's got a very nice wife. They don't have any children but have a fairly big house, I guess." He looked down. "Actually, they included me in the offer."

"That's a nice thing to say to me."

He looked up but would not meet her eyes. "I didn't say I accepted."

"What is going on?" his mother asked. Now she was more plaintive than angry. "Why would this subject even come up? *This* is your home. Since when has there been any doubt about that?"

"Well, I'm staying," he said, with a certain sense of shame, for if she had challenged him on the subject of Erle, he would have had the courage to tackle the matter of Gena. But as it stood now, how, out of the clear blue sky, could he bring it up? He had never in all his life said one word about sex, even the normal kind, to his mother. What pretext, what provocation would he need to air this perverted thing? And yet neither could he continue to evade the issue.

"When's he moving in?"

His mother sighed and sat down in the chair. He had to admit she did not look happy at the prospect. He had always avoided thinking too much about her relations with Erle — quite a different thing from the matter of Gena — because there was really nothing he could do about it one way or the other. It was really his father's business, and his father had run away to war, deserting them all.

She said, "He wanted me to tell you."

"Why?"

"He wanted to know your reaction."

Orrie threw his arms in the air. "For God's sake, a lot he cares about that!"

"Don't talk that way," said she. "You matter most with us all."

There was an element in her tone that touched him, even though he could assume it was the kind of sentiment a mother believes she must voice on occasion. He rubbed his nose. "I don't see that it has much to do with me."

She was ill at ease. "Well, it does. He'll need a room, and of course with you at school . . ."

For an instant Orrie was almost happy: that was the pitiful truth. Only now did he realize that he had tacitly been assuming that Erle would move in with her. He shrugged. "As you say, it's his house." But then he hardened. "I'm not going back to school yet." He patted the sofa beneath him. "I'll bunk on this." He spoke quickly to counter her imminent objection. "No! I'm going to do this my way." He sprang to his feet. "When's he coming?"

His mother's expression was grim. She too stood up. "He wanted first to hear your reaction."

Orrie shook his head. The idea that anyone would seriously ask for an opinion of his was novel indeed. He might have been flattered had he believed for a moment that Erle was sincere, even though he could not have identified a likely reason for the man to be hypocritical in this instance. Why should Erle curry favor, now that he was their only hope? Orrie was never a cynic except when it came to Erle: nor could he have explained that state of mind. He was about to leave the room when his mother detained him. She indicated the box that occupied the place on the drum table which had always belonged to the vase. "Would you ask Ellie if she'd like to have these?"

She had correctly assumed that he himself would have been embarrassed by the offer and was therefore careful not to make it to him.

His sister could not be found anywhere on the second floor, yet he had not heard her leave the house. The only place left then was the attic, which could be reached through the last door at the end of the north side of the hallway, and then on up one straight flight of stairs. It was the kind of place he would have adored as a younger boy, but they had not lived in this house until he began adolescence and was too old for hideouts for make-believe.

Ellie was there now, examining a collection of pieces of luggage, all pretty old and shabby: he had already helped himself to the best of the lot when he went off to college.

"You're getting prepared to move to the Terwillens'?" he asked disingenuously.

She shook her head. "But I'm getting out of this place."

"You'll have to get past me first." Orrie histrionically squared off before her. "I'm not letting you hit the road."

"Then come along."

"Maybe I will be ready for that when the time comes, but —"

"For God's sake, he's *moving in!* What time are you waiting for? Isn't that the limit?"

The fact was simply that Orrie still could not make up his mind as to what he should do, but he could no longer afford to let her know that, for she would only consider it as a weakness — which perhaps it was.

"If we leave now, though," he said, "he's won, hasn't he? We don't have anything on him but your word. Not that that's not good enough for me, but it isn't enough to take to the police. If we stay, we can keep him under surveillance. If we do it the right way, I mean not too obviously, he'll be lulled into a sense of false security."

He lowered himself onto a middle-sized trunk that had come down from one part of the family or another.

Ellie began to like the idea. Perhaps she had seen the same movie he had taken it from. She sat down alongside him. "If only," she said, "we could plant a secret microphone some-place where they would talk."

Orrie knew she was quite serious. To give her something to think about, he said, "You know you can listen through a wall to conversations on the other side by means of a water glass: you put the bottom of the glass against the wall and the hollow end against your ear. It really works." As a high-school student he had once seen some of the other guys doing that on the wall between the respective locker rooms of the boys and the girls, though apparently nothing memorable was heard.

Ellie nodded. "But it still would not be legal evidence, would it, unless it could be recorded somehow? It would just be my word against theirs. And they're adults."

He could see she was not going to make it easy for him. "Maybe not, but what it would do is confirm your suspicions. I mean, if you heard Erle talking about murdering Dad, you'd know you were right that he did it."

Ellie leaned away from him and said, with spirit, "I don't

need anything like that. I *know* they did it, both of them."

He found it chilling when she spoke in such a fashion. To change the subject, he said, "Mother thought you might like to have Dad's ashes." It was out before he realized how inappropriate a subject it was to bring up just now.

But as it happened, Ellie's reaction did not seem negative. "I'll get something nice to keep them in, something really nice."

He preferred her in that mood. "Remember Mr. Swayne, who lived next door to us when we were in the other house? Once his brother came back from a visit to Cuba and brought him a box of expensive cigars in a real cedar box. He gave me the box when the cigars were gone. It had a nice smell of tobacco and real cedar. I loved that smell. I still have the box, keep just junk in it. After all these years it still has that great aroma, real masculine, you know? You can have it if you want."

"Well, thanks," said Ellie. "But I've got some money from birthdays and Christmas and all." Some of this came from Orrie himself. When she was younger he had given her girls' books about horses, nursing, and the like, but nowadays, being pretty ignorant in the area of the tastes of high-school females (except for those of which he disapproved, e.g., pretty-boy crooners), he gave cash. "Friedman's has some handmade brass boxes from India."

"I didn't mean to insult you," Orrie said soberly. "The cigar box is real cedar. I didn't mean I kept junk in it that's really *junk*. My debating medal's there and some cufflinks that belonged to Grandpa and a snapshot of all of us, when you were a little bitty kid, at Lake Mohocan, Gena and us all."

"I've got some old pictures of Daddy," Ellie said. "I found them in here." She pointed down at the trunk on which they sat. "*She* put everything to do with him in there, just as soon as he went away to the Army. She never wanted him to come back."

It occurred to him that Ellie must have spent some previous time in the attic. Near the dirty window that looked onto the street were an erected card table and folding chair. On the tabletop was a stub of a candle, stuck with wax into the inverted cap of a pickle jar. At the other end, away from the window that gave onto the back yard, pushed as far as the sloping beams of the roof allowed, was an old mattress that looked scarcely thicker than a quilt.

"You use this place?"

"Sometimes," said she.

"God!" He rose. "I'm sweating like a pig right now, and it's not that hot a day."

"Neither was it the day that Daddy supposedly put on the fan before he took a bath."

He did not care to hear anything more on that subject at the moment. He went to the front window.

Ellie said, "If you want to save anything of Daddy's, you better take it, because one of these days I just know she'll throw everything out now he's dead."

Orrie examined the window and saw that it had a movable sash that could be opened to let in air. He slid it up. But there was no screen.

"Do you really stay here all night?"

"I tried it, but it gets too hot on sunny summer days. Also the mosquitoes get in."

"Well, if you don't mind, I'm going to have to move up here for a while anyway. Erle's taking my room."

"That son of a bitch."

Orrie was enraged. "I don't want to hear you talk like that! I'll wash your mouth out with soap. Listen, I swear

I will! You're not too old for that." There was little he detested more than a foul mouth on a female of any age. He had once had a crush on a little blonde named Donna May Waters, but lost it when he heard her utter an indecency in a nonextreme situation.

Ellie made no acknowledgment of his admonition. She said, "I naturally thought he'd shack up with *her*."

This was not much better than her previous comment, even though it echoed an earlier assumption of his own. He renewed his glare. "You really ought to try to be more ladylike and not use the smutty language of G.I.s. Erle's got a right to move in. The house belongs to him."

"That's right," Ellie said nastily. "You just go around taking *his* side."

A big horsefly zoomed past his left ear, sounding like an airplane. But a person could suffocate up here with the windows closed. Ellie tried his patience. "You ought to watch your mouth. She said she might have to send you away."

"Good! I can't wait."

But in the next moment his heart went out to her. "Come on down to the kitchen. We haven't had any lunch, if you noticed. I'll make you a fried-egg sandwich with ketchup on it, just the way you like 'em." When their mother was away at weekend lunchtimes, but once in a while even when she was there, it would be Orrie and not Ellie who prepared the food. He could not cook anything but fried eggs, so it would be those, or cold cuts or canned soup. He found it gratifying that these were the only times he ever saw his sister eat with apparent satisfaction.

"I got the funeral guy to open the coffin," Ellie said. "I took Daddy's ribbons to keep. They would just have got burned with the rest of him. You think that was okay or was it, uh, sacrilegious or something?"

"It was okay," said Orrie. "Dad would have wanted you to do that." It was the least he could say.

The way she had been sitting on the trunk, she might have been a little old lady with back trouble, but she sprang up with energy. "I'm going down to get Daddy's ashes before she dumps them in the garbage."

The abusive statement provoked no remonstrance from Orrie, who was weary now. He had chided her enough for today, with absolutely no visible effect.

Ellie stopped at the head of the stairs. "You shouldn't be the one to move up here. You're now the head of the family. I want you to take my room."

"No," he said, "I like being up this high." It was true, though it had only just occurred to him. Looking out the back window, he could see the sturdy branch of the old elm, which he had never before realized, in his earthbound way, was so tall. Some of its limbs seemed to go on past the peak of the roof. Beyond the Mencken yard was an uncultivated area of weeds and the trashy kinds of trees that might actually be bushes or vice versa. Orrie could vaguely remember his father's talking about how smart it would be to buy that land and make it into real-estate lots, but he had not had the money, in fact only moved to this house because he had none. It was definitely on the wrong side of town, less than three blocks from the river and the broken-down buildings along the shore, some of which were hardly more than shacks. The people who lived there were said to be a mixture of Indian, Negro, and degraded white stock. The men fished for a living and performed odd jobs. The women allegedly did some whoring but refused to hire out as household help — in any event that was what was said around town. Orrie had no personal experience of them, though in fantasy he had been seduced many a time by voluptuous, swarthy harlots in waterfront hovels. Some of the more supposedly "advanced" high-school boys claimed to have lost their virginity in that fashion, for the price of two bucks each. But those boasts might well have been empty.

The ritzier part of the river was downstream, toward the city. As a younger boy, Orrie had once promised his mother he would become rich one day and buy her a house there. Gena, still home then, said that too was a slum compared with Beverly Hills. She had saved a Sunday rotogravure article on the stars' homes and could not wait to go out there and take the bus tour.

No part of the river was visible from the back attic window. Beyond the area of potential vacant lots was a quarry full of enough rainwater to high-dive into, though it had been denied to local boys by a chain-link fence since one of them drowned there a few years earlier. Had it been accessible to Orrie, he might not still be without sexual experience, for there had been nighttime skinny dipping and everybody knew where that could lead. He was a good swimmer and would have been emboldened by the darkness. Of course Gena was a veteran of the quarry at an early age. His father had punished her for such indulgences, confined her to her room, but Ellie told Orrie their sister climbed out the window and down a trellis to the ground. So far as their parents went, Ellie held her peace. He had heard guys say girls could never hold a secret, would always spill the beans, sell you out. Not Ellie, even with her hand in the fire! But necessarily he owed his first allegiance to their mother: that was a natural law.

He liked being at a height, he who was shorter than most. Up here he was not so defenseless. He could be attacked only via the bottleneck of the narrow stairs, could hold off an army, taking them on one by one. But ventilation could be a problem. Ellie was oblivious to matters of that sort. He tried to open the back window, but it was stuck too tightly. Something with a blade was needed to be run around the sash. He went to look among his father's possessions.

The trunk was seasoned with wear, but, unlike those shown in movies, devoid of stickers from glamorous steamships and oriental hotels. When Orrie made a lot of money he planned to live in an altogether different way from that of his family. In that aim he was at one with Gena though he shared none of her tastes for the flashy. When he traveled, all would be perfection, his companion a wife of exquisite grace who wore a hat and gloves everywhere and effortlessly spoke the languages of the places visited — as of course, by then, would he.

Just inside the trunk lid was a segmented tray, the compartments of which held an inexpensive pocket watch, some tarnished cufflinks, tie bars, a ring or two, a mother-of-pearl penknife, the kind of thing his father when home and alive surely kept closer at hand, presumably in the bedroom. With its short and slender blade, the knife was useless for Orrie's current purpose. He removed the tray. In the belly of the trunk was folded clothing, but folded without care for the configurations of the garments. Nor had precautions been taken against moths. Fortunately he had borrowed that suit-jacket of his father's during the senior year in high school, when his dad's civilian clothes still occupied the far left end of the closet in the master bedroom, the other side of which was used for his mother's coats, and perhaps the fumes from the mothballs in the pockets of the latter were strong enough also to protect the clothes at the other end. In any event, the jacket suffered no damage. But the first item he now removed from the trunk and shook out of its crumple was a pair of navy-blue trousers that below the fly had been well perforated by the insects, who had gone on conspicuously to damage every formerly wearable garment in the collection except the neckties, a thin leather belt, and a pair of pigskin gloves.

He could use a tie or two. He sensed that Paul did not think much of the plaid one that was his own favorite simply because there it was, always hanging conveniently around the neck of the same hanger that held the jacket. He could use the belt and gloves as well. His current wardrobe for the winter to come was a three-quarter-length corduroy coat, lined with rayon. He dug deeper, looking for the thick woolen overcoat he thought he remembered, and as he did, he felt, not ghoulish as at first he feared he might feel, but really closer to his dad than he had in years, perhaps ever, for clothes are souvenirs more poignant than pictures and much more so than most letters with their received phrases and stilted sentiments.

No overcoat could be found. Maybe his father wore it when going off to war. After all those years, Orrie could not remember offhand which season that had been. But had the Army kept the garment? There was so much about his father's matters that he did not understand, beginning with why his mother so despised the man. Why had his father failed at business while Erle prospered? And he did not even know exactly what business Erle was in. It was supposed to be real estate, but then why didn't *he* buy the land between the house and the quarry and make lots from it? That nonsensical events were commonplace in life went without saying: what was inexplicable was that some of them had enormous consequences while others remained curiosities without implication, and he at least could not tell the difference until it was too late.

At the very bottom of the trunk he found the double-barreled shotgun his father had used that long-ago day to wound a pheasant. Orrie could not bear to watch him put it out of its misery by hand and had run away across the field. That was not the only reason why his father thought him less than manly, but perhaps it was the most memorable. "You eat meat," his dad had said on the drive home. "But you let someone else kill it for you." He had realized at the time that the charge was just, but there was nothing he could do about it. At any rate he would not have eaten a bite of the pheasant, even if his mother had cooked it, which she did not: she threw it into the garbage, didn't know how to roast it, wouldn't have done so if told; food came from the store, not the great outdoors. And Orrie wondered, though did not ask, why kill something when you know you're not going to be allowed to eat it? Was that manly?

The gun was disassembled, its two parts wrapped in the worn canvas of an old brown hunting jacket. Orrie had fired it once, in a practice session before they set out on the hunt for pheasant. He carried no weapon of his own that day, but was to get a boy's beginner gun, a light .410-bore, at Christmas — if his mother approved. Of course she would not have done so, had things got that far, but even before the matter of the downed bird, it was clear that he was not the boy to arm. The recoil of the twelve-gauge had almost knocked him down, though as forewarned he had braced himself, and despite his having kept the butt pressed firmly against his shoulder, it had somehow pulled away only to slam back with massive force when the shot left the barrel. His bruised shoulder had stayed sore for days. He was manly enough not to complain, but he gave the gun back to his father without discharging the second barrel (and was criticized for the lack of proper safety procedures in so doing), and never touched the weapon again until this moment.

His father had taken care of the gun: when Orrie picked

up the business end and, as if he were an old hand with ordnance, squinted through the barrels, he saw they glistened with oil after all these years and, owing to the jacket in which they had been wrapped, showed little dust. It did not take much knowhow to join the barrels with the stock. Put into proximity, they virtually did the job themselves. Pointing the weapon at the window, by the light of which he had inspected the interior of the barrels, he squeezed the near trigger and then the farther, remembering too late that his father had warned, years before, against doing that and so jeopardizing the firing pins, which had a tendency, when futilely striking not metal but rather empty air, to shear off. Orrie saw that as unlikely even when his father explained by analogy: there was less strain on the arm when a fist hit a punching bag than when it missed. "But what about when it hits something hard?" Well, it anyway happened with firing pins, metal having laws of its own. Orrie never really believed it then, but he did now. Not that he had learned anything more about guns in the years since: it was just that he realized Dad had surely known what he was talking about and deserved to be taken on faith by a son who knew nothing at all in those days. . . . And had learned little enough later on. He was feeling worse now than he had at any time since first hearing of his father's death, in some sort of delayed reaction, brought on by the clothing and especially the gun, the peculiar odor of which, blued-steel and oil and maybe even a touch of the polished walnut stock, he had not smelled since the pheasant hunt on which he had so let down his dad.

Just above one of the lower pockets of the canvas jacket was a series of narrow tubular pockets for the carrying of ammunition, and three now held brass-topped, red-shafted shells. Just one would do the job, of course, but with the muzzle in his lips, his arm was not quite long enough to reach

the trigger, even with his finger extended to the utmost —
unless he forced it so far down his throat he would gag and
maybe throw up before he could blow his head off — how
disgusting that would be for his mother and Ellie. Nevertheless, there was no hope for him in life. For a moment that
truth was so exquisitely clear as to be beyond pain, beyond
sorrow, and even beyond regret.

12

Coming back from the crematorium, E.G. had dropped Esther off at home and then gone on a few errands (picking up some meat, collecting rents). He had regretted killing Augie since the moment the deed was done, and could not now remember quite how she had talked him into participating in it. After all, at stake was only ten grand in insurance money, and all of it would have gone only for her upkeep, unless he wanted to provide more from his own pocket. Augie's monthly allotment checks had run through her fingers like sand, and what did she spend it on? She fed the kids on cold cuts and canned junk. When he took her to the track, she expected him to finance her bets and then let her keep the rare winnings. The truth was, he had never really liked Esther. As a kid she had been an easy lay, had practically ripped his fly open the first time he found himself alone with her. She had always been addicted to him, and it was hard to avoid someone who thought so highly of you: even when you cannot return the favor, you must recognize the good taste of such an addiction.

Esther had always been crazy about him while having nothing but contempt for Augie, which if you thought about it was the goddamnedest thing imaginable, the way it all eventually worked out, and it was not over yet. E.G. never had anything against Augie. If he ever pretended to have, it was Esther who provoked him. Throughout all the years he had maintained a connection with her for one reason alone: his son. That he had never yet been able to establish much rapport with the boy was disappointing, but the situation was not hopeless. After all, they had never, he and Orrie, yet lived under the same roof — Esther had even insisted he go home early on those evenings he came to dinner (bringing the steak), or if he and she went out to eat, to return her at a reasonable hour and then leave. Furthermore, on the latter occasions, by always inviting both Orrie and Ellie to come along in the family unit, such events could not be defined as "dates." For a long time now the children could be counted on to decline the invitation and dine from cans at home, leaving Esther and him to get takeout, or maybe eat nothing at all, and go to a tourist cabin. He could still service her effectively after all those years, even though she was not his type and maybe never had been.

Gena on the other hand, when she reached puberty, embodied his ideal: blonde, blue-eyed, and with flesh so young and radiant that it glowed in the dark, yet he could never begin to arouse her. His money bought him nothing but a negative: she would not stop him from doing what he wanted. It was as if she left her body with him, as she might rent out a piece of clothing, and went away somewhere until he was done with it. She was saving up for enough money to go to Hollywood, as she reminded him frequently, lest he think her just a common prostitute. If he knew anything about life after considerable experience of it, she was hustling the streets out there — if she ever got that far, for though on the money he had given her alone (plus God only knew what from others: he had no illusions about being unique in her career), she could have taken the Super Chief, she was a stingy, greedy little bitch and decided to save the fare and hitchhike, earning maybe more money en route. More likely, as he assured her, she would get robbed of the funds she carried in her underpants, when they were ripped away by the driver who raped her and maybe even slit her throat when done. E.G. told her: "You're just a small-town kid." She looked at him and snorted. "Oh, *yeah?*" He had never once seen her without a sullen mouth. You certainly couldn't buy a smile from those lips, which remained cool under no matter how hot a kiss. She could have got anything out of him if she even pretended to like him more. He had too much pride to make that point to her, but for her sake he hoped somewhere along the line she would realize that for a girl like her to get anywhere at all, she had to submit to men, not just fuck them, with or without pay; to have some real respect. Being pretty was not enough, not anywhere, and certainly not in Holly-wood, where those baldheaded old Jew producers could get any kind of quiff they wanted, didn't have to kowtow to some little chippy from nowhere. But listening to anything he said would have interfered with her sense of herself as royalty untouched by human hands even though you might errone-ously believe your cock was up to its hilt in her belly.

One day Gena up and left, without goodbyes for anybody, unless she told Ellie, that skinny, creepy little thing — though he basically felt sorry for her: her sister had got all the looks, leaving none for her, and nobody could have convinced E.G. that brains were a suitable substitute when it came to females. Esther didn't miss Gena for a minute. Maybe she suspected what had been going on. Though different on the surface, underneath it all they had certain similarities, she and Gena, namely the whoriness, though the kid seemed to find the act distasteful and cared only for the money, whereas her mother couldn't get enough of either. Especially as she got older, Esther verged on the nympho, but always had her hand out too, though she lived in the house free of charge except for the utilities and phone. He saw it as a point of principle that he not pay for the enormous supplies of hot water used by her and Gena for their incessant baths or for the latter's overuse of the telephone, which he suspected might well be for business. But no doubt he ended up footing such bills indirectly. Aside from his dick, Esther had no other purpose for him but as a source of money, and though he complained, he generally supplied her needs because of Orrie.

He admired his son. Talk about brains, Orrie had enough and then some. Straight A right through school, at college on a scholarship. This was a terrific honor, though while proud as he could be, E.G. regretted he would not be paying for the boy's education. It would have been the vicarious fulfillment of one lifetime dream. He had himself been a good student and was certainly smart enough to have done well at higher learning, but his dad hadn't had the funds to send him to college, and in those days nobody heard of scholarships. So he had never been a college man, could not fly the pennant at homecoming football games, had no ring with the university seal, no access to the social circles of the educated classes, something he would have liked as he became more comfortably fixed financially and could with suitable encouragement have entertained values beyond the narrowly material. But now this would be possible for Orrie, along with so much more. As a great surgeon, there would be no limit to how high he could rise. Everybody, including presidents and kings, was at a doctor's mercy.

But Augie's murder cast a shadow across such projections. They should never have gone through with it after the electric-fan trick had flopped, a failure that was altogether *her* fault. He could not get over her ignoring his warning to check the length of the cord. He should have dropped out at that first definite proof she lacked basic respect for him. He had planned so carefully, establishing exactly where a blow to the bedroom wall would communicate an effective vibration to the other side: right at where, if the plaster had been scraped away, you could find the stud, to the other side of which the little bathroom shelf was attached. A blow elsewhere, on plaster without rigid support, would likely be harmlessly absorbed and not reach the bathroom side with any force.

But all his care had gone for naught. As it turned out, they might as well have dispensed with the plan and simply burst in and drowned the poor drunk bastard without preliminaries. It would even have been more merciful. As the days went by, E.G. had begun to associate himself more with Augie than with Esther. They were both her victims, in more ways than one, and Orrie might well be the third male she destroyed. What would it mean to his scholarship if the truth were known even in a partial form? That his supposed father had been murdered by his mother, who had been given some assistance by his real father, whose mistress she had been for almost twenty years? And as to the boy's subsequent career, if indeed he got that far now, what prosperous patients would put their lives in the hands of a doctor from a family background like that?

E.G. hated her for jeopardizing Orrie's future. It was absolutely essential now that he himself be permanently installed on the premises. God knew what she might do behind his back. Maybe even, if she feared the authorities were closing in, she would sell him out for their promise to go easy on her. He could not allow himself to be lulled into a sense of false security by the apparent lack of police suspicion: it could be they were just biding their time, waiting for him to lower his guard. Howie Gross could be smarter than he looked, not to mention that, given Augie's recent association with the military, the FBI might be eligible to come in. It might even be that Augie had not yet been formally discharged by the time of his death, in which case they were in the worst trouble of all. The murder of a soldier, a war hero, still on duty?

You could know a woman for two decades and foolishly believe all the while that it was you who had the upper hand, and then suddenly find the situation was precisely the reverse and that furthermore she was thoroughly evil. Moving into the house thus took courage on his part. If she would murder one man for nothing, what about another who could implicate her in a capital crime? He felt then he was laying his life on the line for Orrie, the son who as yet, it had to be admitted, despised him. But as yet Orrie did not know who his father really was.

13

It took Orrie longer to move into the attic than he had anticipated. His clothes were easily transferred, the few hangered items going on nails into the beams and the smaller stuff in two cardboard cartons. But he had to deal with the complex matter of his other possessions, some of which, like the Indian flint blade so large it must have been a spear tip and not a mere arrowhead, he had owned since quite early in life and expected to keep forever. But now the status of some had been altered by his removal to the third floor. The spearhead was of historical interest and scarcely the kind of gewgaw that could be lightheartedly discarded, though perhaps its proper place was in the natural-history museum in the city. He had not found it himself but had been given it by a man his father knew, who had been presented it by a relative of his own. But the letter opener, supposedly a small replica of King Arthur's Excalibur, made in Japan, he had purchased himself in a novelty store that had since gone out of business. The combination pocket compass and folding magnifying glass he had bought through the mail, from an ad in a boys' magazine. The fencing foil had been a gift of his Latin teacher, who had used it in college but never since, living in a place where no one else practiced the sport, so he gave it to Orrie, in lieu of wages, for helping him clean out his basement one Saturday. Orrie used it only to thrust at imaginary opponents in brief fantasies from swashbuckler movies, but had kept it against the day he himself went to college. Now he was there but had not as yet checked into whether there was a fencing team, and the foil meanwhile stayed home — for he had not wanted to arrive at school with it under his arm and be thought some sort of snob by fellow students whose game was football.

The books in the case included those he had received when barely old enough to read, some with only a few words on each page, below the pictures. He would have been embarrassed to be asked by a contemporary why he hung on to such and would probably have professed simply to have forgotten they were there, on the lowest shelf where you normally did not look and where dust formed a blanket (for Orrie was supposed to do his own cleaning, if any was done). But the fact was that he kept them because they had been given to him by his mother, who furthermore had, in the earliest days, when letters were yet incomprehensible to him, read aloud from the books, with his small body against her warmth, her scent his atmosphere. And then a few years later on, it was *he* who, showing off his new skill, would read to *her*. Looking back now, he recognized that her patience with him had been inexhaustible, at a time when his father, and of course his older sister, had no time to spare from their own concerns. He could recollect little about his associations with them except being complained about. But there had never been an occasion on which his mother did not receive him as if there were no more important an event in all the world.

Surely she would still be that way; it was he who had changed. When you reached a certain age, you couldn't go running to your mother, especially if you were already worried about your dad's low opinion of your manhood. And that your dad, at an older age than most, went off to fight in a war made your problem even greater. While his father was in combat, Orrie belonged to the high-school dramatic club (and in a one-act farce once played a girl in lipstick and rouge) and served on the debating team. But he would fight if pushed too far and once had an encounter with a boy who was so much larger than he that simply standing up to him brought more respect than anything Orrie had to that point accomplished in life, some of it coming from the bruiser himself, who afterwards called him a pal.

Despite the sentimental value of some of the stuff in the old room, he would have left much of it behind had the new tenant been anybody but Uncle Erle. The childhood books were especially cumbersome, for there were no shelves in the attic, and it did not seem right to move up the little bookcase itself and so denude one wall of its only furniture: Orrie could honor principle in such matters of order, but he would leave behind nothing of a personal nature, including the only decoration, an unframed charcoal drawing of the head of an Irish setter, done by himself in high-school art class, the only thing he had ever done that even distantly approached his own standards. It was Ellie, and not himself, who thought so highly of his talent — if this example could even be called art. The conception was not at all original: he had copied a photograph, though not in the sense of a tracing. He had used charcoal because he could not cope with water colors. Maybe he should give her the picture now.

But as it was his best, and given the likelihood that he would never again produce anything that could be called art, he really ought to present it to his mother, who furthermore was so partial to dogs. It was with her in mind, in fact, as he now remembered, he had undertaken the project, which was to be a gift at some bygone Christmas. But when he was done, back then, the drawing had just not seemed good enough for the purpose, though it was his best. He had always resisted taking advantage of a mother's natural partiality towards her child: he did not want an approval that was obligatory. By now, however, the quality of the drawing seemed to have improved considerably, he could not say why. He had not really looked at it in years and had little memory of doing it, apart from the banal recollection that your fingers got dirty using that medium and could mark up your face if like him you often touched your features while deliberating: others in the art room would stare at him and giggle. Maybe he cared too much about public opinion, but, given his family, he was often conscious of it, while telling himself it didn't matter, that what did matter in life was not what you came from but where you were headed.

He was all at once captive of a powerful emotion, one that was in effect anti-Ellie, but he could not help it; it was natural enough. He decided to go downstairs and give the drawing to his mother, after all these years, even though it was unframed. She would understand and be touched. It was a positive act on an otherwise negative day that had begun with a funeral. Nevertheless, he felt guilty as he prepared to pass Ellie's room, taking pains to keep the drawing on his far side, though it was too large to be concealed entirely. But his sister's door proved to be, uncharacteristically in daytime, closed so firmly as to give the impression it was locked.

When he was opposite the open door to his own room he

saw Erle inside and was instantly almost asphyxiated with rage on the assumption that the bastard was already moved in.

Erle's face had shown a desolate expression in repose, but he assumed the usual smile when he recognized Orrie. "Hi, fella!" he said, waving though they were so near each other. "I just came looking for you."

Orrie advanced on him by instinct, as if to protect the room against further pollution though he had already completed his personal removal and had neither obligation nor, technically speaking, current license to perform such duty.

"Look," Erle said, "I understand from your mom you got the wrong idea about me coming to live in the house. I'm not going to take your room away from you, for gosh sakes!" Trying to be charming, he was at his most obnoxious. "I wouldn't ever try to do anything like that."

Orrie at last managed to speak, but his throat was still constricted. "No, no!" He coughed. "It's all yours."

"Why, I won't —"

Orrie shouted, "I've moved out! If you don't want it, it will be empty!"

Erle continued to smile, but he was obviously under tension. "It's good news you've decided to go back to school. That's what we wanted. But you'll certainly need your room for when you come home weekends and holidays, which I sure hope you will, because I'm looking forward to us getting acquainted on a new kind of basis now. All these years we've known each other, and yet we really don't *know* each other, as I bet you too would agree." The look in his eye that Orrie had always hated most — the one that was always begging for something was worse than the know-it-all — was now more exaggerated than ever. There was not anything about the man that he did not despise. He detested the eternal five-o'clock shadow, which looked worst of all when Erle's cheeks were newly shaven and powdered, the curve of his nose, his one crooked eyebrow, and the long simian upper lip.

"I'm *not* going back to school, at least not for a while, I can assure you of that. I'm staying here. I moved into the attic."

Erle grinned at him. "Come on. Don't try to kid a kidder." He looked as though he wanted to deliver a joking finger to the bellybutton, as had been his practice when Orrie was younger.

"I'm living up there for the moment," he said levelly. "I'll be on hand."

"Well, that's good news," Erle said, with what seemed an effort at enthusiasm. "But maybe you'll reconsider after a day or so, before you get too far behind in your studies. That's all that concerns me. I mean, I really like you being close by. Maybe we can have some good long talks one of these days. I mean, with Augie gone —"

"The sheets are in the bathroom cupboard," Orrie said, in a louder voice than necessary. He had stripped his own off the bed and transferred them to the attic, but left the blanket and spread.

"You know," Erle said. "This is a good big room. Plenty of space over there by the window for an extra bed and even a bureau. Supposing I buy those pieces: we could share the room. I wouldn't be here much at all, and no matter what you say, I know you'll want to go back to college soon, you're too levelheaded to do otherwise. The last time I shared a room was with your dad, many years ago. Our grandpa — your great-grandfather — had a place down at the shore. Sometimes Augie and I would double up in one of the rooms for a week at a time. We got along all right. If one of us snored, it didn't bother the other!" He acted as if this was a funny comment and grinned smugly. "How about you? How're you getting along with that roommate? I wasn't fortunate enough to go to college myself. On the other hand, I guess I was lucky in not having to go into the service. Though Augie seemed to make a go of it there, didn't he, with those medals and all?"

It did not seem right that he used a father's first name when speaking to the son. But he was anyway babbling. There was really nothing to the man. Molesting young girls was his speed. "My dad was a hero," Orrie said. "I wish he could have lived longer." Tears might have come to him at this point, had he not refused to show any weakness to this inferior creature.

Erle's importunate look grew excruciating. "What's that you have there?" he asked, indicating the charcoal drawing, which Orrie had momentarily forgotten he still held. "Is it that terrific dog picture you did in school?"

Orrie felt outraged. "How do *you* know about that?"

"I sometimes glance in your room," Erle said sheepishly. "I don't mean I'm snooping or anything. I'm always interested in how you're getting along. We're relatives, after all, and I've been close to your parents since before you were born." He gestured at the drawing. "I want to buy that picture. There are people I'd like to show it to, people who are art collectors. Of course, we still think you should keep heading for medical school. But having artistic talent on the side can't hurt."

Orrie simply could not listen to any more of that without reacting in some extreme fashion, so he made his exit. The idea of giving the drawing to his mother now had been ruined. He went into the bathroom, closed the door, tore the picture into bits small enough for the drain, and flushed them down the toilet.

He stopped at Ellie's door, tapped on it, and identified himself. She threw the bolt open and let him in.

176

"I need a pillow and blanket. It'll begin to get cold soon, even up there. I thought of Gena's."

"Oh, sure," said Ellie. "I'll bring them up and make your bed for you."

"I'll do it."

"You're a boy."

"I'm sure Dad had to do it for himself in the Army."

She lowered her eyes and began to take away what was probably four years of her junk from Gena's bedspread. The room was in another kind of mess than in her sister's day, when dirty underwear was always in evidence and the dressertop laden with cosmetics. Ellie's clutter was largely one of books and papers. He helped her now, transferring to the top of the desk several stout volumes, the uppermost of which was a work on the reptiles of North America.

"Since when are interested in snakes? I thought you were scared of them."

"I am," she said. "But I thought that might be only because I didn't know much about them. You know, there are only a very few types of poisonous reptiles in the country. They're the only ones to fear. The other types really do a lot of good for mankind in keeping down the rodent population."

Ellie was certainly brainy, but that would never get her far with the boys — which however, in view of Gena's lamentable ways, might not be the worst fate. At least one of the zoology professors at college was a woman, and there was an instructor in English who was so young and attractive that at first he took her for a coed.

"So I've heard," he said. "But I guess it takes a special sort of girl to think about that when she sees a snake." He hoped she would take that as the approbation he intended it to be.

"You know what might make a lot of sense?" she asked

brightly. "There isn't any good reason why we couldn't share this room. If you wanted your privacy we could hang a blanket on a rope from there to *there*. You'd have a real bed to sleep in and if I moved her clothes out of the closet and took them up to the attic, there'd be loads of room for your stuff."

Orrie shook his head reprovingly. "Come on, Ellie, you know that wouldn't be right."

"You mean just because of the ideas of other people," she said with scorn. "So what do we care? We're nothing like other people anyway."

"What's that supposed to mean?"

"Do you know anyone else like our family?" she asked bitterly. "Everybody looks down on us as it is."

"That's not true! Didn't the Terwillens just invite us to move in with them?"

"Because they pity us! That's not respect."

He moved past her and, having peeled the bedspread off, claimed the underlying pink blanket and the caseless pillow in its striped ticking. After all these years Gena's scent could still be detected, though what as a younger boy he had found nauseating was no longer blatant.

"I'm not saying you're right," he said, adjusting his armload of soft stuffs. "But let me tell you something: if you are, then the way to fight back is not to do anything weird, but to be as normal as possible, to do every single thing in the regular way approved by all. Not to throw away all standards and just do what you feel like! Can't you see that?"

"I suppose it's normal to sleep on the floor in the attic of your own home?"

He smiled in pride. "In certain circumstances, yes." He might have added that she would understand such matters only when she was older, but was restrained by the thought that she might not. He was aware they had different ap- proaches to life, but could not have said whether that was due to their opposing sexes or altogether to a natural variation in individuals even of the same blood.

He had not closed the door after Ellie had admitted him. Now their mother came into the doorway, though no farther.

She seemed to be speaking under a strain. As always, when he was in Ellie's company, she addressed him only. "Erle came back to take us all out to dinner. He wants to save me the labor of cooking on a day like this." She made a little quick mechanical smile. "He wants you to name the res- taurant."

"I'm not hungry," Orrie said. He expected Ellie to chime in with the same message, as she had always done in the past, but she remained silent.

"Well, I wish you'd do me the favor of going," his mother said.

"I don't look at it that way."

She took note of his burden. "I'm told you have moved up to the attic. That's really foolish of you. I don't want you up there. It embarrasses me."

He sullenly avoided her eyes.

"He's not moving in right away!" She continued to stand in the doorway. Was what she was saying largely for the benefit of a listening Erle?

Ellie had sat down at her desk and opened the book about reptiles.

"He can move in whenever he wants," Orrie said at high volume. "The house belongs to him, doesn't it?"

His mother winced. "You won't even honor my request that you come to dinner?"

"It's not the kind of thing you should be asking. There's no honor in it." Orrie was immediately sorry he had added the final phrase, but was too proud to withdraw or even soften it.

After a long pause, she left.

His sister rushed to the door, closed and locked it. She came to Orrie's side. Her voice was lowered. "It's not smart to be antagonistic. How can we get anything on them if we avoid them one hundred percent?"

Orrie wished that honor would have allowed him to escape from the entire matter. He remained essentially alone, even with regard to Ellie.

"When they leave," he said, "we'll go down and have some fried eggs."

"If there *are* any eggs," Ellie said, looking skeptically from the tops of her glasses. "I think I forgot to get any."

He climbed to his lair and dropped the blanket and spread on the wadded sheets from his old bedroom. When they moved out of their former house, the one he had known since birth, his mother discarded or gave to the Goodwill a lot of extra stuff that might have made this attic more comfortable. Empty as it was, it could scarcely be called cozy. But how long was he going to live there? The question made him uneasy and he dismissed it, for the main purpose of moving up was to find a place of refuge in which he could establish a relative peace of mind in which to formulate his plans. He did not need still another question. He would stay as long as he had to: he was not taking anything away from anyone else.

Ordinarily he left beds unmade. At home, his mother took care of that when it occurred to her or ignored it, but at college he had been chided so much by Paul that he had already got into the habit of emulating his roommate and stretching sheets and blankets taut, then folding the corners into a crisp arrangement that Paul had been forced to learn at the military academy he had been sent to at one unruly stage of his life. Such established practices were therapeutic for the troubled spirit, providing standards to live up to without added moral effort. Orrie now made up the floorbound mattress as if it were a complete bed. He would lie only a couple of inches above the rough attic floor and such vermin as coursed there when night fell: a thought that in other situations would have been even more unpleasant than here, where it was merely a distraction and even welcome enough as such. If rats and roaches were his only problem, how sweet an existence it would be!

When the bed was made, clothes hung from the rafters, and the books and other possessions on or under the card table, he had established residence and could find no further excuse for avoiding the issue of why he was here at all: not why the attic, which was self-evident, but why was he staying home from college? To protect Ellie. But how long would that job go on, and how much of his life could he afford to spend on it? It was degrading for him even to think that perhaps he was foolish to discourage her from running away from home. The proposal of the Terwillens was useless, however generous, for even if Ellie agreed to it and his mother consented — two impossibilities — it would violate all standards of decent conduct for his mother scandalously to live alone in the house with Erle while her daughter was taken elsewhere as an ophan.

Furthermore, what would "protecting" Ellie consist of, in practical measures, if he was in the attic? Surely locking her door, which she could do herself, would be effective absolutely. Erle would hardly break in by force in the wee hours. But supposing one night she forgot to turn the key, or, improbably, Erle could pick locks, or intended to waylay her on her way to or from the bathroom? But to make the last-named at all likely would mean Erle had the capacity to predict when she might feel the call of nature in the middle of the night. Orrie had no sense of that himself, and he had known his sister all her life.

But supposing anyway that Erle got his dirty hands on or too near the girl, and Orrie caught him. What to do then? Call the police? . . . *Mother must be kept out of it.* It would be too shocking for her. If she found out at all, it must be by degrees, after much preparation. Whatever the exact nature of her own association with Erle, she had a regard for him, which might be misguided, but it was genuine enough. Orrie must protect both his women, each in another way.

His father's shotgun was propped vertically against the trunk, where he had left it. He wondered whether, if he revealed to Erle he had the goods on him, the man might want to do the right thing and commit suicide. If so, the means were at hand!

It was an asinine fantasy, and Orrie sneered at himself for having had it. When would he grow up? . . . The fact was that the shotgun could provide the answer, if he had the courage to use it, not of course actually to fire at Erle but to threaten him. Let Ellie alone or get shot! . . . But that too was ridiculous, which he realized as soon as he tried to imagine actually doing it, pointing a gun at this person he had known all his life. While never liking him, he certainly had not dreamed of threatening him with a lethal weapon.

Orrie lifted the gun, pointed it towards the rear window, and, feeling like a fool, lowered the barrel. A sensible idea came to him: how about writing an unsigned letter to Erle, saying that the writer had evidence he had been in the criminal habit of molesting female minors and could turn it over to the police but decided it would be better for all involved, especially the bereaved family of the late Captain August Mencken, if a warning would suffice. Cease this vicious behavior at once or go to jail! There would be no second warning.

But he had no implements or materials with which to write such a letter, and did not want so soon again to apply to Ellie, believing that his presence tended to influence her emotions towards extravagance. He would not go downstairs until his mother and Erle left for dinner. He lay down on his new bed, through which, compressed as it was, he could feel the hard floor against his back. It was even harder on his hip and shoulder, when he turned. The mattress would not have been relegated to the attic had it been in serviceable condition. Perhaps the same thing could be said of himself.

14

"Nobody's hungry," Esther said. "They don't want to go out to eat, and neither do I."

She expected an angry reaction from E.G. but no longer cared about such things. He however surprised her with a lack of response. He was preoccupied.

"I can't get over Orrie thinking I wanted to take his room away from him. I couldn't seem to talk him out of it."

Though Esther herself was dismayed by Orrie's move to the attic, she now felt pride. "He's always been independent. There's *his* way and then the wrong one. No compromise."

She was disappointed to see that the statement had sweetened E.G.'s mood. He began to smile faintly. "Yeah. Well, I can see the similarity at that. I was the same myself at his age. I guess I should keep in mind how young he is."

Esther remembered Augie's telling her more than once that his cousin as a boy had already got a good start at becoming the master manipulator he proved to be later on, and of course she had her own memories of a younger Erle. Orrie resembled him in no way. As to who was Orrie's father, she could not have said. By now the matter was of no concern: it was exclusively herself whom she saw in her son and nothing of either of the two weaklings who could have provided the seed.

She enjoyed repeating the earlier announcement that nobody wanted to go out to dinner.

In his brightening state E.G. said, "I figured that might be the case. This has been a hard day on all of us. So I brought back a big steak a guy was aging for me. It's got to be two inches thick."

"Nobody wants to *eat*," Esther said, though Orrie had not gone so far as that.

It was some satisfaction to see the spark go out of his eye once again. "Everybody's got to eat some time." He glanced resentfully at the ceiling. "Hell, they didn't see him for four years. There's no difference in their lives." He got up from the chair beside the drum table, that which Esther had lately used when in the living room, though she would not have called it "her" chair, having little feeling of proprietorship for particular inanimate objects: that was a male emotion. As soon as he went into the Army, she had thrown out Augie's chair, a thick, graceless leather thing in which he sat to brood about the raw deal he had got from life. Esther was proud of her gift for interior decoration. With any encouragement she might have made a career of it, but there had never been enough money to purchase the fine things with which she could furnish only the rooms of fantasy.

E.G. went to the kitchen and came back with a bottle of whiskey, which he displayed to her as though it were a new baby. "Red Label. Prewar. Years since you could find that in any liquor store." He used a thumbnail on the seal. "There hasn't been a time throughout the war I couldn't lay my hands on meat, gas, booze, and I got a whole set of new tires in the middle of 'forty-two, if you recall. The rationing didn't slow me down any."

"While Augie was dodging German bullets," Esther said, though in a nonjudgmental tone.

"Or so he claimed anyway."

"He was wearing the medals to prove it."

"Hell," E.G. said, "you can buy a chestful of those on any street corner in the country." He gestured loosely. "Go get glasses and ice. And that bottle of club soda on the sink."

She had vowed to stop serving him but, with the children upstairs, did not want to start a row.

She returned from the kitchen to see that he had not only opened the Scotch but had apparently already drunk some of it from the bottle, which was empty to well below the neck. She had never, over the years, known him to be a drinker. That was Augie's vice.

"He wouldn't even sell me that picture," E.G. said. "I sincerely offered to buy it."

"What picture?"

"The dog." He seized a glass from her and splashed Scotch into it, holding onto the bottle when done.

"You want ice?" It was in a bowl, on the tray with the bottle of soda.

He ignored the question. "I can't let him move up to the attic. He'll resent me more than ever."

Esther lowered the tray to the coffee table. She had brought no glass for herself. She had no interest in E.G.'s supposedly paternal feelings.

"I've been thinking," said he. "It's been eating at me. It's the only thing that could justify the other night —"

She jerked her head in fear and chagrin, violently pointing at the ceiling.

He poured himself a refill. "I guess I just thought you weren't really serious at first, but one thing led to another and on and on —"

In a strident whisper she said, "Will you shut up! Voices carry in this house."

"Nuh-no," said he, touching his lips with his index finger. He was suddenly acting drunker than he possibly could yet be on what he had drunk from the bottle.

Concerned by his performance, she said, "Sit down with your drink."

He sat on the sofa. "I got this feeling that for some reason you're not going to get anywhere trying to collect that G.I. insurance money."

"That's ridiculous. He was in the service, wasn't he?"

"Who knows what Augie might do? Maybe he just didn't take any out."

"I heard it was compulsory."

"Yeah, but . . ." He looked at the carpet and went to another subject. "I'm feeling my age. God damn it, I'm not going to last forever. I tell you I want that boy to know who his real father is."

"Will you keep your voice down?" she cried, though in an undertone.

He shouted, "I've waited long enough!"

She thrust both hands at him. "Are you crazy?"

He gestured at her with the glass. "I did it for *him*. At least I can say that much. I didn't do it for the money."

The slur infuriated her, but she still kept herself under control. "On second thought, I *would* like to go out to eat."

"I want to get this settled."

At last she sat down beside him, not in companionship but with a purpose to lower the volume of the conversation. "You've had all these years. Why now?"

"Augie was alive."

She could have laughed at that statement, but given his emotional state, did not.

He took a quick drink, and said, "You don't have any idea of what being a man is." He seemed in some kind of burgeoning despair. She felt no sympathy for him. She could not remember what she had ever found attractive in him, after wasting twenty years. He sighed and continued. "My dad used to kick the living shit out of me for the least little thing. Augie, never to my knowledge anyway, ever got punished for anything. Maybe you could say he never did anything to get punished for." He swallowed some Scotch and narrowed his eyes as if in speculation. "You could say that. Now you can sneer at this, but let me tell you something: I even admit Augie might be a better father than I could ever be. Maybe I hated my own father too much, you see?"

She finally asked, "Aren't you drinking more than usual?"

He brandished his glass at her. "You can't stand to hear this kinda thing, can you?" And added almost as an after-thought, "You fucking bitch you."

Because of the offhand nature of the abusive term, she was not as angered as she might otherwise have been, but she would not let him get away with it.

"Don't take it out on me if you're having trouble being a man." She sneered and drew away.

He stared into his empty tumbler. "Augie should have whipped your whore's ass from the beginning." He looked up, smirking, his eyes focusing on something, or nothing, past her shoulder. "Old Augie always suspected you were giving it to everybody in town *except* me."

"Why?" she responded, smiling poisonously. "Because he thought you were queer?"

"You're lying!" E.G. shouted. Then he strangely became very quiet and mumbled as if to himself, "You're trying something I'm not going to let you get away with."

"Pull yourself together," she said with disgust. "You're just going to feel worse with all that whiskey in you."

"You don't want me to say *anything*, do you?" He leaned over to the bottle on the coffee table and poured himself more Scotch. His hand was steady enough. "I got news for you: I'm going to say it anyway. You broke Augie's balls all those years. I don't know how he could take it, but he always felt a responsibility for his family. Even when he finally left, he still sent back those support payments."

"They came from the Army, not *him*," Esther pointed out. "I didn't owe him anything at all. The truth is, he *didn't* support us. But you know that. Why are you defending him, all of a sudden?"

E.G. reared back in indignation. "For Christ's sake, isn't there a decent bone in your body? We just picked up his ashes. I'm trying to speak well of the dead."

She forgot herself for an instant to ask, "After what we did?"

His eyes were hollow. "That's exactly why I want to tell the boy who I am. It might not make it right, but —"

"Then why don't you just go and do it?" she asked. "Don't keep whimpering to me. Why not try to prove for once you're not the gutless wonder you seem?"

He had lately replenished his glass without drinking from it, and he now threw the contents into her face. The alcohol made her eyes smart. It was a moment before she could shake off the effects and find the bottle. Her purpose was to brain him, kill him if possible, and she swung the bottle as violently as she was able, but she was a woman, unused to this type of effort and without sufficient strength to move the heavy weapon (he had not drunk more than a third of its contents) with a force that matched her rage. Also, in their relative positions she could not establish good leverage. Therefore the blow he received was glancing, but struck the sensitive temple.

He dropped the glass and clasped his face, moaning at first but soon going into a full-throated howl of fury.

He leaped to his feet and pulled her up. He threw a punch that could have destroyed her nose, but she was swinging the bottle again at that moment, and his fist was deflected somewhat but still caught her in the right eye.

She missed him entirely with her second swing. He was still making vocal noise, but she was utterly silent, and his next punch crushed her mouth.

With her good eye she saw Orrie in the doorway to the foyer. He carried that gun of Augie's that she always hated. He screamed at E.G. and when the man turned, shot him with a great blast of fire and sound. E.G. buckled but remained on his feet. It was obvious that Orrie would shoot him with the other barrel as well, perhaps killing him, making incredible any argument that it was accidental or in self-defense. It was concern for the son she adored and not her quondam lover that moved her now to hurl her body between the two.

She took the second charge between her breasts.

PART

III

1

The attic had not been sufficiently secluded to meet all of Ellie's requirements for privacy, and therefore during the preceding summer she had found, in the patch of woods behind the house, a little hollow walled by bushes and with a big slab of stone to lean one's back against. In dry weather she could sit there and think in peace. Should this refuge be found by a wandering tramp, she carried along, concealed in a ring notebook, the knife of Orrie's which she had told him she kept as defense against a sexually importunate Uncle Erle. She had no regrets about so lying about Erle when he was alive: he had been a wicked man, an adulterer and finally a murderer, and any measure that would bring him to punishment was justified, though she had had nothing specific in mind as to the form such vengeance might take. Certainly she never envisioned his being shotgunned point-blank in the living room, and by her brother, who she could have sworn had not taken her seriously. "My God," she had screamed when she reached the living room and saw what was there. "*You did it.*"

Ellie had looked once at her mother's body and then never again: it was too awful and not at all what she had had in mind. If she allowed herself to think about such matters she could not survive, and therefore she avoided the subject by exerting what she had always considered her superhuman will, which was like bringing down a steel shutter of the kind she had seen protecting closed shops on her only trip to the city.

Orrie just stood there, holding the gun. The shots had been so loud that they seemed to continue to echo throughout the house. She expected people would come bursting through the front door at any moment, and not to help but rather to arrest her brother and perhaps herself as well.

She told him to put the gun down.

He dumbly did as ordered, going to some pains to find the rare place on the floor that was not soaking with blood.

He raised his hand and tried to speak, but Ellie quickly anticipated him. "Nothing can be done for them," she said. "We have to get out of here."

He protested incoherently and tried to go to their mother's body. But he had become so weak that Ellie was able virtually to strong-arm him into the hallway.

"I know it was justified," she said. "But who else will believe that?"

Suddenly he spoke clearly. "She ran right into it."

"It's done now," Ellie said. "I know why it happened, but —"

"No, you don't!" Orrie cried with a strength he could not transfer to his body, for she was still able to keep him moving towards the kitchen. "I didn't do it because of *you!* He was beating her to a pulp, the dirty son of a bitch. I'd do it all over again to *him*. But she *ran right in the way*."

They could not leave the house, with him all but screaming now. "Will you be quiet?" she said. "I've got to call the ambulance."

He tried to pull away, crying, "I've got to go back to her."

"No," Ellie said conclusively. "You'll only make things worse." She could not, if challenged, have explained just what she meant by the phrase, but it had its effect on Orrie. He sank to his knees and clasped his hands at the level of his chest, and asked God to forgive him. Despite her great regard for her brother, Ellie had always believed him wrong in becoming agnostic at the age of sixteen. Her own faith, which had little to do with the organized creeds, had never wavered, and had God not now decisively proved He would bring down retribution on criminals whom human beings refused to punish?

All the same, in the midst of this moral smugness, she could sense that a tremble had begun to develop down in the arches of her feet. Unarrested, it would climb upward to claim her entire body, and if that happened Orrie would have no one to protect him in his own delicate state. Whatever his protests, he had honored his promise to her to avenge her father's murder and she was therefore responsible for him.

"We have to get out of here," she told him. "They're not going to believe us. The police chief wouldn't listen to me before any of this happened. It could have been prevented. I wanted them to go on trial for their crimes, but *no*." She found a flashlight in a drawer of the kitchen cabinet and pressed its switch. The batteries were weak.

"Here, hold this." She handed the flashlight to him, with an idea that it might give him a chore on which to focus while she called the ambulance. But at that moment someone began to pound loudly on the front door and shout in a kind of voice that sounded official. So the shots had been heard, and the police were at hand.

Ellie pushed her brother out the back door and caught the screen that would have banged behind them. At the bottom of the yard she looked back and could see above the house the police car's red light against the high foliage on the opposite side of the street. She went in front of Orrie and, seizing his hand, led him off their property and into what, after a favorite childhood book, one in fact that Orrie had given her, she privately called the Wildwood. Though it might be short on trees and overabundant in weeds, it was as close as she could come locally to an enchanted forest. The flashlight grew even weaker with use, and they wandered for a while, making too much noise in the brush, before she found her hideout, the depression in the ground behind the glacial boulder.

She pulled her brother down. They sat side by side, backs against the rock. Fortunately the night was warm. But she wished she had had time to bring along the remainder of the loaf of bread and the rest of the baloney. He would be hungry by morning. Maybe she could sneak back to the house, once *they* were done there.

"I *killed* her," Orrie said pitifully.

She put her arms around him, partly to suppress any tendency he would have to raise his voice, but also to arrest her own trembling, which had begun again.

"She ran right in the way," said Orrie. "Why did she do that? *Why?*"

Ellie knew it was to protect Erle, but this was not the place to make that point.

"He was punching her," Orrie said. "God knows how long he had been doing it before I heard the screaming."

Closer to the scene and ever alert to what went on when Erle and her mother were together in the house, Ellie had of course heard it too and felt vindicated: the murderers were at each other's throats. She said, not untruthfully, "I didn't think it was that serious."

"You should have seen him," said Orrie. "The way he was hitting her. I don't know why I brought the shotgun along. It was just the way she sounded, I guess. I really didn't know Erle was still there. It could have been one of those Rivertown people who broke in . . ."

"You don't have to explain it to me," Ellie said, hugging him fiercely. But he kept repeating the same thing, all night long. All she could do was to hold him.

2

Paul Leeds had just returned to the dorm from Spanish 101 when a fellow from a neighboring room shouted through the door that there was a phone call for him.

The telephone was at the end of the hall, near the firehose that hung coiled behind a glass window.

Paul assumed his father had called to complain about some forwarded bill, and he answered sullenly.

But it was a girl's voice. "My name is Ellen Mencken. I'm Orrie Mencken's sister. I saw you outside school the other day with my brother . . . ?"

"Oh, sure," said Paul. "Hi. Has something happened to him?"

"Not exactly," Ellie said, "but he sort of does have a problem."

"How much does he need?"

"It's not exactly money. What he needs most is someplace

to stay and somebody to calm him down for a while until the problem is solved."

"You can count on me," Paul said. He had wished Orrie would introduce them, the other day, for he liked the way she looked: nothing cheap about her. She looked smart, and her conversation now, clear and straightforward, not the devious kind of thing he believed characteristic of young girls, confirmed him in his first impression.

"I guess I better leave it to Orrie to tell you about the problem," Ellie said.

"Sure," he said. "I still am hanging on to the car I rented the other day. I thought it might come in handy before long. If I start now, I should get there between seven and eight."

"That will be really nice of you."

The compliment pleased him. "All right then, I'll see you soon."

Ellie told him where to meet them. At first he thought it odd that he would not be coming to the house, but no doubt Orrie's problem had something to do with that. "Okay. I can remember it without writing it down. I'm pretty good with directions. 'Just pull up by the fence of the quarry': you'll be there?"

"Just wait a minute," Ellie said. "We'll come out." The operator came on the line, saying the three minutes were up, and Ellie rang off. He wondered whether the cloak-and-dagger stuff was justified, though Ellie seemed much too sensible to go in for make-believe, unless of course she was humoring her brother.

Eager to be of some use, Paul made even better time than he had predicted, perhaps because after having just made the round trip only a few days earlier, he knew the route so well, and he stopped only for gas and fed, while rolling, on candy bars and peanuts. Therefore he was early in reaching the quarry road, which he found easily, and had to wait awhile in the car before the two of them showed up.

Orrie looked almost comatose and said nothing. Ellie was furtive. She kept looking around as if for pursuers. Paul felt it would be out of order to ask questions, but was disappointed that she avoided his eyes. He had after all in response to her plea come a considerable distance and gone without real food for most of the day.

Ellie bent the passenger's seat down so that Orrie could climb into the back. It pleased Paul that she herself chose to sit next to the driver. But from what she said, he gathered she would not be going very far.

"There's some people named Terwillen," she said. "They offered to take us in when my father was killed. You can get the number from Information and leave messages with them. I'm asking you to hide Orrie out for a while. I leave the details up to you." Finally she looked directly at him. She was haggard and her clothes were rumpled, with bits of twigs and dead grass on them, but he still thought she had a sweet face. He liked the feminine fragility that eyeglasses gave a girl. "You're Orrie's friend and I trust you."

"Well," Paul said, "I hope you consider me your friend too."

She frowned. "It wasn't his fault. He was only doing his duty and isn't guilty of any crime, but *they* won't believe that. I don't trust the police, so meanwhile if you'd keep Orrie under wraps somewhere where he won't be seen?"

"I can do that," said Paul. He turned and looked back at Orrie and asked him, "Are you sick or anything?"

Ellie said quickly, "Would you mind starting up? The sooner this is done, the better."

"Wait," Orrie suddenly cried, with clarity. "I didn't know

she called you. But now you're here, you should know what it was I did." He took a gasp of breath and related the terrible story.

Paul had never heard anything like this firsthand, and listening to it, he felt his scalp flex and then stretch so tight he expected it to tear away at the temples. There was absolutely nothing he could do to meet his obligation as a friend to minimize the event or mitigate Orrie's agony, which was only appropriate. It was by far the worst thing he had ever heard or heard of. He could easily have changed his entire sense of Orrie, had he let it get to him in a certain way.

But Ellie had seized his wrist. "It was self-defense! Nobody can blame him for anything."

"It was murder," Orrie said. "I didn't mean to do it, but it was murder."

"Wait a minute," Paul said. "That doesn't make any sense. If it was an accident that you didn't mean to do, then it *can't* be murder. Talking like that won't do any good for anybody."

Ellie squeezed harder on Paul's wrist. He wanted her to rely on him.

"You listen to Paul," she said, twisted to look back at her brother. "He knows what he's saying. He's older."

Paul, who was almost twenty, was flattered. "I'm just trying to talk sense," he said. "What's done maybe can't be undone, but we also can't let it take everything else to ruin with it. You're not a criminal. You can't tell me anybody's going to think you are when they hear the explanation." Ellie was now shaking his arm, so he started the engine.

"That's what I've been telling him," she said. "For all the good it's done. If you can just hide him out for a while . . ."

"I can," said Paul. "You just leave it to me. But why don't you come along too? Two heads are better than one." He was now speaking as if Orrie were not conscious. "I think together we can eventually straighten him out." He began to back the car around. When she made no reply, he said, "I can't just leave you here on your own."

Ellie looked straight ahead. "I've got something to do here. I'll be okay."

She had let go of Paul when he started the car. He wanted some other connection with her. He took his left hand off the steering wheel and got out his wallet. "You anyway ought to have an emergency fund in case of need. Maybe after a day or so you'll want to come join us, and you'll need the fare." He would have thought of more reasons had she protested, as he expected, but she said nothing and passively accepted the bills he gave her.

Ellie seemed preoccupied, but when they reached the edge of the business district she gave him precise directions. Where she wanted to get off proved to be the village hall, at the POLICE sign over the side door.

"I'm going to try again to get that chief to listen to me." She made a firm little mouth.

Paul had never known a girl like her. "Good luck," he said. "If there's anything I can do —"

"Better get going," she said, "before somebody spots Orrie." She opened the door and hopped out before Paul could say anything else to fortify their connection. But obviously she thought well enough of him to entrust him with her brother.

3

Bob Terwillen kept shaking his head. "I told May I felt something awful was going to happen in that house. I didn't know what, but I knew it would be bad. Of course, if I had known it was going to be this bad, I'd have taken those kids out of there by force." He sat alone at the bar, the time being the dinner hour for most, but May was under the weather with a stomach upset, so he had made weak tea and toast for her and for himself heated a can of chicken-noodle soup, finishing the entire sequence, including scouring the pot he had burned, early enough to reach the Idle Hour by not much after six.

"Chief Gross called in help from the county," said Herm. "He was leery about going down to Rivertown without reinforcements."

"He thinks it was revenge, right? Somebody with a beef about rent or something?" Terwillen shook his head more violently, the light reflecting off his glasses. "I don't believe it.

I've been down there with the lifesaving squad a couple of times: once a kid almost drowned, another time a guy got a chicken bone stuck crossways in his throat." He smiled briefly. "We took care of both of them, before the doc showed up. I never saw anybody who seemed so bad they would shoot two people down in cold blood and kidnap kids. And not steal a cent: E.G.'s wallet was still there, full of cash."

"Then again," Herm pointed out, "you don't know what anybody might do with enough liquor in them, or, down there, reefers or worse."

Terwillen shrugged. "I just don't believe it."

"So," asked Herm, who had not yet served him anything to drink, "your theory is what?"

"I don't know what to think. Maybe the two of them had a fight, Esther and him, and shot one another. The kids got scared and ran away." He frowned forcefully, the thick eyeglasses rising on his nose. "But that's pretty farfetched." Terwillen stopped shaking his head for an instant of immobile deliberation.

"Maybe the chief is right, then."

"Howie Gross makes a good town cop," Terwillen said, "but how often has he had a case like this to deal with? Why would anybody kidnap those children? Where would the ransom come from? Everybody they're related to is dead now. No, I tell you they ran away."

"But where would they run to?" asked Herm, at last delivering the beer he had drawn.

"You should have seen that place, with the blood all over. Kids having to see a scene like that! Jesus Christ, to find your mother . . . I think they ran away because they were scared. Maybe they thought they would be next, or maybe just because they lost their heads. Poor kids!"

"Well," Herm said, standing back with his chin angled in concern, "I just hope they can be found before anything else happens to them. I hear they're real nice kids."

Terwillen hardly knew them, but he said, "The best!"

Joe Becker came in, walking more slowly than usual. He had aged in the last few days. He put a hand on Terwillen's shoulder, but sat down two stools away. To Herm he said, "This kind of stuff happens with the scum down in the big city. It's not supposed to happen up here."

"So what do you think, Joe?" Terwillen asked. "You agree it's not likely they've been kidnapped?"

Becker turned his head very slowly to face Terwillen. "The girl turned herself in to Howie Gross about an hour ago. She claims she shot them both for murdering her father. Says her brother tried to stop her, but after she did it he ran away so it would look like he was the one who was guilty, says he wanted to take the rap for her."

Herm said, "My God."

Terwillen's eyes looked as vulnerable as they did when his glasses were off. "She kept saying that, the day we were called in for Augie: that those two murdered him. It was awful to hear a little girl talk that way. But Christ Almighty, I never thought she might do something like this."

"She didn't!" Becker barked. "How could a little girl like that lift a twelve-gauge and pull the triggers?"

"Damn," Herm said incredulously. "She claimed that?"

"Then who did it?" Terwillen asked.

"Well, there *is* that theory about the Rivertown bunch," said Herm.

"Naw," Becker said. "Huh-uh. And it's got nothing to do with the racketeers which Erle Mencken might or might not have been connected with when he supposedly lived down in Florida." He turned to Terwillen. "You were there yesterday,

Bobby. Wasn't Esther pretty beat-up on the face? I mean, other than the shotgun wound."

Terwillen lowered his head and murmured, "Sure was."

"Now who would have been punching her?" Becker asked. "Young Orrie? Little Ellie? You saw her. I didn't. But according to Howie Gross, her one eye had really been hit hard, and her jaw was broken on the left side, teeth knocked out and all."

Herm leaned across the bar and asked, incredulously, "Erle beat her up?"

"Looks that way now. Howie's got a detective from the prosecuting attorney's office to help him, and that's their theory. Nobody came in from outside, that's pretty sure. The girl can be believed so far as that goes, anyway. There's no fingerprints of anybody else, except those on the shotgun — other than Augie's old ones: it belonged to him. But not *one* of little Ellie's. She's got no answer for that. Just sticks to her story."

"What's her version of how her mother got so beat up?" asked Bob Terwillen.

Becker threw his hands out. "No answer! She swears they got along beautifully: they murdered her father and were happy about it. In fact, they were gloating over it at the time she shot them: that's why she did it." He slapped the bar top. "As for her brother, he had already gone back to college, according to her. But the fact remains that nobody at school has seen him for the last four-five days."

Rickie Wicks came from the direction of the men's room. Apparently he had been there all the while. Herm drew him a beer. He stared into it awhile without drinking, listening to the others. "Getting so bad," he said at last, "you never know each day what worse thing can happen up there, and then it does."

Terwillen said, "That little girl never shot anybody. But she *is* cracked on the subject of her dad's death."

"I don't think she killed them," Becker said. "But maybe her theory as to Esther and Erle isn't all wet. I'm sorry, I don't like to speak that way of the dead, usually, but you know what was going on up there for years. Erle was always basically a skunk, starting out as a kid, and didn't change when he decided to call himself by the fancy initials. He was a shit as a boy. Hell, I've known him as long as I knew Augie. Never liked him."

"I'll tell you how it could have happened," said Herm, having been thinking. "I'm not saying it did, but Esther could maybe have been threatening him with the gun, and it went off . . ."

"I don't think we're going to get the straight story till Orrie turns up," Becker said. "*If* he's willing to talk. But I think he will, once he knows what his sister is saying. Those kids stick up for each other. You can see that."

"I like that in brothers and sisters," Wicks said, but for much of his life he had been on bad terms with his younger brother. At the moment they had not spoken to each other for more than a year, though, as residents of the same small town, they often crossed paths.

Molly McShane was coming in at the door. She always made a certain ceremony of her entrance, and Becker had time to whisper to Terwillen and Herm, "Don't say anything about Ellie turning up. It's none of *her* business." Terwillen nodded, but Herm looked noncommittal.

As it happened, Molly made no reference to the Mencken mess. She said nothing till she got settled on the stool and inspected the bar top by lowering her head and squinting to catch an angle of vision that would reveal any liquid Herm had failed to wipe up. As if that were not enough, she also slapped about with flat hands. Finally she brought up the big purse from the floor.

"Glad's arthritis kicked up," she said. "It's this weather we've been having lately, in my opinion. Too hot. Summer lasts longer every year. Some might think that's great, but I say it isn't healthy." She had directed her words thus far to Herm, who had her sherry ready before she got her purse situated.

"Couple reporters were in here earlier," Herm said, and the men all stared at him resentfully, for he had reserved this information for Molly. "This might be national news, due to the nature of it. I mean, it's not every day a series of tragedies occur in the same family."

Molly seemed miffed and just said, "Oh?" and took the first sip of her wine.

Becker said angrily, "You didn't mention that."

"Just plain forgot," Herm replied with a straight face. "Howie Gross sent them over. Said we know more about Augie and his family than any other sources. Pity it was too early for you guys to be here, but they got papers to put out and couldn't wait."

"I could tell them a thing or two," said Molly, with a grunt. "But I don't speak ill of the dead." She grunted again. "I guess they'll all get to be famous, now it won't do anybody any good."

"You sound jealous," Becker said. He signaled to Herm with an index finger. "I guess I will have a drink after all."

"Jealous?" Molly snorted. "No thanks. There's enough sin in the world."

"Since when are you so religious?"

"How would you know whether I go to Mass, since you're never there?"

"I don't see where religion comes into it," Terwillen said.

He was Dutch Reformed. Rickie Wicks too was Protestant. Some thought Herm was a Jew, but if so, he never admitted as much and abstained altogether from any discussions of religion.

"I'll tell you how it does," Molly said in response to Bobby Terwillen, though she did not glance his way. "Immorality. And that's all I have to say on the subject, period."

"You mean, Esther and Erle got what they had coming?" Terwillen asked, though with no evident moral implication.

"I didn't say that!" Molly now stared at him. "I don't judge people. I leave that to —" She poked her free shoulder towards the heavens.

Becker had asked the others not to reveal to Molly that Ellie had turned up to claim responsibility for the killings, but he now proceeded to do so himself, if only because the former irked him with her hypocritical self-righteousness, and he added, "I don't believe it for a minute. I don't care what she says."

Molly was badly shaken for an instant to be the last in this group to have heard the news, and tried to rally by saying through her teeth, "Don't put your money on it. She might be a chip off the old block. The other daughter sure was."

"That little girl never shot anybody," Terwillen said. "I know her. She's the sweetest little thing in the world."

4

Ellie had to steel herself to go back into the house. Now that Orrie was not at hand to take care of, she had no distraction. But it was necessary for her to demonstrate to a skeptical Police Chief Gross and the detective how she shot down her mother and second cousin, for that was what Erle had been legally.

The chief had brought along the unloaded shotgun. She had already, at the police station, revealed her ignorance of how the shells were inserted into it. But she insisted that it had been already fully loaded when she found it in the attic and brought it down to her room to use should Erle make any more attempts to molest her.

"That's why you shot him?" the detective asked, smoking another of the cigarettes he had been sucking on since he showed up that morning. She could taste smoke in her throat.

"How many times do I have to tell you I shot them both for murdering my father?" Ellie cried. "I'm just explaining why I happened to have a weapon in my possession." She tried to use as much official jargon as possible, but thus far had not succeeded in getting the superior smirk off the detective's ugly face.

Chief Gross was more sober, but gave her no reason to believe he found her account credible. "Now, Ellie," he said patiently, "you know you never had any evidence your dad's death was anything but an accident. And you're fibbing about what happened to your mother and Erle. You're trying to cover up for your brother, aren't you?"

"I keep telling you that Orrie wasn't even there."

"And *I* keep telling *you* that the neighbors saw him looking out the window not long before the shootings."

"I don't mean he wasn't in the house at all. But he was upstairs in the attic."

She had demanded to be taken to the scene so she could reenact the events of the day before. But there was another reason why she wanted to get back to the house, which the police had locked up: in the haste to save Orrie, which after all had to take precedence, she had left her father's ashes behind.

"Okay, little lady," said the smoking detective, who was keeping his gray hat on indoors. He handed Ellie the shotgun, which seemed even heavier here than it had at the station. "Show us what you say you did."

With an effort she hoisted the weapon waist-high and felt for the trigger. There turned out to be two triggers, and she got her finger wedged between them, but finally managed to get it free and pull one, which produced a click.

"You just fired the second barrel first," said the grinning detective.

"Honey," said Chief Gross, who had kept his cop's hat on too, "your story isn't holding up."

She lowered the heavy gun to the carpet. Just beyond the muzzle began one of the extensive dark patches of blood, not all of which looked quite dry. "What difference would it make that one side fired before the other?" she asked.

"See, what you don't know," said the chief, "is that one barrel is what they call more choked than the other, meaning narrower at the end, so the cluster of shot will travel further before falling apart. That's because when you're shooting at a flying duck or whatnot, the animal is further from you by the time you fire the second barrel. The shot's got greater concentrated force, so it travels further all bunched together. Take my word for it your mother was shot second, with the second barrel."

The subject could not have been more painful. One of the few things she had shared with her mother was a detestation of the firearms that were so attractive to the male sex, with the exception of a few special people like her brother. That it was he who had done this killing was absurd, perverse, unbearable by any standard: that fact must be concealed forever. She simply had to do a better job with her imposture.

"What I do today doesn't have to be exactly what I did yesterday. I was all upset then, all worked up. I don't remember exactly which trigger I pulled. They were laughing about killing my dad, you see, and I couldn't stand to hear it. So I just ran up to get the gun, and came back down and shot it at them."

"You didn't aim?" asked the detective, with the usual implicit derision.

"I just wanted them to stop!"

"Your mom was standing where?" the chief asked, and now finally he took off his cap. Ellie told him. "And E.G., where was he?"

She pointed with her left hand.

"Honey," said the chief, "give me the gun." He tucked it under his heavy arm as if it were weightless. "Let's call an end to this foolishness. Not only didn't you shoot them. You probably didn't even see them shot. Now just tell us where your brother is. We're not going to hurt him."

"Please," Ellie said, "can I go up to my room and get my father's ashes? You can come along if you want: I'm not going to try to escape."

"Go ahead," the chief said. "We trust you."

She came down with the cardboard box. "All right, I'm ready to go to jail."

The detective snorted. Chief Gross said, "Go back up and pack a suitcase with the clothes you'll need for the next couple of days. You'll be staying on at my house. Later on, the court will decide where you'll live."

"I want to stay at the Terwillens'," she said. "They invited us."

The chief returned the cap to his graying head. "But wasn't it nice last night, bunking in with my daughters? I know they'll be glad to have you stay on for a while longer."

The Gross girls had already gone to sleep in their twin beds by the time she was led to the empty cot in the corner of their room, and in the morning she had got out of there before they were up and waited on the screened-in porch.

She stubbornly repeated her previous statement.

"You sure it would be okay with Bobby and May?"

"You just ask them."

The Terwillen house was altogether different from either that Ellie had lived in, with a well-trimmed lawn in front and neat flower beds on both sides. Mrs. Terwillen, wearing a frilly green-and-buff apron, asked the chief to stay for coffee and doughnuts, but he declined with thanks and the excuse that he had to watch his weight.

Ellie too, having no appetite, turned down the version of the refreshments offered her, which included chocolate milk. Mrs. Terwillen led her to a room on the second floor. Everything in it, bedspread, little round rugs, and curtains, was flowered, and on the bed, its head on the fluffed-up pillow, was a flaxen-haired doll dressed in a long, old-fashioned dress made of flowered fabric.

Ellie knew from the sudden hush that came over Mrs. Terwillen that the room was supposed to evoke an expression of surprised pleasure and therefore she did what she could, so as not to be rude to this kind person.

"This is as nice as can be."

Mrs. Terwillen touched her shouldercap lightly. "It's always been waiting for someone just like you."

At home, finding a trip to the attic unbearable at present, Ellie had not been able to find anything in which to transport her clothing but an old paper shopping bag from Gena's end of the closet, which turned out to be full of dirty underwear, after four years. She put the bag on the bed. Mrs. Terwillen immediately removed it to the flowered chair in the corner.

5

Orrie could not recognize his surroundings. He lay fully dressed, including shoes, on a narrow bed of which the unoccupied twin was less than three feet away. Sunlight came through a dusty screen onto a rag rug between the beds. The door to the room was only a step or two beyond his feet. On one wall hung a calendar: the picture above the name of the funeral parlor it advertised showed a trio of kittens. A narrow waist-high chest of drawers stood so close to the entrance that the door probably could not be opened flat, and on top of it was a variegated-blue enameled bowl with a matching pitcher inside it. A bar of soap, worn away to half its normal thickness, lay melting in a wet saucer. No towel was visible.

He swung his feet to the floor, which was bare wood except for the tiny rug. For a moment he had no memory of anything though he had the sense of sleeping for some time . . . but without rest. It was as if he had been unconscious through not his own doing but rather that of an assailant who had left him for dead.

The door opened and Paul entered, carrying a paper bag. "You're awake finally," he said, frowning at Orrie. "I was getting worried." He looked impatiently around the tiny room and could find no place to put the bag but, pushing the bowl-and-pitcher back, on top of the dresser. "What a dump! It was the only thing I could find the other night. It got late, and we were out in the middle of nowhere. Then you slept all the next day, and I didn't want to wake you up. This morning I was getting worried." He opened the bag. "I got coffee and doughnuts from a beanery in a little town a couple of miles away. I wanted something more substantial, seeing you haven't had any food for all this while, but they wouldn't make orders of bacon and eggs to go because they would have had to put them on their regular dishes, not having any paper plates, and even though I offered to buy the dishes, they wouldn't do it. It was just that cheap restaurant china. Damn hicks! Who would have thought things could be so backward only sixty-some miles from the city, wherever we are exactly. I got lost. I don't have a map."

"I slept a whole day?"

"Yeah." Paul looked at the bowl-and-pitcher. "We don't even have running water. Got to go to the office for hot water, which is in this guy's kitchen." He reached into the bulging pocket of his jacket. "I got a toothbrush and a razor for you. There's an old-fashioned general store in town." He deposited those items next to the paper bag. "The toilet here's an outhouse in the back yard. And they've got the nerve to call it a tourist court."

"Why are you doing this?" Orrie asked.

Paul flexed his shoulders and tried to make light of it. "It's exciting being a fugitive from justice." He smiled sadly. "I hope this razor's okay with you."

"I shave maybe twice a week," Orrie said. "I'm not really a grownup." He immediately regretted making the statement. He asked, desperately, "Do you think I'm a coward for running away?"

Paul did him the honor of not disparaging the question. "I'm doing what Ellie wants me to do."

"Shows you what a state I'm in," Orrie said. "My little sister is running things."

"She's a fine person," Paul said quickly.

"I always tried to look after her. My dad was never around. I wasn't that close to my older sister. Maybe I shouldn't say this, but I never liked her that much. I never liked my father, either. Well, 'like' is probably the wrong word for what you feel about close relatives: it's not as it is with other people. Whatever your likes or dislikes, you've got the connection, you can't get away from it." For the moment he was obsessed with stating the obvious. Perhaps by this means a temporary salvation could be found. It was imperative to gain time.

"Don't feel you've got to explain everything to me," said Paul.

"I think I'm trying to figure it out for myself. This might sound crazy, but right now I actually believe I could go back there and find everything back to normal. They" — he had momentarily forgotten their names — "all of them would be there, safe and sound and on good terms. You see, that's what did it: him hitting her, beating her up, but I could have jumped on him, you know, or just hit him with the gun, or just yelled something, but I didn't, I didn't utter a sound. For that matter, why'd I bring the gun along at all? I just heard screaming. It could have been anything at all, a fire or something, anything." He frowned, in genuine bafflement. "I grabbed the gun and even loaded it, I guess while running downstairs. I wouldn't have thought I knew how to load a gun, just saw my dad do it many years ago. I hated hunting: I couldn't stand shooting living things."

"How about drinking some of this coffee anyway?" Paul asked. "Before it gets any colder." He poked in the bag. "I had one of these sinkers: I can't honestly recommend them."

"Listen," Orrie said, "I'm sorry about this whole thing. You shouldn't have been dragged into it. Now, Ellie" — he realized he was at the threshold of incoherence and forced himself to bring order to what he said. "My sister Ellie — I think you saw her the other day, she's just a kid in high school . . . wait a minute, yeah, we mentioned her earlier, didn't we?"

Paul put his hand into the bag. "These containers feel ice-cold already."

"I wouldn't pay any attention to what Ellie says, if I were you: I mean, in case she's been talking about her theories. What I did . . . it wasn't because of anything she might have said. You know, that's the only time I ever saw him touch my mother? I mean it, never in my whole life. I never saw them even shake hands. . . . For that matter, I never saw him touch Gena, either, and he's supposed to have messed around with her, according to Ellie. But I tell you, I could have predicted that kind of thing would happen sooner or later with Gena, I mean, the way she went around." He looked solemnly at Paul. "I oughtn't be saying these things, but look where my family is now. All the grownups are dead." It occurred to him that grief was the most appropriate emotion, but he was still too confused to feel anything identifiable.

Paul put the bag down. He said, "Ellie is claiming she did it."

"What?"

"She went and turned herself in to the police. I just talked to Mr. Terwillen on the phone." Paul punched his fists together. "I promised her I'd hide you out, but I didn't know she'd do this. He said they don't believe her, but still."

Orrie was on his feet. "My little sister! What kind of man am I? I killed my mother, and I'm going back to pay for it."

6

Chief Gross was alone in the police station, which was too small to have even a one-cell jail. In the rare event he had to lock someone up, the chief used the county facilities, twelve miles away. Orrie came in just before noon.

"All right, son," he said after the boy had blurted out the confession, "you just sit down in the chair there and catch your breath."

"Is my sister in jail?"

"No, and she never has been," said Gross. But he saw that in the fashion of people who are distraught Orrie had not listened to him and was about to rant on the subject of the same imaginary outrage, so the chief raised his voice. "Hey! I said she's not in jail. She's staying over with Bobby and May Terwillen. Now, *sit down.*"

Orrie obeyed the order. He looked as though he had not combed his hair for a while and had slept in his clothes, but underneath it all was the same clean-cut young fellow encountered at the schoolyard the other day.

"Where's that college pal of yours?" the chief asked, to break the tension a little. "He go back to school?"

It took Orrie a moment to understand the reference. "Oh, Paul . . . he left me off here. He didn't want to, said I oughtn't come except with a lawyer, so he went to find one somewhere, but that won't do any good, I can tell you." His eyes were feverish. "I did it by myself. I'm guilty as hell. I shouldn't have run away. Arrest me."

"Your friend's got the right idea, Orrie. You shouldn't say things like that without an attorney." The chief rubbed the stubble on his chin: on arising he had thought he could get away without shaving until lunchtime. "In fact, I'm going to pretend you didn't say it. At least for a while, until I understand exactly what happened up there at your house the other night."

The boy stared between his feet. "I don't want to hide anything."

The door opened at that point and Dick Flint came in. He was the detective from the county prosecutor's office. He greeted the chief but after a cursory glance was ready to ignore Orrie insofar as it was possible to do that in so small an office.

Gross told the boy to hang on and asked Flint to step out the back door into the alleyway behind the station, where the cruiser was parked: about the only privacy available on or near the premises. He identified Orrie for Flint and told him what had thus far been said.

"So we've got our killer," Flint said. "I knew the girl was just protecting him."

"Well," said Gross, "I want to get his story before I call him a criminal."

Back inside, Flint confronted Orrie. "You confess to the murders of Esther Marie Mencken and Erle Grover Mencken?"

When Orrie said he had fired the gun, Flint asked Gross to handcuff him. The chief was still not ready to make an official arrest, but he could not argue with the detective in front of the boy, so after a bit of trouble, having used them very seldom in his job, he put the manacles on Orrie.

Flint lighted a cigarette, throwing the match to the wooden floor: Gross resented that. The detective rested one buttock on the edge of the desk in front of Orrie, blocking the chief's line of vision. Gross sat in his swivel chair.

"You proud of yourself?" Flint asked.

"The only thing I'd be proud of," said the boy, his head hanging, "would be to have the guts to kill myself, but I haven't."

Flint blew smoke. "Let's drop the grandstanding. Just tell me exactly how you murdered your mother and your cousin."

Orrie raised his chin. "I guess it was murder, but I didn't intend to kill either one of them."

"Oh, come *on*," Flint groaned.

Gross leaned so he could see around the detective. "Orrie, you just tell what happened so far as you remember it, every single detail you can recall."

"I was up in the attic," Orrie said. "I was going through some old stuff of my father's in a trunk there. He just died, and these things were all left behind. He had been away in the war for many years, and he just got home when —"

"We all know that," said Flint, projecting smoke at the ceiling. "This doesn't concern your dad. You're telling me how you killed your mom."

Gross winced at the coarseness of his associate. He asked

Orrie in a kindly voice, "What were your dad's things? Clothes and so on?"

"And the shotgun . . . I was just looking at it when I heard this yelling and screaming from downstairs."

"That was an awful long way away, wasn't it?" Flint asked. "Three floors? Must have been *real* loud."

"Warm day," the chief pointed out. "Orrie, were the windows open?"

"I guess so," Orrie said. "I heard it, anyway, and I ran downstairs. I didn't even realize I was still holding the gun until I got into the front hall. I could hear my mother still screaming, and I guess I just lost my head. I didn't realize Erle was still in the house. In this split second I didn't recognize him in the living room, with his back to me. I don't know, I was all confused. All I could think of was my mother's screams. In that instant I thought it was a burglar, somebody who had broken in —"

"He was doing something to her?" Flint gestured violently with his cigarette.

Orrie shook his head. "Believe me, I've been trying to understand it ever since. Maybe it was the angle I was at. . . . Erle was a close member of the family. We always called him Uncle. He helped us out a lot, especially after my father went to the Army."

"Yeah," Flint said with obvious irony, "we know about E.G. Mencken. He and your mother were real close, weren't they?"

Orrie said quickly, "We all were. He was very good to us all."

"But you shot him down like a dog," said Flint.

Chief Gross stepped in here. "You couldn't recognize him? That's hard to believe, Orrie."

"I had been taking a nap," Orrie said. "Sleeping up in the attic, on an old mattress up there. I stayed confused for a while after I woke up because of the screaming."

"Now you're taking a nap?" Flint asked indignantly. "Just a minute ago you were supposedly looking at this shotgun." He put a finger between his forehead and the inner band of his felt hat and scratched. "Which was it, nap or shotgun?"

"I guess I fell asleep after looking at the gun."

"Okay, you didn't know Erle G. Mencken from Adam, this guy who was a member of your family and around there all the time — in fact, he more or less lived there, didn't he?"

"He had his own apartment in the city."

"All right, so much for him at the moment. You not only did not recognize him, you emptied one barrel into him, point-blank. But then what about your mother? You didn't know who she was either? So you nearly blew her apart with the other barrel."

The chief thought Flint was being too hard on Orrie, though it was pretty obvious the boy was not telling the whole truth.

"There *is* no excuse for what I did," Orrie said quietly. "I want to be sent to the electric chair."

Dick Flint got off the desk and strolled behind Orrie. "More grandstanding," he said to the back of the boy's head. "It won't be you but a judge and jury who will decide what punishment you get, and insofar as you killed both of them, that's never been in doubt, so you haven't told me anything yet. *Why* did you kill them? That's all I want to know. Why?"

From behind the desk the chief said, "We just want to get to the truth. Was Erle beating your mother up for some reason?"

Orrie shook his entire trunk. "No. I guess they were just discussing something."

"Then why was she screaming?"

"I've thought about that a lot." He had not once shown any discomfort with the handcuffs, though wearing them must have been a unique experience. "She might have been laughing."

Dick Flint, still behind Orrie, struck the back of the chair with a sharp blow of his hand. "You trying to make a monkey out of me, you little twerp? *Laughing?*"

"No, sir," said Orrie. "I mean it. At least it's a possibility. My mother didn't laugh much, but when she did, once in a great while, it was really high-pitched."

"You're insulting my intelligence," said the detective, and came around in front of the boy. "And you'll be sorry for it."

Chief Gross spoke in his usual calm tone. "Would there be anything to laugh about, though, Orrie? Your dad's funeral was just that morning."

"I know. I can't explain it."

Flint returned to the desk top, but he suddenly softened his manner. Leaning towards Orrie, he asked, almost sympathetically, "Erle wasn't hitting your mom? Then why'd you shoot him?"

"I don't know. I guess I thought this guy, whoever he was, was menacing her somehow, maybe holding a gun, a pistol on her. His back was turned to me when I came into the room."

"He was hit in the left side."

"He started to turn."

Flint sucked on a tooth. "So much for E.G." He closed his eyes to slits. "You dropped him with barrel one." His voice began as almost a whisper, but became a shout as he finished the question. "Why did you proceed to empty *the gun into your* MOTHER?"

"She ran into the line of fire," Orrie said levelly.

Gross asked, "You don't mean she was trying to save Erle?"

Orrie closed his eyes.

Flint leaped off the edge of the desk and pushed his finger within an inch of the boy's face. "Enough of this lying crap, you little punk. You killed them because they were having an affair, weren't they? And you couldn't stand it. You never liked it, but now with your father coming back and dying as he did, there was nothing in their way. Maybe they were having a lovers' fight of some kind. Her face was covered with bruises. He *was* punching her, whatever you say. But that was just your excuse, and it won't work, I'll tell you why: nobody brings a loaded twelve-gauge to stop a fight unless they want to kill somebody. You were looking for just such an excuse to kill him. But what about your mother? Why'd you give her the other barrel?" Flint took away his finger and put his nose in its place. "Let me tell you: you hated her for screwing Erle, didn't you?"

"That's a dirty lie," Orrie cried, at last struggling against his bonds. "You son of a bitch! I'll kill you."

Flint turned and smirked at Gross, who, right in front of Orrie, asked, "Aren't you going a little too far, Dick?"

"He shot down two human beings point-blank," said the detective. "Maybe he had cause. If so, he can make his case in court. He won't be railroaded. This is the U.S.A."

"You mean, try him as an adult?" Gross thought privately this would be a shame.

Flint shook his jowls, smoke drifting from his lips. "Look, I'm not speaking for myself. I'm just doing my job. But I'm pretty sure what Bernie will say: 'He's old enough to be in the service, killing Japs and Germans. Instead he's home here, shooting down his family.'" He referred to the prosecuting attorney of the county, Bernard J. Furie, who was known as a hard man on lawbreakers.

7

"I'm Anthony Pollo. I'm your attorney."

Orrie was at the county jail but in a room with a table and several chairs, and not in a cell. The guard had told him the sheriff decided he would be safer there till he was bailed out than with the other prisoners currently on hand, all of whom were larger, older, and seasoned criminals. If he needed the men's room, he was supposed to knock on the door. It was expected that he would be bailed out soon, but Orrie had decided otherwise.

The lawyer chose a chair on the side of the table across from him.

Orrie said, "I don't have any money."

"Your friend Paul Leeds hired me," Pollo said in a tone of reason and authority. Orrie started to protest, but the attorney stopped him with an upthrust hand. "I know you refused to let him put up bail, but I want you to rescind that decision right now."

"It's no business of yours."

"Come on, stop acting like a smart-aleck and thank God for having such a friend as Paul and such a devoted sister as Ellie. And this town is full of people who are on your side. Can't you see you're letting them all down if you won't accept any help?"

The unfair argument did serve to evoke from Orrie another emotion than that which had occupied him exclusively for as long as he now could remember. He was astonished to discover that he could feel indignation. "It's nobody's business any more, not even Ellie's. It's no longer a family matter, in the sense of a living family, which is why I don't have anything to say to Ellie. It's between me and those I killed, you see." He was sure nobody would ever understand, but he was closer now to Erle than he had ever been in life. He and his mother and Erle were intimates. He had hated the living Erle but felt a kind of affinity with the dead one, for whom he was responsible. Outsiders could never understand that. If he tried to tell them, they would think him deranged. As to his mother, he believed that if he was faithful to the principles she had taught him, he might finally earn her forgiveness. He could never now live to be a doctor, but at least he could die as a man, taking what he had coming. Killing Erle was no mistake, and he was not ashamed of the deed. Had Erle been the only victim, Orrie would have defended himself with every resource at his command. It was against his mother that he had committed the crime. Who among the living could have understood that it was all the worse for being an accident?

The lawyer pushed the chair back and got to his feet. He was a heavy man, but his paunch was no thicker than his chest. He paced the floor on his side of the table. "Once you pulled the triggers — which I gather you admit doing — it was no longer private. Society has to stick its nose in when somebody dies even of natural causes: the state always requires a doctor's certification." He halted and looked down at Orrie. "Ever think of this? You can usually live more privately than you can die." He resumed his pacing. "Here's something to consider in this case: unless you tell what you know to be the truth, people are pretty likely to have their own theories. It might be your privilege not to care what happens to yourself, but it's not fair to those who can't tell their own stories."

Pollo came around to Orrie's side of the table and loomed over him. "You owe it to your mother, and you know it." The lawyer moved away when Orrie began to weep. The tears were not those of grief: he had other ways of mourning. It appeared that any serious effort he made towards atonement would be opposed by the world — and for the best reasons, kindness, sympathy, understanding, just what he could not bear. The inevitable truth was that he should do away with himself, but how to do so without further obscuring the point was beyond him at this moment, hence his access of self-hatred. He was guilty of course, but in quite a different way from what would be inferred upon his suicide. He was guilty of having done nothing in the matter of Erle before shooting him to death. He was guilty of having panicked, losing control, using a man's weapon without a man's authority to wield it. His father had undoubtedly tried to teach him about apprenticeship, but he ran away, refusing to listen, rejecting instruction in manhood, horrified at the death of the pheasant, a wild creature that lived by Nature's law and expected to be prey of any creature larger and not of its own blood.

Pollo returned to him after a while and said, "Let's get you bailed out. Whatever your situation, insofar as I see it, staying here will not help. Think of it: you're a smart fellow, I hear.

And you should remember this: you can tell me anything and it won't go further if you don't want it to. I'm not *allowed* to tell anyone else. This is an even more useful system than Confession, because I won't ask you for penance. I'm obliged to defend you, notwithstanding what you did or what you're charged with — which incidentally are usually two different things even with professional criminals." He touched Orrie's shoulder. "Frankly, I suspect at this point you yourself might not be absolutely certain what happened or why."

But the lawyer had now gone too far. He was being patronizing, and while Orrie saw no alternative but to accept his immediate suggestion, he could not really trust him.

8

The money that Paul Leeds spent to help Orrie was not his own but rather his father's, and with the lawyer's large retainer (Pollo was renowned in his field), it exceeded the sum he would have gone through had he been normally profligate, and he did not dare to tell his old man where it went, though the irony was that for the first time in his life he was doing something other than serve his own proximate pleasures, something in which he could take pride, and furthermore, he knew he was doing it well, for the person for whom he cared most had told him so.

The recognition that he was in love with Ellie took some time because though at twenty he had had experience with women, it was only of the kind associated with being handsome, well-born, and affluent and for his part had little to do with feelings much deeper than the generic sexual urge. What he felt for Ellie was foreign to sensuality. She was an ethereal young girl, a saint in her selfless regard for her brother, and with so delicate a physical presence that she seemed to exist on air rather than food, and she had no personal interest in him whatever, which seemed only right, for otherwise he would have felt like a creep, given the difference in their ages. It was good of her to commend him for the help he was providing Orrie.

"I hope you understand it's easier for me to thank you than for Orrie. Please don't think he's not grateful."

The fact was that as the weeks went by Orrie had tended more and more to avoid his friend, and when he could not, he was frequently all but disagreeable. Ellie's implication concerned her brother's pride — and she was always worth listening to — but Paul had begun to wonder whether her devotion made her altogether blind to what he had begun to suspect was an unattractive element in Orrie's character, a tendency first to reject offered assistance and next to accept it with reluctance and then finally resent those who gave it. Paul still felt sorry for his friend, but by now the main reason he continued to adhere so loyally to his cause had more to do with maintaining Ellie's respect than serving his original friendship, for which after all he had done more than a bit, to the degree that he stayed away from college and, after his father had consequently cut off his funds, went so far as to take the first job he had ever experienced, namely, that of temporary clerk for the holiday mail, at the big main post office in the city (parking on the street all day, collecting tickets and losing hubcaps and antenna), which he discovered was no means to wealth. He had never been so admirable a person in all his life, but it was a fact that neither had he ever been so uncomfortable and lonely, for everyone seemed to assume he had limitless funds and concerns of greater magnitude than what they saw him doing, neither of which was the case, but he did not dare reveal the truth even to Ellie, lest it cause her to reflect unfavorably on his value if he no longer had money.

Owing to his financial state, his quarters were necessarily mean and therefore could not be in the immediate area lest he be embarrassed. He still kept the car he had rented from the garage man upstate, who had known him only when he was prosperous and had not yet questioned his credit. He drove to one of the neighboring towns and got the off-season rate for a little room and bathroom privileges in a tourist home operated by a widow in her fifties, who usually did not have paying guests in the cooler months when nobody came to swim in the lake, and was therefore unaware of how inadequately that area of the house was heated. After a few weeks of this and meals at a lunch counter whose bill of fare never changed, Paul no longer believed (if he ever had) that living modestly was any more "real" than having the wherewithal for the pampering of oneself, yet his resolve to stick to his mission was firmer than ever, for though he might by now have been tempted to abandon Orrie, he had this fealty to Ellie, by which he could continue to rise above himself.

Both Orrie and Ellie were living with the Terwillens, under a temporary legal guardianship arranged by Anthony Pollo. Paul would greatly have enjoyed being a welcome guest in this house that usually smelled of Mrs. Terwillen's no doubt delicious cooking, but when he came to see his friends, he had yet to be invited even to enter the living room from the little vestibule just inside the front door. He always asked for Orrie, but invariably nowadays it was Ellie who came out to say that her brother was indisposed, a state of affairs Paul would not have deplored had he been able to spend the time with her, but with one or both Terwillens circulating nearby, he was reluctant to suggest going elsewhere should it sound like making a date. He suspected their coolness towards him took its source in an assumption that a guy his age (furthermore, one with money) could have only one intention when frequenting a penniless female orphan — and in all fairness, they would have been right if dealing with an earlier Paul, who had always found girls from more humble circumstances than his own more sexually attractive than those of his own milieu.

Christmas promised to be an exceptionally bleak time for him. He might even have found his father briefly bearable had he not alienated the man forever by his apparent failure at still another school. Even his landlady would be out of town, visiting a daughter in the Midwest, and his only comfort in remaining alone in the house was that he could control the thermostat. The local eating places would all be closed on the twenty-fifth. To feed in public he would have to find some hotel dining room in the city. The alternative would be canned soup and sardines in the widow's otherwise empty kitchen.

After paying his rent, he had had just enough left from the money he had earned sorting letters at the P.O. to buy gifts for Ellie and her brother, and on Christmas morning he went to deliver them, which, so as to avoid anyone's embarrassment, he decided to do discreetly, putting the packages on the doormat, ringing the bell, and leaving before the summons was answered. But in putting the plan into action, making too hasty a departure, he slipped on the icy sidewalk and had just got to his feet when the door opened and Mrs. Terwillen appeared.

"Why, Paul," she said, in a much warmer tone than usual, perhaps because of the holiday. "Merry Christmas. Did you hurt yourself?"

"It was nothing."

She picked up the two little packages, which he had wrapped himself, no doubt awkwardly, but he had never done such a thing before. He had even remembered to attach little cards for the recipients' names. "Well, won't the children be happy." Her smile grew warmer. "Come in and have some coffee. Bobby's out delivering the church baskets to the needy, but everybody else is here."

"Thanks, but I got to be going," he said for his pride's sake, but by the time he reached the car, Ellie had come out and was shouting to him.

"Merry Christmas to you, too," he cried in return.

"I said, can't you come in?"

Now he accepted the invitation. The Terwillens had what looked like a really pleasant house, with everything flowered, walls and slipcovers and pictures and even little figurines. Ellie led him into a solarium off the living room, where the windows of many small panes were continuous. Mrs. Terwillen brought a plateful of pastries and asked him whether he drank coffee: suddenly she seemed to think him younger than he was.

When they were alone Ellie thanked him for the present, which, still wrapped, lay beside her on the flowered sofa.

"Maybe you'd better open it. I don't really know what you like or don't like. I'll change it for something else if it isn't right." Her hair was brushed to glisten today, with a bow-shaped barrette at each ear, a well-fitting burgundy-colored dress of velvet, and what looked like new plastic-framed eyeglasses. He suspected Mrs. Terwillen was responsible for the changes, which may have gone too far, Paul preferring the Ellie he had known.

She lowered her head between rising shoulders, as young girls do when admitting their deficiencies, and said, "I don't have anything for you, and I'm sure Orrie doesn't either."

"That's all right."

"He'll be out in a minute, I know." Mrs. Terwillen had left Orrie's gift on a table near the front door. It was a fountain pen of the type Paul himself used, which Orrie had noticed once, in their dorm room, and admired because of the way it filled.

"Go ahead, open it," Paul told Ellie.

She untied the ribbon and peeled away the paper more carefully than he had ever seen anyone do. He admired all her ways.

"Oh, gosh," she said, taking the little gold wrist-chain from its box. "Isn't it *nice*."

"Are you sure?" Paul asked. "I didn't know how you might feel about it."

"I've never had any real jewelry before."

He would not have called it exactly jewelry, such a simple thing without even any precious gems, but would say nothing to diminish it now that she appeared so pleased.

She draped the chain over her left wrist.

"It's not too big, is it? I could get a few links taken off."

"No, it's just right." She kept smiling at the bracelet.

He did not know what to say to a girl like her when they were not discussing her brother, and was reluctant to break the current mood by bringing up the subject of Orrie, which no doubt she would return to soon enough.

"How about a refill?" asked Mrs. Terwillen, coming in with the pot. She stared into the cup she had brought earlier. "But you haven't touched any of *this*."

Ellie displayed the bracelet, and for an instant Paul was worried lest the woman misinterpret his motives, but Mrs. Terwillen beamed at him with her motherly plump face and said, "That's the nicest thing I have ever seen!" He hastily drank most of the coffee, which was cool enough by now to chug-a-lug, and she replenished the cup. "I just wish you could stay and have Christmas dinner with us, but I'm sure you —"

"I'm free," he said hastily, almost spilling the cream he was adding to his cup from the tiny pitcher. He forgot his pride and added, "I'd really love to stay."

He was further rewarded by Ellie's saying, "That's just great." But as it turned out, her enthusiasm for his remaining had mostly to do with her brother. When Mrs. Terwillen went away to tend the turkey she said, "Maybe you could talk to Orrie man-to-man. He won't listen to me any more."

Paul nobly agreed. "But what should I talk about? He hasn't even come out the last few times I've dropped in."

"I don't know. What do boys talk about when they're together?"

Paul said, "I've been thinking, there are these doctors that specialize in treating people who are in a depressed state of mind."

"No." Ellie shook her head. "I know he would think that would mean he's crazy."

"But it wouldn't," said Paul. "My mother's not crazy and she goes to a doctor of that type and she's not exactly even depressed but nervous and drinks and smokes too much." He was amazed at himself, making these revelations to a high-school girl in a little town upstate.

But Ellie kept her narrow focus on her brother. "He just sleeps all the time. At meals he hardly eats a bite."

Paul rose and got rid of his cup and saucer, which he had been holding in his lap all the while. "I'll go see him."

Ellie said, "It's upstairs, third door on the right." She shook her raised wrist with the chain. "I've got to help Mrs. Terwillen with the meal, so I'll take this off and leave it here."

Paul was touched by her concern that he might be offended if she was not wearing the bracelet next time he saw her.

He took Orrie's gift from the table where it had been left by Mrs. Terwillen and climbed the stairs.

Orrie was sitting on the edge of his bed, tying his shoes. Paul said, "Ellie told me to come on up."

Orrie lifted his head. "She's always got ideas about what I should do."

Paul did not like this, but said only, "She's worried about you."

Orrie glared at him. "I just want her to let me alone."

"She's your sister."

"So was the other one. Gena got the hell out and stayed away. So did my dad — then made the stupid mistake of coming back."

Paul still stood in the doorway. "You oughtn't talk that way about your family. It's Christmas."

Suddenly Orrie's look was beseeching. "You know, I never dream of it. Right after it happened I didn't dare close my eyes at night for fear that's all I would see, and then finally I would fall asleep against my will, just get so tired, and not once ever dream about it. It's during waking hours I can't think of anything else, but when I fall asleep it's like nothing ever happened. That's not right."

"Whether it's right or not is beside the point," Paul said. "It's natural. It's not something you decided to do. Furthermore, it's something you can't do anything about. So you just have to accept it." He went into the room and gave Orrie the little package. "Now, come on downstairs. You've got to eat something. You're all skin and bones." Paul felt for his friend, but he could not wait to get back near Ellie, in whose presence he glowed. But he did not yet have the courage to reveal that about himself to anyone, including her.

9

Cassie was buried by her parents three days after Christmas. She had died early on the twenty-sixth, of sudden complications in a seemingly routine case of the flu that had been going along the assembly line at the plant. But her mother was convinced that the girl had died of a broken heart, after weeks had gone by without Augie's return or so much as a word of explanation from him, not even for Christmas. Of course Cassie, the self-styled clairvoyant, had predicted the trip would have dire consequences, but as usual no one took her seriously. While she insisted that Augie must have met with some terrible though unspecified fate, both her parents, knowing more of life, were sure the man had simply run off after having enjoyed himself with her and getting a lot of free meals during the time he was in local residence before going back up North. From the first they had considered him much too old for her, but had said nothing, for she had no other suitors, all the eligible younger men being away at war. It had been her father's considered opinion that Augie's disappearance might work out for the best, for with the war over now, more appropriate men would soon come marching home.

Her parents' only consolation, and their pastor told them it should be a profound one, was that their daughter died a virgin.

10

Ellie was always flattered to be consulted privately by Anthony Pollo. Fortunately there were glass doors between the solarium and the living room, because the Terwillens, though kind people, tended to be nosy. Mrs. Terwillen seemed to be none too pleased when she saw Ellie closing the doors, but the latter reminded her, as respectfully as could be, that the lawyer-client relationship was sacrosanct.

"I wanted to see you again apart from your brother," the lawyer said, choosing the chair rather than the sofa. He put his stout briefcase on the floor. "It's good news, but the way Orrie has talked, I don't know how he'll take it. Furie's finally decided to try him for manslaughter. There was never the slightest grounds for a charge of murder: that was just his bid for the headlines — well, not quite: your brother himself keeps using that term. I'm worried about Orrie. I think he should see a doctor. But he doesn't want to listen to me even when it comes to the law."

"That's Paul's idea too," Ellie said. "But I can't get Orrie to do anything. As far as he's concerned, he's the big brother."

"What about Paul?"

"He went back to college at the end of Christmas vacation. I insisted on that when I found out his main reason for being down here. He really helped us, but I don't want him to jeopardize his education and fight with his father and all. I didn't understand him for a long time. I thought he was just this rich kid who hadn't anything better to do than hang around with people like us." She smiled. "He had a little too much eggnog at Christmas dinner, I guess — Mr. Terwillen gave him some of it with real rum in it — and told me a lot of things about himself I didn't know. Do you realize he ran out of money and had to work at the post office, in the city, during the holiday rush?"

Pollo smiled paternally. "I know he's Orrie's devoted friend. Isn't that why he was here?"

Ellie was not the boasting type, but the matter of Paul was too extraordinary to keep to herself as she had felt she had to do thus far: she did not dare upset Orrie, and it was not the Terwillens' business. "This might be hard to believe, but Paul asked me to marry him."

"*What?*"

"Don't worry, everything was on the up and up. He wasn't trying to make a fool of me, though at first I did think it was some kind of dumb practical joke. When I saw he was actually serious, I said, 'Well, I like you too, but what I wish you'd do is go back to school and work hard and get good grades instead of just getting by or not even that, and then two years from now, when I'll be eighteen and finish high school, we can talk about it — if you're still interested, which frankly I doubt.' "

Pollo looked relieved. He said, "You're a levelheaded young lady. I don't think we have to worry about you."

"He really is nice, but I think maybe it was because he felt so sorry for us. Anyway, *I* would be crazy to think about getting married right now. I haven't ever even had a date!" Her face fell. "But what's going to happen to Orrie?"

"He's out of the house at the moment?"

"Mr. Terwillen took him to see my mother's grave. That's the only place he'll go."

Erle Mencken's will had revealed a sentiment that Ellie considered sickening: he had some years earlier purchased a cemetery plot big enough for himself and his cousin's entire family including the missing Gena. Ellie supposed she should be grateful to them for having cremated her father instead of putting him into that polluted ground. As to her father's ashes, at last they had found a proper place of repose. She had exchanged Paul's bracelet and added her savings to obtain the finest box Friedman's offered, one with a top of etched silver.

"My biggest problem in defending your brother," said Pollo, "is not Bernard J. Furie but Orrie himself. He's left me with nothing but that preposterous story of mistaken identity. It's obvious that Erle was giving a savage beating to your mother. I assure you no jury in this country would convict a boy who killed someone who was striking his mom. That in the course of his defending her she herself got killed was a tragic accident. Why in the world does he continue to deny what happened?"

"He's got this idea that the only reason Erle would be hitting her was a lovers' quarrel," said Ellie, "and he could never admit that."

"I just would hate to see his life ruined," said Pollo. "Young as he is, first offender, the peculiar nature of the case, he might not be sent to prison if he's found guilty, but he'd certainly have a record, with all the consequences that could come from that. Did you tell me he wanted to become a doctor? Can you see that happening unless he's cleared of this?"

"I'll say this about my brother," Ellie said. "It's always hard to tell what's going on in his mind at any given time, but what he finally does can surprise you."

Pollo moved his large head. "I don't like surprises. Please keep trying to get him to reveal what really happened that evening. It could only help him."

Ellie no longer tried to tell people that her mother and Erle had murdered her father. Nobody but Orrie (whatever he said) had ever believed her. But Orrie had been enough.

The mailman was coming up the walk as she let the lawyer out. Mrs. Terwillen was suddenly at hand, having probably never been far away.

Ellie sensed that for her to take the mail from the postman would have been considered as a gesture more forward than politely helpful. She was halfway up the stairs when Mrs. Terwillen said, "Oh, Ellie, here's a letter for your family. . . . Maybe I should save it for Orrie?"

Ellie went down to her, taking two steps at a time. Mrs. Terwillen had got somewhat touchy throughout their weeks of residence, what with Orrie's brooding in his room and Ellie's mostly rejecting the kind of maternalism she offered. Ellie did what she could not to offend the kind woman needlessly, but this letter was unique. She snatched it and ran upstairs.

The envelope was addressed to "The Mencken Family" and had been sent to the house where her parents and Erle had died, but at least Orrie was sufficiently well known so that the post office had not even bothered to alter the street and number for delivery to the Terwillen home. The postmark said California though the city of origin was smudged.

She peeled away the flap with a thumbnail.

Dear Mom, Dad if he's back, Orrie & Ellie
also Erle too —

Supprise! I guess you got tired waiting to here from me, maybe even thought I got too high & mighty to remember where I came from. I wont go intos the whys and wherfores of all I did since I last saw all of you. It hasnt all been beer & skittles believe you me — theres a big world out there which maybe you dont know about if youve never been there, but I did and lived to tell the tail!!!!

The movies dont amount to all that much. Fact is, I got somewhat dissilusioned by the kind of people associated with them. Phonier than you might think and I mean the most important folks in that game and Jews every one of them too. I had quite a few offers, so its anything but sour grapes but the pay isnt as good as you hear and for that matter — but why go on, you know I always try to look on the best side of any situation and keep smiling and I made a go of it didnt I, and never wired you for a cent. Well, why dwell on what never worked out. I look on the bright side so just let me tell you what I did. I guess you wouldnt ever have thought of me as a religious person in your wildest dreams, the way I always avoided Sunday school but maybe that was because of the kind of so-called religion there which was just hippocrictical — to show you what I mean, when I did go one time the "reverent" Mister Wilbert tried to get too friendly back in the cloakroom if you ask me, with his fat old wife right out in the other room serving cookies and punch.

Anyway, what Im talking about is the Temple of the Loving Spirit. I guess what I like most about it, its more than a religion — its a Way of Life, because affecting everything, like not eating any red meat which produces rage and every other kind of negative feeling — well that wasn't hard for me to give up, I never liked greasy hambirgers or stakes anyhow, if you can still recall after all these years and I sure hope you can, because I think of you all a lot and just hope all of you or any can come out here sometime and see what Im talking about and maybe get some spiritual help for yourselves, because Im going to be frank maybe but thats what I do now, I've found my so-called vocation and am First Sister of Love at the Temple now dont laugh because its serious like a nun or priestess you might say, and give spiritual instruction to those who come to us in need of loving faith all races and colors and creeds, mexicans, colored, cathlics, all kinds, and we all live in the Temple and share and share alike including our Teacher, who we arent supposed to call by any other name, so I wont except to say that last week I was quite proud to present him with a new son 7 lbs 14 oz who we call Chrisanthemum. You can all figur what relation this makes yourself, granma, uncle or whatnot . . .

But what I was saying was, all or any are invited to come visit and maybe learn something that will change your life the way I did and put aside the corruptions of the flesh and vanity and anger and greed — and you can say which apply to your own case individually. Now I can just hear your screams but maybe after you calm down you will think about the matter and see maybe Ive got something. Meanwhile I miss each and every one of you, even though I might not have gottn in touch for quite a time but I did want you to know Ive had this kid who sends you all the love in the world and by the way could use some baby clothes. Not to mention it was just Chrismas and by the way he was born just two days later which must give him some connection with Jesus, who we respect as one of the Great Love Givers along with Budda, Confewshus, Jehovah, and Islam. Ill be sending a Kodac of him when I take one — cute little tyke. And Erle, maybe you could send a donation to the Temple? Be good for your soul. We do a lot of good for the human race.

With fondest regards,
Gena Mencken

It was typical of Gena that she failed to include a return address on either letter or envelope. Ellie read the text a second, quick time and then tore the several sheets of paper into thin strips and flushed them down the bathroom toilet.

When nosy Mrs. Terwillen later on asked, "Not bad news, I hope?" Ellie said, with simulated exasperation, "Some charity, wanting money. I don't know where they got our name."

"Imagine," said Mrs. Terwillen, "all the way from California for that."

"I guess it was really for Erle. I don't know why it was addressed to the family. It should have gone to his lawyer."

Mrs. Terwillen groaned. "*That* crook."

"Well, Mr. Pollo can handle him," said Ellie. "He's going to clear Orrie's name and Orrie's going to inherit Erle's ownings and have enough money to go on and finish college and medical school."

"I certainly hope you're right, sweetheart."

"I've been right so far," Ellie said. She saw Mrs. Terwillen's eyebrows rise, but did not elaborate. She had already decided that this trashy news about Gena and her illegitimate child would only make Orrie feel worse, and anyway there was no means by which to get in touch with their sister, so it made sense to pretend the letter had never arrived.

11

The trial opened, at the county courthouse, during a mid-January thaw, with ankle-high slush in the parking lot. Paul had come down from college but at Ellie's urging had brought his books along so he could study at night for the exams at the end of the month. He was also gratified by the Terwillens' insistence that he stay with them and sleep either on the solarium couch or on a cot in Orrie's room, depending on Orrie's reaction. Paul did not want the question put to his friend and took the sofa, which was anyway the better idea, the solarium providing the privacy he needed for the memorization of terms required to pass zoology. Every day he drove Orrie, Ellie, and Mrs. Terwillen to the courthouse, Mr. Terwillen not being able to get off work.

Having returned to school and indicated that his attitude towards his studies had been remarkably transformed, and as yet concealing the attachment to Ellie, Paul was in more fragrant odor with his father than he had been for years and therefore had enough money to have bought an engagement ring, but Ellie was not ready to accept such.

"Don't get me wrong. I really appreciate the offer, but I'm just too young right now to talk about that subject."

Paul said, "I haven't known anyone more mature, whatever the age."

"My mother got married when she was sixteen and look what happened to her."

"But was that the reason?" Paul asked. "Anyhow, we don't have to get married for years, if you don't want. I'd just like to make some sort of connection between us, if it's only for you and me to know about."

"Well, if that's all, then I guess I could agree." She shook hands with him on it, but still declined the ring. "It would just be something to worry about. And I hope you're serious about the 'for years,' because I've pretty much decided on a profession. I want to be a lawyer. Mr. Pollo said he'd help me get into law school when the time comes."

Paul scowled. But from the expression on her face he saw she would not take kindly to opposition, and he could not let Pollo, on whom she had a crush, get the advantage. "Yeah, okay, if that's what you really want."

Ellie looked smug. "We have a lady judge, after all."

Nor did that fact thrill Paul, who doubted that the Honorable Thea Palliser, a middle-aged woman with iron-gray hair in a bun, could be fair to a defendant who had killed his mother, whether or not she had offspring of her own.

12

Of the Idle Hour gang, only Joe Becker, who was his own boss, and Molly McShane were able to attend the trial. The other men all had to work, and Gladys was laid up with a badly sprained ankle and was just lucky not to have broken anything. Molly would have spent the time with her and not in court, but in fact Gladys wanted to keep up with the news of the trial, so most days the former rode the bus to and from the county seat. Molly managed to live in her modest way on her late mother's insurance. She would not ask Becker for a ride, and for his part he would not offer her one unless she asked. In the courtroom they avoided each other. Becker sat with Ellie, Mrs. Terwillen, and Orrie's friend from college, Paul Leeds.

At the bar, the evening of the day the case went to the jury, Molly was exasperated by what Becker was saying.

"I don't know where you get that," she protested. "Bernard J. Furie's just doing his job."

"He's a bum," Becker said. "He didn't have any evidence except that so-called confession, given when the poor kid was all confused and horrified by what happened."

"You're wrong there!" Molly crowed. "Orrie didn't confess till noon two days later. He ran away the night of the killings and left his little sister to take the rap."

Becker's lip curled. "You're going to sit there and say he should go to prison?"

Under the disapproving stare of the men (except Herm, who was busy rinsing glasses), Molly changed direction but was scarcely more amiable. "You always twist everything to fit your own warped mind. I got a lot more real sympathy for that poor kid than you have, any old day. What I'm doing, as any fool can plainly see, is saying how it *could* look to an innocent bystander. Bernard J. Furie was only doing his job. For heaven sake, the boy gave an official confession, signed it, and used the word 'murder.' It's not up to the prosecuting attorney to prove he didn't mean it."

Becker seemed to speak to his glass. "Orrie shouldn't ever have been brought to trial, and you know it. Nobody can say what went on up there that night, except him, and he's not going to tell, but not because it would reflect badly on himself: that's one thing I'm sure of. He'd rather go to prison to protect his mother's reputation. He's got the same kind of character as Augie: stand on your principles, regardless of the consequences. You don't see much of that any more." He was a little drunk.

From the last stool on the left, Al Hagman asked, "What's he say was Orrie's reason for using the shotgun?"

Molly corrected him. "You mean 'motive.' "

Becker snorted. "I'm no lawyer, God knows, but that's where Furie's case was weakest. According to him, Orrie got in a big fight with Erle and Esther and lost his temper."

"Got mad enough to shoot them down?"

"The pity is, Orrie said all kinds of things in that so-called confession that can be interpreted in different ways. He said he didn't like Erle, though Erle had been good to the family. He said he had more or less decided to drop out of college, but his mother argued with him about that. He said Erle had taken his room. Most damaging of all, he kept using the word 'murder' for what he did. And Furie got some witnesses from school, a couple of kids who Orrie had fought, and some old-maid teacher and that principal, uh, Maxwell. They testified he lost his temper sometimes, for no good reason according to them, and got into fights. So what? Is that abnormal for a kid? Especially with little guys like that, you know they're sometimes quicker to put up their dukes than certain big fellows. My dad used to call the type 'little banty roosters.' Got something to prove, I guess. But the boy was an honor student all the same. He's no hoodlum. Furie was just trying to influence the jury."

"Old Maxwell?" Rickie Wicks asked derisively. "He still around? That old stuffed shirt? I got hauled down his office once for fighting and he had me shake hands with the other kid and promise to be friends." He grunted. "So we did it — the other kid was Cliff Moran — and then went out and took right up where we left off, only off school property. We used to fight all the time, hated each other's guts. Nowadays I like Cliff well enough when I see him, which ain't all that often though. Funny about kids."

Becker went on impatiently. "But this Pollo is really something. You can see where he gets his reputation. When he'd get hold of the witnesses he'd be real nice to them — he was only sarcastic when it came to Furie — but he'd always make them sound sort of weakminded. But he was best with Orrie. 'Did you love your mother with all your heart?' 'Yes.'

'Would you ever have done anything knowingly to hurt her?' 'No.' 'If you had a choice between saving her life or your own, what would you have done?' Orrie was crying by then, and you could hardly hear his answer, so Pollo asked him again. 'I would do anything,' Orrie said. 'I don't care about my own life.' And Pollo said, 'That's why you called it murder, wasn't it? You blamed yourself for this terrible, terrible accident. You blamed yourself so much you wanted to be punished, you wished you were dead. So you said the worst thing about yourself you could think of, that you had murdered your beloved mother — isn't that why you used that word?' " Becker lifted his glass. "I don't think there was a dry eye in that courtroom, including mine — including the judge's, I'll bet."

Herm renewed Wicks's beer, being careful to put almost no head on it. "You think the boy's going to make it?"

"Dammit, I did when the jury retired this morning." Becker still held the glass without drinking from it. "But when they didn't reach a verdict by lunchtime, and then not all afternoon . . . Now nothing can happen till tomorrow morning: they've been put up in that little hotel over there. I don't mind admitting I'm worried. I don't know what's the trouble."

"If you'd think about it, it might just occur to you," said Molly. "Esther wasn't the only one who was killed. And Orrie's version of how he came to shoot Erle is really hard to swallow even if you're on the boy's side as I am and didn't think Erle was worth anything as a person, as I do, having known him just as well as you since we all were kids."

Al Hagman nodded to Herm, who had pantomimed asking whether he wanted a refill, and said to Becker, "Orrie stuck to that business about just not recognizing him? I'd think Pollo could get him to improve on that story."

Molly nibbled at the rim of her wineglass. "You and me both, brother."

Becker blinked rapidly. "Not if it was the truth. You know, I sat with little Ellie in the courtroom — by the way, I actually think that made Paul, Orrie's college friend, jealous. If you ask me, he's sweet on her —"

"He better watch himself," Molly said sourly. "She's jailbait. He's this big grownup college man."

"You got a dirty mind! He comes from a good family, in case you don't know. His dad is a real important man in the business world. This boy doesn't have to come up here in the sticks to find some little girl to take advantage of, for God's sake."

As always Herm was the pacifier, coming up quickly with, "What were you saying about Ellie?"

"Just that she swears it was true Orrie didn't know it was Erle until after he shot him."

"You mean she swore to you," Molly said. "She didn't get anywhere near the stand."

Suspecting that the statement would touch Becker off again, Herm asked, "Why would that be, Joe? Why wouldn't she be a witness for Orrie? She was the only living person other than Orrie who was at the scene of the crime, and she sure would be on his side. I mean, you can see why Furie wouldn't call a sweet little sister to testify against her brother, but what about Pollo?"

Becker had at last tasted his highball. He lowered the glass now. "My own theory — and it's not the kind of thing I would mention to anybody involved — my own theory is that Pollo didn't have her testify because Furie could have cross-examined her, and Pollo was afraid of what that might lead to. She might claim her mother and Erle murdered Augie.

Underneath all that sweetness she's a tough little character. I doubt Pollo could shut her up."

"Would that be bad?" Herm dried his hands on a towel and immediately wet them again in replenishing the ice in Becker's drink. He would add whiskey when asked but meanwhile provided dilution. He was concerned about Becker's temper.

"Be playing with fire, to do that in court. The law doesn't allow you to take revenge as a private person," Becker said. "Much as I for my part might think it would be okay in certain cases."

Molly made an ugly smirk. "Killing a mother for killing the father would be okay with you?"

Amazing everybody present, Becker did not take visible offense at the question. "What I think doesn't matter in this instance. Nor your opinion, or anybody else's except the jury's."

"And then the judge's," Herm said, again wiping his hands. "If they find Orrie guilty, he'll be the one to impose sentence, right? What's the term for manslaughter?"

"She," Molly said. "The judge is a woman."

Herm snapped his fingers. "Sure, she is. I keep forgetting."

"Well, you shouldn't." Molly assumed an even more self-righteous expression than she usually wore when addressing her male bar-mates. "She's done a great job, and don't let Joe Becker tell you different."

Becker laughed off this crack, saying, "The lady has done all right. This might sound funny to say when you're as prejudiced as I admit I am, but if anything the judge has been easier about objections on Pollo than on Furie. And in her instructions to the jury she kept harping on how legal guilt must be without a shadow of a doubt, that it wasn't their job to say anything about *innocence* so-called: trials don't determine if the accused is *innocent*. That's up to the Almighty. What a jury does is find whether the prosecution has proved its case for the defendant's *guilt*. If it has not, beyond every reasonable doubt, then the verdict *must* be not guilty: there's no choice."

Hagman spoke up. "Maybe being a woman, she's taking pity on a young boy like that, and also thinking of the little girl: Ellie's brother's all she's got left of a family."

Becker raised his eyebrows. "I'd sure like to think so."

And Herm chimed in. "That's the way it ought to be."

Molly was sneering. "You fellas just can't admit that maybe a woman could make a better judge because she's *fairer*."

"That's a new one on me," Hagman cried, but in good humor.

Bob Terwillen came in the door. "Had a bad one tonight, down in Rivertown. Kid overcome by gas fumes from a heater that got blown out. Little three-year-old boy might not make it. We took him to Good Samaritan." He stuffed his knitted cap into a pocket of the plaid mackinaw and found a place for the coat on the one free hook on the wall rack beyond Molly. He took a stool between Hagman and Becker and asked Herm for rye. He said, "These are the ones you hate." He gave more details.

"You've been overworked lately, you guys," Herm said, delivering the whiskey in a shot glass. "I never have known a time when there were so many bad accidents around here all at once."

Joe Becker put a hand on Terwillen's sweatered forearm. "Maybe this isn't the time to ask, but it's been bothering me, and Herm talking about accidents and all. Ellie lives there with you — does she still say anything about Augie's death not being accidental?"

Terwillen gulped the rye in one fluid movement. He shook his head. "She didn't mention it to me again after her mother and Erle died." He held the shot glass to Herm for refilling. "And I'm sure glad she didn't, because it's not right to talk that way." Before swallowing the next, he asked Molly about Gladys and then said to Herm, "I haven't seen Phil in ages. He all right, you think?"

"On the late shift," said Herm. "I think by now he's about given up on them locating his brother."

Terwillen drank half the ice-water chaser and stood up. "Got to get home before bedtime. Tomorrow's the verdict, and I want to do what I can for Orrie. Having this happen, and him without a dad!"

When the door had closed behind him, Becker said, "They don't come any better than Bobby Terwillen. I never realized that until just lately." With Augie gone, he really needed to have someone to think of as best friend.

13

All of the jurors, male and female, were ready to exonerate Orrie in the matter of the death of Esther, for no boy who looked like him, waited tables in a college dining room, had been an honor student in high school, and had recently lost his father could possibly have killed his mother except in a second tragic accident.

But unanimity had not been reached as to the death of Erle Mencken. Two men balked at finding a lad of draft age, old enough to be tried as an adult, entirely guiltless in the killing of the male victim.

"All right," said Harry Warnicke, after a discussion of some length, "at the very least, his judgment is terrible, or his eyes are bad, or something. He shoots down somebody he's known all his life because he doesn't recognize him?"

"It could happen," insisted Grace Cudahy. "Come on, you know it could. That's what I hate about guns. It's the unloaded ones that always kill people."

No one challenged her on the irrationality of the statement. She was a housewife and mother, and like the other women on the panel could have got excused from jury duty for the simple reason that she was female, but in fact had eagerly accepted the summons, assuming it would exempt her from some household chores for the duration of her service. But as it turned out, her teenagers proved to be absolute shirkers and she had to do all the usual work when she got home late each afternoon.

Warnicke was a salesman of wholesale paper products. As most of his income came from commissions, he was losing money every minute he spent in court, so was making his moral point at some material cost. "What I'm saying is, suppose it *was* completely by accident: can we send this kid out to maybe do it again, next time he wakes up from a nap and hears some funny noises?"

Frank L. Perkins was the other holdout, and his argument was sterner than Warnicke's. He had flatly announced as at least a possibility that Orrie had killed Erle by intention.

Margaret Rayburn, an unmarried schoolteacher in early middle age, said angrily, "Then you go out and tell Mr. Furie he should have made the indictment first-degree."

Perkins was thirty-two years old and a bank teller. He had fair hair and a somewhat darker mustache. "Isn't there something here that wasn't brought out in the trial? First place, his father died under circumstances I'd call suspicious. Then, don't you think it's more than possible something was going on between Esther and Erle? You know what I mean: I don't have to spell it out."

Miss Rayburn was about to reply, but Ralph Ames, the foreman, said quickly, "The judge told us we really shouldn't consider anything that wasn't brought up in court, and that wasn't."

"Both sides seemed to be avoiding it," said Perkins, "though it seemed like something anybody would think of immediately. And all these violent deaths in the same house, within a few days of each other? Isn't it just common sense to at least consider the possibility they were related?"

Ames chuckled. He was a plump man in a drab gray suit, but with a very bright tie. "Hell, our business here ain't common sense, Frank. It's the law. The judge made that clear enough."

Some of them snickered, but Margaret Rayburn said angrily, "Hasn't the poor boy suffered enough by now? That's what matters here, so far as I can see."

Perkins squinted at her. "I guess I feel sorry for the boy too, but we can't just let everything be ruled by sympathy. There is such a thing as truth, and sometimes it's unpleasant, maybe even unfair, lousy, wrong, but it's still the truth. Both sides went to the trouble of picking us —"

"And you, like the rest of us," said Miss Rayburn, "swore you started with an open mind."

"I still have one. I just say it's our job to ask certain questions and not just rush into a verdict so we can get home more quickly."

Margaret Rayburn happened to be one of the two jurors who had misrepresented their objectivity during the process of selection. Having heard of Esther Mencken through a colleague who taught at Orrie's school, she knew the woman's reputation as a slut. And Vincent Cardone, a plumber, had failed to reveal that he had done some work for E.G. Mencken, years back, in the squalor of Rivertown, and had never been paid. His resentment was such that he did not worry about the consequences of being found out: he was in the right.

Jerry Baum, whose thickset physique seemed at odds with his profession as an accountant, wrinkled his nose at Perkins, across the table from him. "You don't mean you want to send the boy to prison?" Others made sounds of disapproval.

It was Harry Warnicke who responded. "No, of course not. But suppose we let him off entirely. Suppose he goes on to live a perfectly decent life for years. We'd be glad to hear that. I know I would. I'd like to keep tabs on a fellow whose fate I had something to do with. I'd feel responsible for him in a way. I'd sure want him to keep out of trouble, to do real well. Poor kid!" He looked at Margaret Rayburn. "I agree with you he's suffered plenty. But what about the rest of society? If he's capable of flying off the handle and shooting someone supposedly by accident . . . I don't want to send him to jail, but shouldn't we do *something*? Just think how we will feel if he might do it again, many years from now."

Miss Rayburn shook her trim head. "All of this is theoretical. Who knows what anybody will do in the future? You're just playing with words. This boy has his life to live, and without the help of any adult relations. Then there's the little sister to think of."

"Speaking of her," said Perkins, "don't you think it's funny Pollo never put her on the stand?"

"Orrie said he was alone with those two. His sister wasn't there."

"And you believe that?"

Miss Rayburn set her teeth. "You know better? Were *you* there?"

Two of the jurors, a young single woman and a married man a few years older, had developed a romantic interest in each other and yearned for a verdict to be reached so that they could leave the courthouse. Neither contributed to the discussion except to murmur an assent to every argument in favor of total acquittal.

Sally T. Hemphill, the fourth woman on the panel, had lately served in the Women's Army Corps, rising to the rank of Technician Fifth Grade in a payroll office. She had said nothing throughout the deliberations except to vote with the majority. James Donovan, who worked in a canning factory, and Carl B. Ridley, driver of a gravel truck, were also recently discharged veterans. Donovan had been a mechanic in the Air Force; Ridley, a combat infantryman who had been captured by the Germans and held in a prison camp for seven months, a fact the prosecutor did not know, else he would have excused Ridley by peremptory challenge, on the assumption that the man would have an instinctive bias against any authority that had the power to take away an individual's physical liberty. Oscar Ventura worked in a dry-cleaning plant. He resented the effort by Perkins to be better than the others in intelligence and morality as well. But he kept silent because of his accent, which he knew made a certain kind of person look down on him.

Warnicke said, "Maybe if he could be found not guilty but given some kind of special —"

Perkins broke in, with a derisive snort. "Like let off with a warning?"

This offended Warnicke, who had after all been a partial ally of Perkins. He flushed now and told Miss Rayburn that he withdrew his objections and voted for acquittal.

Ames asked Perkins whether he wanted to be responsible for a hung jury. "Now, that's unfair," said the latter.

Ames raised his hands. "It's your right to do what you

will. Nobody's taking that away from you. But it's simply a fact that unless we arrive at a unanimous verdict, this will all have to happen all over again with another twelve people."

"Maybe not," said Perkins, with a slight smile. "I don't think Furie's heart's been in it from the first. I think maybe he indicted the boy only because it more or less had to be done in a case of this kind. Maybe he wouldn't bother a second time, and could save the taxpayers some money."

"That's just silly," said Miss Rayburn in her most severe classroom manner. "You are just trying to get out of making up your mind. There'd be another trial, and those poor children would have to go through all of it again, and twelve more jurors would have to listen to these awful things and be shown those terrible photographs of the bodies. How can you say you're a decent human being and let that happen?"

Perkins was wounded. "I am as decent a human being as you," he cried. "That's precisely why I have been taking my time. I don't call it decent to immediately jump to some foregone conclusion when other human beings have lost their lives in a tragedy that for my money remains unexplained. It doesn't behoove you to question my motives."

Miss Rayburn closed her eyes briefly while saying, "I assure you I did not mean it as personal."

But even that statement was put in a superior tone, and Perkins could not see it as an apology. He had been on the verge of capitulation to the majority, had resisted thus far only to insure that there would be some real discussion of the essential matter, as he saw it: two people had died violently under conditions that were irregular, disorderly, outside the perimeter of normal behavior: that was the reason for having a trial in the first place. But apparently he was the only responsible person on this jury, for he regarded Warnicke's point as being capricious and exhibitionistic, whereas his own position was one of conscience. He intended to hold out until that truth was acknowledged.

But he told Miss Rayburn, "I didn't take it personally. I assure you all I care is to see justice is done."

Down at the end of the table, Jerry Baum groaned.

"All right," Perkins said testily, "be cynical, if you want. *I'm* not."

"Who's cynical?" Baum asked. "I just think maybe you might have your own private idea of justice."

"You people should talk about private reasons." Perkins shook his head in resentment.

The comment alerted Vincent Cardone, who was suddenly worried that Perkins might know of the plumbing bill never paid by the late E.G. Mencken.

"Hey," Cardone said. "Come on. Don't light into us. We're all in this together."

"If you really mean that," Perkins said, "then let's think about the point I raised." He was trying to calm himself by unscrewing the cap of his fountain pen and then screwing it tight again.

"I *have* thought about it," said Miss Rayburn. "You'll never be able to make me believe that Orrie shot anybody with malice."

"But how about if Erle was fighting with his mother, hitting her? Didn't Furie suggest that?"

"The child denied it." Miss Rayburn assumed her coldest expression, lengthening her upper lip. "*He* was there, and no one else was who is still alive."

"Is that your idea of conclusive proof?" Perkins asked, with a prosecutor's edge to his voice. "It hasn't ever occurred to you that people on trial tell their own versions of the truth?" He was still smarting from her questioning his humanity, and went for blood: "Are you *that* simple-minded?"

Having taken such a turn, the deliberations would continue.

14

Orrie stopped to lay the white rose on his mother's grave, the earth of which still looked raw after weeks of rain and snow. The headstone had not yet been delivered: the Terwillens were preparing to complain to the masons.

Mr. Terwillen had discreetly left him there and gone off elsewhere in the cemetery, perhaps to a family plot of his own. It occurred to Orrie that he knew very little of a personal nature about the kind people who had given shelter to himself and Ellie. He should do something about that, talk to them more about themselves. He must also be nicer to Paul. No one ever had such a friend. Paul had even gone so far as to include Ellie in his kindness, and Orrie was most grateful, being aware that, occupied as he had been, he had neglected the little sister who now had no one but himself in all the world.

His failures had been many, but could be corrected. His crime would remain what it was forever, though he had been exonerated by a jury of, not his peers but rather his elders: most of the eight men, four women were old enough to be his parents, some undoubtedly having children of their own. Mr. Pollo had expended a great deal of his notable energy in selecting these people, and went enthusiastically to shake their hands when they brought in the right verdict, urging Orrie to join him in the expression of gratitude. But Orrie declined. It was bad enough that he had had to tell the preposterous story about not recognizing Erle before shooting him to death. That the people who believed it were to be congratulated on their gullibility was too much. If they had not given it credence but proceeded to find him not guilty because they felt sorry for him, which in fact he thought more likely, his complicity in their malfeasance would be even more shameful.

"If they served the cause of justice," he told Pollo, "then they did no more than their duty, and I've got nothing to thank them for." They should be insulted by a show of gratitude. Orrie did not expect the lawyer to agree with his point. He and Pollo though associated in this peculiar intimacy had very little in common. He hoped in future to avoid attorneys-at-law, whose sense of morality, being essentially linguistic, was so basically at odds with his own.

He should thank this cruel jury for sentencing him to a lifelong term — of life? While no doubt believing they were doing him a kindness: another pain to add to all the others, for everybody was kind to him. When the verdict was announced, people burst through the gate to come to him, persons he did not recognize, perhaps even strangers, to wish him well, shake his hand, sometimes both hands, and there were women who went so far as to hug him and kiss him on forehead or cheeks. It was extraordinary that killing his mother had made him so popular. Even Mr. Furie, who had supposedly tried so hard to convict him (though, in Orrie's secret opinion, not really), gave him a handclasp and said, "I hope you understand I was only doing the job that is my sworn duty to the citizens of this county and this state." He wished Orrie a brighter future. The prosecutor seemed to want to be thought a kindly person: he showed that sort of smile. As Orrie was too young to vote, he had to assume Furie was sincere, but he wondered why.

"I used to think I knew a whole lot," he said now, aloud, and there was nobody to hear him but his mother, who was dead, "because I got good grades in school. What a reason! But then I was only a kid. Now I'm as old as a man can be, and I don't know anything at all. . . . But maybe thinking that way is arrogance too, because I do know I wanted in that split second to rid the world of Erle. But there's the arrogance again. *The* world? Hardly. *My* world. That's one motive I couldn't ever confess to anyone alive." Nor did he look towards Erle's grave, at the far end of the plot: someone had rightly seen that it would be no closer to his mother's. "And now that I'm the heir of everything he owned, you're the only person on whom I would have wanted to spend it."

A bright but heatless January sun was shining. The snow had disappeared in the unseasonable thaw, but the air had turned cold once more. Orrie wore the thin corduroy garment, no better than a long jacket, that he had been seeking to replace with his father's overcoat when he found the shotgun instead. He was prosperous enough now, with his profit from killing Erle, to buy himself the belted camel's-hair polo coat that had figured in his fantasies of winter elegance, no doubt derived from the movies. But though what he had done had been condoned by a jury of twelve decent human beings, he could not consider spending gains so ill-gotten. Even the pious thoughts of renovating the shacks in Rivertown while reducing the rents for the poor souls therein, which he had shared with the charitable Terwillens because he knew they would be pleased, seemed phony as he stood here. Could he play the philanthropist with blood-money?

No living soul was nearby on the bright but bleak morning in the garden of headstones, in which, in the absence of a tree or tomb for an acre, he was the highest eminence, short as he was and probably, having arrived at his current age, would always be, which meant he would likely go through life always looking younger than he was and thus attracting unwanted sympathy, particularly from older women.

He addressed his mother again. "I do think it's right to get Ellie everything she needs. She's got it coming — even now I don't want to tell you why, unless of course you already know, but if so, then saying anything on the matter would be pointless. What better use for the money than to get her the college education she could not have gotten otherwise, even though her grades have always been better even than mine. If she wants to go on to study law, she can do that too, though I don't personally care for the profession. But then maybe somebody like Ellie could improve on it.

"What I won't ever be able to do, however, is admit to her I think she was right about you and Erle." It would take a great deal of strength for him to continue, and he sought to collect it while looking up and away from the grave. By chance he saw Mr. Terwillen heading back. He had to hurry with what he had to say, but that was just as well.

"I think you and he did murder my father, and that was why you were fighting each other so savagely. . . . But I will always believe I killed you by accident. . . . I had to say that once. I will never mention it again. I will always love you and try to make you proud of me." And finally he added, though he was not clear as to just how much he intended the phrase to include, "*I will never get over it.*"

On the way home in the car, while waiting for a traffic light to change, Mr. Terwillen turned and looked at him through the thick glasses. Orrie by now was used to what, in the early days with the Terwillens, had seemed a suspicious stare.

"I hope it will be okay with you: May's invited this niece of hers to come have Sunday dinner. She's a real nice girl. They live just over the state line. May's brother Buster is a little stuck up, even she will admit that. But he's goodhearted underneath it all. And the girl's more like her mother, quiet but smart, you know? I think she's a senior now."

Orrie made a melancholy smile. "Am I supposed to be getting fixed up?"

The green light came on. Mr. Terwillen looked forward and put the car in motion. "No," he said, somewhat miffed, "nothing is expected of you. She's just coming to dinner, is all. By herself, because her folks are going into the city to see the outdoor-sports show. Her dad's big on hunting and fishing."

Orrie could not remember when last he had thought about girls, though in the old days they had been an obsession. He was now sexless and totally incapable of any new emotion: only in such a state could he live a subsequent life that would be blameless. He could not endure a return to hell.

"I'm sure she's very nice," he said, "but I don't feel much like meeting anybody."

"Orrie," Terwillen said, his big hands manipulating the steering wheel, "you're going to have to come out of it one of these days."

"No, I'm not," Orrie said defiantly. When they got home,

he hopped out and opened the garage doors, then went immediately inside the house via the rear door. He slipped through the kitchen and up the back stairway before Mrs. Terwillen, at the stove, could turn.

Ellie came out of her room before he reached his. She spoke in the subdued tones of a conspirator. "You should see what's downstairs."

"I know," he said impatiently. "Their niece. He told me." He did not intend to dwell on the subject, for his sister was always too eager to make common cause with him against an outside world that had been notably benevolent towards them.

"Christ," Ellie said. "A bleached blonde!"

It had been a long time since he had chided her about her language, having been in no position to find fault with anybody else, but now he was moved to do so. "Will you stop using profanity? You just got home from church."

As usual she disregarded the admonition. "And you know what her name is? Hermione, for God's sake."

Mr. Terwillen had said the girl's father was stuck-up. No doubt this was an example. "Well, so what?" he asked. "My name is really Orville, isn't it? Kids get stuck with fancy names. It's not their fault."

"So what do they call her? Minnie? Minnie Mouse?"

"You're being nasty for no reason," he said. "And really impolite. Why aren't you down there, talking to her? You're both high-school girls, probably with a lot in common."

"Are you kidding?" Ellie said, making a mouth. "I don't have anything to say to somebody of *that* type."

"You really ought to do something about the prejudiced way you look at people," said Orrie. "How do you know what she's like unless you talk to her? She's supposed to be smart."

"Then *you* go talk to her."

"All right," he said. "I will."

But that was worse. "You will? *Don't*." She glared at him.

He realized she was just being jealous, but decided that to be forthright was better for all concerned. "I'm telling you for the last time: don't try to run my life. I'm your big brother."

He went downstairs and in the solarium encountered a girl who stood in the center of a cloud of gold, an effect that after a moment he realized was produced by the winter sun coming in the window behind her fair hair and white angora sweater.

"Hi," he said. "I'm Orrie."

"Hi," she replied in a voice that was both soft and luxurious, rather like her sweater. "My name is Hermione. I know that's too much for a lot of people to say, so sometimes I'm called Sonny."

"But Sonny's a boy's name," Orrie said. He was about to add, with respect to her fantastic figure, that she was anything but masculine, but decided it might have an obscene implication. "I like your real name. It's something special." He remembered his manners. "Won't you have a seat?"

She sat down on the couch, but he remained standing.

"I hear you're in college?" Her hair was, unlike Gena's, blond all the way to the roots.

"Yes, I am."

"I guess it's pretty tough?"

He shrugged and finally chose the chair that was most distant from her, though fortunately the room was not all that wide. "A lot more reading assignments than high school, but that's about all." She looked as if she were made of peach ice cream. There was not a pimple on her face. She wore golden bangs, and on either side of her face the hair fell straight and smooth and shining to her shoulders.

274

She raised her perfect eyebrows. "Maybe I'll see you up there next year — that is, if you're still going?"

That she might be dubious about his continuing to pursue higher education was insupportable. "I will certainly be there. You can count on it. I'm in premed, you know."

"Gee, that's great," Hermione said. "A couple of guys from my class are going, but they're just big dumb guys on football scholarships. It'll be nice to know somebody intelligent who's already there. I don't make new friends easily." Her smile made the sun seem dim. "I've never been away from home except maybe to stay overnight at a friend's house."

Orrie smiled back. "That's just about the way I was too, when I first went. You'll be just fine. Everybody has to leave home eventually, and college is probably one of the nicer ways to do that."

"I really like your sister," Hermione said brightly. "I myself am an only child."

"She's just a junior in high school right now, but she wants to go to law school when the time comes."

"Sounds like a smart family."

Suddenly they were respectable. That should please Ellie if she had any sense. He wondered how much Hermione knew about himself, but the whole story had been in the newspapers and on the radio and anyway as the Terwillens' niece she could hardly be in the dark — and yet she apparently found him an acceptable human being, even seemed to be implying that she would welcome his friendship, though of course before jumping to any rash conclusions he should probably get the advice of Paul, who was so wise in the ways of women.

Mrs. Terwillen came into the doorway at that moment

and exclaimed, "You've already gotten to know each other! Well, dinner's on the table."

Hermione frowned beautifully. "Now, Aunt May, you said I could help."

"But you're the guest, sweetheart."

"Then I'll do the dishes!"

Mrs. Terwillen simpered at Orrie. "When I was her age, I did everything I could to duck out of any work." She patted his shoulder. "Would you please go get your sister, dear? I hate the way shouting sounds."

Orrie was embarrassed to remember that Ellie seldom volunteered for household chores. But going up the stairs, he reflected that he might soon have the pleasant responsibility of looking after another younger member of the female sex, one to whom he was not related. Surely there was nothing that could make you feel more of a man.

FOR THE BEST IN PAPERBACKS, LOOK FOR THE

In every corner of the world, on every subject under the sun, Penguin represents quality and variety—the very best in publishing today.

For complete information about books available from Penguin—including Pelicans, Puffins, Peregrines, and Penguin Classics—and how to order them, write to us at the appropriate address below. Please note that for copyright reasons the selection of books varies from country to country.

In the United Kingdom: For a complete list of books available from Penguin in the U.K., please write to *Dept E.P., Penguin Books Ltd, Harmondsworth, Middlesex, UB7 0DA.*

In the United States: For a complete list of books available from Penguin in the U.S., please write to *Dept BA, Penguin,* Box 120, Bergenfield, New Jersey 07621-0120.

In Canada: For a complete list of books available from Penguin in Canada, please write to *Penguin Books Canada Ltd, 10 Alcorn Avenue, Suite 300, Toronto, Ontario, Canada M4V 3B2.*

In Australia: For a complete list of books available from Penguin in Australia, please write to the *Marketing Department, Penguin Books Ltd, P.O. Box 257, Ringwood, Victoria 3134.*

In New Zealand: For a complete list of books available from Penguin in New Zealand, please write to the *Marketing Department, Penguin Books (NZ) Ltd, Private Bag, Takapuna, Auckland 9.*

In India: For a complete list of books available from Penguin, please write to *Penguin Overseas Ltd, 706 Eros Apartments, 56 Nehru Place, New Delhi, 110019.*

In Holland: For a complete list of books available from Penguin in Holland, please write to *Penguin Books Nederland B.V., Postbus 195, NL-1380AD Weesp, Netherlands.*

In Germany: For a complete list of books available from Penguin, please write to *Penguin Books Ltd, Friedrichstrasse 10-12, D-6000 Frankfurt Main I, Federal Republic of Germany.*

In Spain: For a complete list of books available from Penguin in Spain, please write to *Longman, Penguin España, Calle San Nicolas 15, E-28013 Madrid, Spain.*

In Japan: For a complete list of books available from Penguin in Japan, please write to *Longman Penguin Japan Co Ltd, Yamaguchi Building, 2-12-9 Kanda Jimbocho, Chiyoda-Ku, Tokyo 101, Japan.*

FOR THE BEST IN CONTEMPORARY AMERICAN FICTION

FOR THE BEST IN CONTEMPORARY AMERICAN FICTION

☐ **THE WOMEN OF BREWSTER PLACE**
A Novel in Seven Stories
Gloria Naylor

Winner of the American Book Award, this is the story of seven survivors of an urban housing project — a blind alley feeding into a dead end. From a variety of backgrounds, they experience, fight against, and sometimes transcend the fate of black women in America today.

192 pages   ISBN: 0-14-006690-X

☐ **STONES FOR IBARRA**
Harriet Doerr

An American couple comes to the small Mexican village of Ibarra to reopen a copper mine, learning much about life and death from the deeply faithful villagers.   *214 pages   ISBN: 0-14-007562-3*

☐ **WORLD'S END**
T. Coraghessan Boyle

"Boyle has emerged as one of the most inventive and verbally exuberant writers of his generation," writes *The New York Times*. Here he tells the story of Walter Van Brunt, who collides with early American history while searching for his lost father.   *456 pages   ISBN: 0-14-009760-0*

☐ **THE WHISPER OF THE RIVER**
Ferrol Sams

The story of Porter Osborn, Jr., who, in 1938, leaves his rural Georgia home to face the world at Willingham University, *The Whisper of the River* is peppered with memorable characters and resonates with the details of place and time. Ferrol Sams's writing is regional fiction at its best.

528 pages   ISBN: 0-14-008387-1

☐ **ENGLISH CREEK**
Ivan Doig

Drawing on the same heritage he celebrated in *This House of Sky,* Ivan Doig creates a rich and varied tapestry of northern Montana and of our country in the late 1930s.   *338 pages   ISBN: 0-14-008442-8*

☐ **THE YEAR OF SILENCE**
Madison Smartt Bell

A penetrating look at the varied reactions to a young woman's suicide exactly one year later, *The Year of Silence* "captures vividly and poignantly the chancy dance of life." (*The New York Times Book Review*)

208 pages   ISBN: 0-14-011533-1

FOR THE BEST IN CONTEMPORARY AMERICAN FICTION

☐ **IN THE COUNTRY OF LAST THINGS**
Paul Auster

Death, joggers, leapers, and Object Hunters are just some of the realities of future city life in this spare, powerful, visionary novel about one woman's struggle to live and love in a frightening post-apocalyptic world.

208 pages   ISBN: 0-14-009705-8

☐ **BETWEEN C&D**
New Writing from the Lower East Side Fiction Magazine
Joel Rose and Catherine Texier, Editors

A startling collection of stories by Tama Janowitz, Gary Indiana, Kathy Acker, Barry Yourgrau, and others, *Between C&D* is devoted to short fiction that ignores preconceptions — fiction not found in conventional literary magazines.

194 pages   ISBN: 0-14-010570-0

☐ **LEAVING CHEYENNE**
Larry McMurtry

The story of a love triangle unlike any other, *Leaving Cheyenne* follows the three protagonists — Gideon, Johnny, and Molly — over a span of forty years, until all have finally "left Cheyenne."

254 pages   ISBN: 0-14-005221-6

You can find all these books at your local bookstore, or use this handy coupon for ordering:

Penguin Books By Mail
Dept. BA Box 999
Bergenfield, NJ 07621-0999

Please send me the above title(s). I am enclosing _____
(please add sales tax if appropriate and \$1.50 to cover postage and handling). Send check or money order—no CODs. Please allow four weeks for shipping. We cannot ship to post office boxes or addresses outside the USA. *Prices subject to change without notice.*

Ms./Mrs./Mr. _____

Address _____

City/State _____ Zip _____